forever & always

by jasinda wilder

This is a work of fiction. Names, characters, places, and incidents are either the product of the author's imagination or are used fictitiously. Any resemblance to actual events, places, organizations, or persons, whether living or dead, is entirely coincidental.

FOREVER & ALWAYS

ISBN: 978-1-941098-01-1
Copyright © 2013 by Jasinda Wilder

Cover art by Sarah Hansen of Okay Creations. Cover art © 2013 by Sarah Hansen.
Interior book design by Indie Author Services.

To PG & GV, who wrote their own incredible love story,
one letter at a time.

somewhere out there

Caden

It's always the hands that mess me up. I can never get the fingers right somehow. It's something about the proportions between the knuckles, and the way the fingers are supposed to curve when at rest. I had an entire sketchbook full of failed attempts.

Even at that moment, in the passenger seat of Dad's F–350, I was sketching out another attempt. My tenth so far, and we weren't even to Grayling yet. This one was the best yet, but the middle knuckles of the last two fingers looked awkward, like they'd been broken.

Which gave me an idea. I glanced over at Dad, who was driving with his left hand, the right resting on his thigh, fingers tapping to Montgomery Gentry on the radio.

"Dad?" A sideways glance and a raised eyebrow were the only acknowledgment I got. "You ever broke your fingers?"

"Yeah, broke most of my left hand, matter of fact." Dad took the wheel with his right and showed me his left hand. The knuckles were bulbous, the fingers crooked. "Didn't get 'em set right, so they've always been kinda fucked up."

"How'd you break 'em?"

The fingers in question scratched at a shaved scalp, the stubble of a receding hairline whisking under his nails. "Me and your Uncle Gerry were out in the back forty, riding the fence line, checking for breaks. My horse got spooked by a snake. He threw me, 'cept my hand was tangled in the reins. Dislocated most of my fingers. Then, when I hit the ground, his hoof landed on the same hand, broke the middle two pretty good. Your Gramps is a hard-ass, and I knew he'd wallop me good if I came back without the job done. So I set the broke fingers best I could. There was a busted fence post, see, way out at the far corner, and Dad's prize Thoroughbred kept getting out. Gerry and I fixed the break and went home. I never told Dad about my fingers, just had my mom wrap 'em for me. Never really healed right, and even now when the weather's shitty my hand aches."

I'd heard the stories of my father's childhood growing up on the Wyoming horse ranch that had been in the Monroe family for several generations. Every summer of my entire life had been spent on that ranch, riding and roping and tagging and birthing and breaking. Gramps didn't accept excuses and didn't tolerate weakness or mistakes, and I could only begin to imagine what it had been like growing up with Connor Monroe as a father.

Gramps was a tall, silver-haired, iron-hard man. He'd served in both Korea and Vietnam before returning to work the ranch. Even as his grandson, I was expected to pull my weight or go home. That meant up before dawn, to bed past sunset, the entire day spent out in the field or in the stables, rarely even sitting for lunch. At fourteen, I was tanned, muscled, and, I knew, hardened to the point of looking older than I really was.

Dad had been the first Monroe son to pursue a career away from the ranch, which had caused a decades-long rift between him and Gramps, leaving Uncle Gerry to take over running the ranch as Gramps got older. Dad left Wyoming after high school, moving to Detroit on his own to become an engineer. He'd started on the floor of a Ford plant, assembling truck frames and attending night school until he'd completed his degree, and eventually he'd been promoted to the engineering department, where he'd worked for the last twenty years. Despite his decades as an engineer, Dad had never really lost the wild-edged intensity of his upbringing.

"Why the questions about my fingers?" he asked.

I shrugged, tilted the drawing into his line of sight. "I can't get these damn fingers to look right. The last two look messed up, and I can't fix it. So I thought I'd make 'em look broken on purpose."

Dad glanced at the drawing and then nodded. "Good plan. The relationship between your angles and curves is off, is your problem. I'm more of a draftsman than an artist, but that's my two cents."

I made a surreptitious study of Dad's broken fingers again, adjusted the knuckles on the pencil-rendered hand, making them look misshapen and lumpy, then worked on the tips of the last two fingers, curving them slightly to the left, zigzagging the fourth finger to resemble Dad's. When I was done, I held up the drawing to show him.

Dad cut his eyes to the drawing and back to the road several times, examining critically. "Good. Best one yet. The index finger still looks a little goofy, but otherwise good." He punched a button on the truck's radio, bypassing the commercial that was airing in favor of a classic rock station. He turned it up when Led Zeppelin's "Kashmir" came on. "I think this summer art camp will be good for you. Interlochen is one of the best art schools in the country."

I shrugged, bobbing my head to the beat, mumbling along with the lyrics. "It's weird to not be going to the ranch."

"Gramps'll miss your help this summer, that's for sure."

"Will he be mad at me for not going?"

Dad shrugged. "He's Gramps. He's always mad about something or at somebody. Somethin' to stew on gives him reason to get up in the morning, I think. He'll get over it."

"He didn't get over you moving to Detroit," I said, spinning the pencil between my fingers.

"True. But that's different. Every Monroe boy since before the Civil War has lived and died on the ranch. I broke a family tradition going back a hundred and fifty years."

Conversation faded after that, and I watched the road and the corn fields and the blue sky spotted by puffs of white, listening to Jimi Hendrix singing "Purple Haze" and twisting the guitar strings into shrieking banshees. I-75 eventually was replaced by M-72, and I felt myself nodding off. A while later, I blinked awake, and Grand Traverse Bay sparkled off to the left, a dozen sails flashing white in the distance.

"Thought we were going to Interlochen?" I asked, rubbing my eyes. The bay was farther north.

"No rush. Thought we'd grab some lunch before I drop you off. Ain't gonna see you for a while, you know."

We ate at Don's Drive-In, a retro burgers-fries-and-milkshakes kind of place, small and cramped, red plastic-leather booths, chrome table edges, and black-and-white checkered tiles on the walls. We didn't talk much, but then we rarely did. Dad was a reserved man, and I'm a lot like him. I was content to eat my burger and sip my shake, worrying internally about spending an entire summer around a bunch of artsy kids I didn't know. I'd grown up around silent, hard-bitten cowboys, men who chewed tobacco and swore and could—and often did—go days without much more than a grunt or two. I knew I was a talented artist, as capable with pens and pencils as with paint. What I wasn't good with was people.

"Don't be nervous, son," Dad said, apparently reading my mind. "Folks are folks, and they'll either cotton to you or they won't. That was my mom's advice to me when I left for Detroit. Just be you. Don't try to impress anyone. Let your work stand for itself."

"This isn't like school," I said, dragging a fry through ketchup. "I know where I fit there: alone in the corner, with my notebook. I know where I belong on Gramps's ranch. I know where I belong at home. I don't know where I belong at an arts camp."

"Wherever you are is where you belong. You're a Monroe, Caden. That may not mean shit to anyone else, but it should mean something to you."

"It does."

"Well, there you go." Dad wiped his fingers with a napkin and sat back. "Look, I get it. I grew up surrounded by thousands of acres of open land, all hills and horses, rarely seeing anyone but Mom and Dad, Gerry, and the other hands. Even school was the same kids from kindergarten to graduation. I knew everybody in my world, and they knew me. When I moved to Detroit, it was scary as hell. Suddenly I was surrounded by all these buildings and thousands of people who didn't know me or give a shit about whether I made it or not."

"People confuse me."

"That's 'cause most people don't make a damn lick of sense, if you ask me. Women especially. Trick with women is to not try and figure them out. You won't. Just accept 'em as they are, and try to go with the flow. Good advice for life in general, really."

"Do you understand Mom?"

Dad let out a rare laugh, but I didn't miss the way the corners of his eyes tightened. Things had been strange and tense around the house lately, but neither Mom nor Dad was the type to talk about what was bugging them. "I've known your mother for twenty-five years," he said, "and been married to her for twenty-two. And no, I still don't understand her. I *know* her, I *get* her, but I don't always understand the way her mind works, how she comes up with ideas or arrives at her conclusions or why she changes her mind so goddamn much. Makes my head spin, but that's how women are and that's how she is, and I love her for it."

All too soon, Dad was paying the bill and the truck doors were slamming, and we were hauling down US-31 toward Interlochen. The ride was quick, and then Dad was parking and unstrapping my duffel bag from the bed of the truck and handing it to me. We stood toe to toe, neither of us speaking or moving.

Dad pointed to the rows of tiny wooden cabins. "That's the cabins. You know which one you're in? "

"Yeah, number twenty."

"All right, then. Well, guess I'll be going. Gonna be a long drive without you snoring in the passenger seat."

"You're just turning right back around and driving home?" I asked, then immediately hated how childish and whiny that had sounded.

Dad lifted an eyebrow in reproach. "You're here for three weeks, Cade. You expect me to sit on the beach and twiddle my thumbs for a month? Your mom needs me home, and I've got projects to finish at work."

I felt the question bubbling up, coming out, and couldn't stop it from emerging. "Is—is everything okay? With you and Mom?"

Dad closed his eyes briefly, breathed in slowly and let it out, then met my eyes. "We'll talk when you get home. Nothing for you to worry about right now."

That sounded oddly like an evasion, which was entirely out of character for my gruff, straight-talking father. "I just feel like things are—"

"It's fine, Caden. Just focus on having fun, meeting new people, and learning. Keep in mind that this is three weeks out of your entire life, and you don't ever have to see these people again." Dad stuck his left hand into his hip pocket and wrapped his right arm awkwardly around my shoulders. "I love you, son. Have a good time. Don't forget to call at least once, or your mom'll have a hairy conniption."

I returned the embrace with one arm. "Love you, too. Drive safe."

Dad nodded and turned back toward his truck, then stopped and dug into his back pocket. He pulled out a folded square of $20 bills and handed them to me. "Just in case."

"I've been saving my allowance," I said. Dad always expected me to earn money, never gave it for free.

"It's…just take it."

I stuffed the money into my hip pocket and shifted my weight. "Thanks."

"'Bye."

"'Bye." I waved once, and watched Dad drive away.

I'd spent months at a time away from my parents, lived on Gramps's ranch for months at a time. Goodbye was nothing new. So why did this one feel so unsettling?

Ever

My twin sister Eden rode in the seat next to me, listening to music, the volume turned up so loud I could make out the lyrics, tinny and distant but totally audible. In the front seat, Dad was chattering into his cell phone as he drove, discussing whatever a Chrysler senior executive discussed at ten o'clock on a Saturday morning. Something more important than his daughters, clearly.

Not that I would have wanted to talk to him even if he'd been off the phone. Well, that wasn't completely true; I would have *wanted* to, but I wouldn't have known what to say to him if he'd been willing to hang up the phone for ten seconds. He'd always been a workaholic, always on the phone or on his laptop, in his office at home or at the Chrysler headquarters. But up until last year, he'd spent time on the weekends with us. He'd taken us to dinner or to the mall. Movie night once a month, Sunday evening, on the big home theater screen in the basement.

And now?

It was understandable, I reasoned. He'd lost her, too. None of us had been prepared—no way to prepare for a freak car accident. But after we'd buried Mom, Dad had thrown himself into work more obsessively than ever.

Which left Eden and me to fend for ourselves. Of course, he'd done the parentally responsible thing and gotten the three of us individual therapy sessions twice a month, but I had quit going after a few weeks. There hadn't been a point. Mom was gone, and no amount of talking about the stages of grief would bring her back.

I had found my own way of dealing with the loss: I'd found art. Photography, drawing, painting, anything hands-on that let me shut down my mind and my heart and just *do*. Currently, I was into oils on canvas, thick glops of vivid colors on the matte white surface, spread around with a bristly brush or bare hands. It was cathartic. The reds would smear like blood, the yellows would blot like sunshine through a window; greens were delicate and crusted like sap-sticky pine needles, blues like cloudless skies and deepest ocean and oranges like sunsets and tangerines. Color—and the creation of something beautiful from emptiness.

In my more philosophical moments, I thought maybe painting appealed to me because it represented hope. I was a blank canvas, no thoughts, no emotions, no needs or desires, just a square of white floating through a loud, chaotic world, and life would paint me with color and substance, smear and spread and colorize me.

I found myself needing more tactile sensations, though. Just before I'd packed for this three-week summer camp up at Interlochen, I'd spread newspapers on the floor of my art room over the garage, laid a huge twenty-by-twenty canvas over them, and tossed mammoth blobs of paint down. I'd used my hands to spread it around in arcs and whorls and streaking lines, then added another color and another, mixing and daubing, smashing gouts together with my palms and tracing delicate lines with my fingertips and aggressive sunburst rays with my palms.

I didn't know or care if I was any good on an objective level. It wasn't about art or expression or any of that. It was avoidance at best, if Dr. Allerton's therapy speak could be believed. Apparently the staff at Interlochen thought I was something special, because they'd been enthusiastic about having me in the program for the summer.

As long as I had plenty of time to paint, I didn't really care what they wanted from me, or for me.

Lost in my thoughts, I tuned out Dad's incessant chatter and Eden's sullen, plea-for-attention silence, wondering if I'd get a chance to try ceramics or sculpture at Interlochen. My junior high's art program had been pathetic at best. I might have been only fourteen—fifteen as of yesterday—but I knew what I liked, and handfuls of cracked old watercolor paints and hopelessly mixed-up oil paints weren't it. They didn't even have access to clay, much less a kiln. I couldn't even get lessons on stretching my own canvases.

Being more mature than your age kind of sucked, I reflected. People either overestimated you and didn't give you any room to be a kid, or they ignored what you were really capable of and treated you like a child. I'd begged to go to a private arts academy for high school, but so far Daddy was putting his foot down, insisting Eden and I go to the same school, and Eden was set on going to the local high school because their strings program was one of the best in the state, and apparently Eden was some kind of cello virtuoso. Whatever.

I'd demand private lessons, then. Or an art tutor. For now, Interlochen would have to do.

After an interminable drive, Daddy pulled the Mercedes SUV to a gentle stop in front of rows of rustic cabins, finally ending his phone call with a touch to his earpiece.

Eden cast a glance out the window and snickered. "*That's* where you're going to stay for three weeks?"

I followed my twin's gaze to the cabins. They were tiny…nothing but little wooden huts in the forest. Did they even have indoor plumbing? Electricity? I shuddered, and then stuffed it down, putting on a game face. "Apparently so. It could be worse," I said. "I could be stuck at home all summer, doing *nothing*."

"I'm not doing nothing, *Ev*er," Eden snapped. "I'm taking private lessons with Mr. Wu and fitness training with Michael."

"Like I said, stuck at home." I tried to hold on to the hauteur, even though I didn't entirely feel it. I was going to miss my sister, and I knew I'd be homesick within days. But I couldn't say any of that. Talking about one's emotions wasn't the Eliot way, not before Mom's death, and certainly not after.

"At least *I'll* have plumbing, and cell service."

"And no life—"

"*Ever*. Enough." Dad's voice, raised in irritation, silenced us both. He hit the button to pop open the hatch.

Eden's gaze reflected her own conflict. She wanted to hold on to the argument because it was easier to snipe and bicker than to admit how scared she was. I could see that in her and feel it in myself. Our identical green eyes met, and understanding was achieved. Nothing was said out loud, but after a moment, I hugged Eden and we both sniffled. We'd never been apart before, not more than an hour or two a day in our entire lives.

"You better not let Michael make you skinnier than me," I said.

"Like *that'll* ever happen." She groaned. "He's gonna try to kill me, not that it'll make a difference."

Eden was slightly heavier than I was, not by much pounds-wise, but enough so that it resulted in a much curvier shape, and she was sensitive about it. Being mercilessly teased all of eighth grade hadn't helped much, so she was determined to get fit over the summer and show everyone in ninth grade how different she was. I had argued that the other girls were just jealous because Eden had tits and an ass and they didn't, but it had fallen on deaf ears. She'd convinced our father to hire her a personal trainer for the summer. Never mind that she was only four-teen and far too young to worry about bullshit like slimming down, but neither Dad nor I had been able to change Eden's mind.

It was part of Eden's grief, I knew. I painted and drew and took pictures, Eden played the cello. But it was deeper than that for Eden. We were nearly iden-tical images of our mother, dark hair, green eyes, fair skin, fine features, beautiful. I was closer to looking like Mom, slim and willowy, while Eden had gotten more of Daddy's genetics—he was short and stocky, naturally muscular. Eden wanted to remember Mom, to be more like her. She'd even taken to bleaching her hair, the way Mom had.

"We'll miss you, Ev," Dad said, twisting in the seat to meet my eyes. "It'll be too quiet around the house without you."

Like you'd notice, I wanted to say, but didn't. "I'll miss you too, Dad."

"Don't be a hooligan," Eden said, an inside joke of ours, referring to our maternal grandfather's favorite phrase.

"You either. And seriously, don't go too crazy with this Michael dude. You're not—"

Eden stuck her fingers in her ears. "LA-LA-LA-LA…I'm not listening!" she sing-songed. Removing her fingers, she said, "And seriously yourself, don't start."

I sighed. "Fine. Love you, ass-head."

"You too, butt-face."

Dad frowned at us. "Really? Are you two teenage girls or teenage boys?"

We both rolled our eyes, and then embraced one more time. I leaned forward and hugged Dad from between the seats, smelling the coffee on his breath. Then I was out of the car and opening the trunk hatch, and trying to juggle my purse and suitcase while closing the hatch. With a final backward wave, Dad and Eden were gone and I was alone, completely alone for the first time in my life.

A few feet away, a boy my own age was standing in the swirling, left-behind dust. He had a huge black duffel slung over one shoulder, and he was standing with his spine as straight as the pine tree trunks rising all around. One hand was shoved into his hip pocket, and he was toying with the strap of his bag with the other hand. One boot-clad toe was digging in the dirt, twisting and scuffing as he peered at the rows of cabins.

I couldn't help sneaking a second look at him. He wasn't like any boy I'd ever seen before. He looked to be about my own age, fourteen or fifteen, but he was tall, already almost six feet, and he was muscled more like an adult than a teenager. He had shaggy black hair that needed cutting, and the fuzzy scruff of a teenage boy hoping to grow a beard.

Until that moment, I'd never really had a crush before. Eden talked about boys all the time, and our friends were always going on about this boy or that boy, gushing about first kisses and first dates, but I had never really gotten too into all of that. I noticed cute boys at school, of course, because I wasn't dead or blind. But painting took up most of my time. Or, more accurately, waking up each day and not missing Mom took up most of my time, and painting helped that. I didn't have much brain space left for thinking about boys.

But this boy, the one standing six feet away from me, looking as nervous and out of place as I felt. There was something different about him.

Before I knew what was happening, my traitorous legs had carried me over to stand in front of him, and my traitorous voice was saying, "Hi…I'm Ever Eliot."

He turned his eyes to mine, and I almost gasped out loud. His eyes were pure amber, rich and complex and piercing. "Um. Hi. Caden Monroe." His voice was deep, although it broke on the last syllable. "Ever? That's your name?"

"Yeah." I'd never been self-conscious about my name before, but I wanted Caden to like my name as much as I liked his.

"It's a cool name. I've never known anyone with a name like that before."

"Yeah, it's unique, I guess. Caden is cool, too."

"It's Irish. My dad's name is Aidan, and my Gramps's name is Connor, and Great-Gramps's name was Paddy. Patrick. Irish names all the way back to my more-greats-than-I-can-remember Gramps, Daniel."

"Was he, like, an immigrant?" I flinched at the way I had unconsciously used "like" as a filler. So much for sounding smart.

"Well, all of our families were immigrants at some point, right? Unless you're Indian, that is. Native American, I mean." He rubbed the back of his neck,

and his cheeks flushed red. Which was sinfully ador-
able. "But yeah, Daniel Monroe was the first Monroe
to come to America. He came over in 1841."

I racked my brain for the significance of that date.
I'd learned about it in my world history class last year.
"Wasn't there this big thing in the 1840s? With Irish
people coming to America?"

Caden set his duffel on the ground. "I think it was
something about potatoes. A famine, or something."

"Yeah."

A long, awkward silence stretched out between
us.

Caden broke it first. "So. Ever. What do you…
do?"

"Do?"

He shrugged, then waved at the cabins and the
campus in general. "Art-wise, I mean. Are you a
musician, or…?"

"Oh. No, I'm an artist. I guess they'd call it a
visual artist. Painting, mostly. For now, at least. I like
all sorts of stuff. I want to get into sculpture. What
about you?"

"Same, although I draw more than anything."

"What do you draw? Comic books?" I regretted
that last part as soon as it came out of my mouth.
It sounded judgmental, and he didn't seem like the
comic book type. "I mean, or—animals?" That was

even worse. I felt myself blushing and wishing I could start over.

Caden just looked confused. "What? No, I don't draw any one thing. I mean, I do, just…it's whatever I'm working on. Right now I'm trying to figure out hands. I can't seem to draw hands right. Before that it was eyes, but I got those down."

"Sorry, I didn't mean—I'm an idiot sometimes, I just—" I was only making it worse now. I grabbed my suitcase by the handle and lugged it around, facing away from him. "I should go. Find my cabin."

A sun-browned hand took the suitcase from me and lifted it easily, which was ridiculous, since it weighed at least fifty pounds and I could barely move it. He had his duffel bag on his shoulder and my suitcase in one hand. "What number are you?"

I reached into my purse and unfolded my registration printout, even though I knew the cabin number by heart already; I didn't want to seem too eager. "Number ten."

Caden glanced at the numbers on the nearest cabins. "This way, then," he said. "I'm in twenty, and these are four, five, and six."

I cut my eyes to the side, watching the way his bicep tensed as he walked with the heavy suitcase. "Isn't my suitcase heavy?"

He shrugged, which made his duffel bag slip, and he hiked it higher. "A little. Not too bad."

After a too-short walk, we came to cabin number ten. I couldn't figure out how to delay him without sounding clingy or desperate, so I let him set my suitcase just inside the squeaky screen door, then waved as he shouldered his bag and strode off, rubbing the back of his neck in a way that made his bicep stand out.

I watched him go, and then realized several girls were clustered around the screen door as well, ogling him. "He's hot!" one of them said. They asked me who he was.

I wondered if the strangely possessive feeling in my gut was jealousy, and what I was supposed to do about it. "His name is Caden."

For the first time in a long time, my mind was occupied with something other than painting.

That afternoon there was a get-to-know-you thing, which was stupid, and then dinner and some free time, all of which passed in a blur. I didn't see Caden again that day, and as I slid into the thin, uncomfortable bunk bed, I wondered if he was thinking about me like I was him.

Somewhere out there, maybe a boy was thinking about me. I wasn't sure what it was supposed to mean, but it felt nice to imagine.

goodbye is not forever

Caden

Between art classes and the requisite camp activities—which were stupid bullshit—the first week of camp passed in a blur.

It was Monday afternoon, all-camp free time, so most everyone was gone somewhere—into downtown Traverse City, to Sleeping Bear Dunes, canoeing on one of the two lakes, swimming at Peterson Beach. There were a few students on campus, most of them doing the same as I was, finding a solitary place to play an instrument, paint, draw, or dance. I had found the perfect spot overlooking Green Lake, sitting with my back to a pine tree, sketchbook on my knees, trying to capture the way a duck's wings curved for landing as they floated over the rippling surface of the water.

I'd been there for over an hour already, the bark scratching my back through my T-shirt, earbuds in and playing my current favorite album, *Surfing With the Alien* by Joe Satriani. I'd drawn the same picture six times, each one a quick, rough sketch, capturing the outlines, the curves, the angle of the bird's body and the delicate arch of its neck. None of them were right, though. Like with my work on human hands, one particular detail was eluding me. This time, it was the pattern of the pinfeathers as the duck fluttered its wings, the way each feather rounded into the next, layered yet separate, while its green head and yellow beak thrust forward, the wings creating a bonnet around its body. I'd stuffed each failed sketch under my foot, using the last as reference for the next. My pencil went still as another duck approached the water. Its wings curved to slow its descent, orange feet outstretched, and then at the very last moment it reared back and flared its wings, braking to a stop and settling on the water with barely a sound or splash. I watched intently, my eyes and mind capturing the moment of wing-flare, watching the tips of its wings, then I glanced down and erased frantically, redrawing, pencil moving furiously now, line overlaying line, adjusting the curve and angles.

"You're really good," a voice said behind me.

I knew without turning who it was. "Thanks, Ever." Had I really remembered her voice after that one conversation?

I wished I didn't feel so self-conscious all of a sudden. Would she think I was stupid for drawing ducks? Watching them land had been fascinating when I was alone, and drawing them had captivated my focus for the last couple of hours, but now that a pretty girl was standing behind me...I was pretty sure it was the nerdiest thing ever.

I closed the sketchbook and set it on top of the pile of discarded sketches, standing up and brushing off the seat of my shorts. When I finally turned my gaze to Ever, I had to blink several times. I hadn't seen her since the day we arrived, despite looking for her in the visual arts classes and at meals. She'd been pretty then, dressed casually in jeans and a T-shirt. But now...she was so beautiful it made my stomach flip and tighten.

She was wearing a pair of khaki shorts that barely made it to mid-thigh, and a rib-hugging green tank top that matched the emerald of her eyes perfectly. Her hair hung in loose spirals around her shoulders, and she had a bulky easel under one arm, a canvas under the other arm, and a wooden carrying case for paints in her hand. A smudge of red paint stood out on her forehead, matching a similar smudge on her left wrist, and green paint was smeared near her right cheek and earlobe.

I felt an absurd compulsion to wipe away the paint with my thumb. Instead, I reached for the easel and took it from her. "Were you just setting up? Or heading back?" I asked.

She shrugged, and the strap of her tank top slipped over the round of her shoulder, revealing the white strap of her bra. "Neither. I was kinda just... walking around. Looking for something to paint."

"Oh. I was just...sketching. Ducks. Obviously." I felt myself blushing as I mumbled, forcing my gaze away from the overlapping green and white straps and the hint of pale skin as she brushed the strap back in place. "I don't really like ducks, I just...I thought the way they looked when they landed was kinda cool, and I—do you want me to carry your easel?" I felt like a spazz, shifting tracks so suddenly and blurting like an idiot.

Ever shrugged again, and the damn strap of her shirt slipped again. I wished she would stop shrugging so much, because it was wreaking hell on my ability to not stare at her. It wasn't just the strap, though, it was her chest, the way it lifted and settled along with her shoulders. I felt my cheeks burn and wondered if my thoughts were visible somehow, like I had a digital marquee on my forehead, announcing the fact that I was staring at her boobs.

"Sure," Ever said, and I had to refocus to remember what we were talking about. "It is kinda heavy."

Oh. The easel. Right. I leaned down and scooped up my sketchbook and papers, then adjusted the easel under my armpit more securely. "Where to?"

I was sensing a pattern now, and managed to avert my gaze *before* she did the shrug.

"I dunno. I was thinking somewhere on that side over there." She pointed to a not-too-distant portion of the Green Lake shoreline.

We traipsed through the woods along the shoreline, chatting about our art classes, comparing notes and complaints. Every once in a while, Ever would move ahead of me, and the way her shorts clung to her backside was so distracting I almost dropped the easel a few times.

This was new territory for me. Girls were just girls. There'd never been one who had grabbed my attention like this before, and I didn't know how to handle it. Of course, there were hot girls at school, and I looked at them, 'cause duh, I'm a guy. But this was different. Ever was someone I could see becoming a friend, and it was tricky having a friend you couldn't stop staring at like some wonderstruck moron. I felt like she had this power of reducing me to a mouth-breathing caveman.

Ook. Me Caden. You woman.

I trotted up to walk next to her, which was only nominally better. The problem was that anywhere I looked, there was something I shouldn't be staring at.

Eventually, she came a stop on a little knoll surrounded by trees with a stunning view of the lake. "This is good," she said. "I could paint this." I set the easel down and unfolded it, then moved away and watched her arrange her canvas on the easel, open her paint case and select a pencil. "You can't watch over my shoulder. That's weird and creepy, and I won't be able to think." She gestured off to one side. "Find your own spot, and we'll critique each other's work when we're done."

"So we're both drawing the same basic landscape scene?" I asked.

She nodded. "Well, I'll paint it. You draw it."

I found a place off to Ever's left, framing the lake between two huge jack pines. I set my pad on my crossed legs and started sketching, and pretty soon disappeared into capturing the scene before me. I didn't entirely forget about Ever, because she was hot even while painting—especially while painting, really. She was messy. She had a tendency to use her fingers as much as the brushes. She would swipe her bangs out of her face and get paint on her forehead and cheeks and nose. Even as I tried to force my attention back to the sketch in my book, she scratched her wrist with one hand, smearing orange paint on her wrist, and then rubbed her jaw with the same wrist.

I must have laughed out loud, because she glanced over at me. "What?" she asked.

"It's just...you have paint all over your face."

"I do?" She wiped at her cheek with one hand, which of course only smeared it worse.

I set my pad and pencils down and moved to stand next to her. "Yeah, it's...everywhere." I hesitated, then dragged my thumb lightly across her forehead and showed her the paint on my thumb.

She frowned, and then lifted the bottom edge of her shirt to wipe her face. At the sight of her stomach and the hint of white bra, I turned away. "Is that better?" she asked.

I turned back around. She had paint all over her shirt, but her face was clean. "Yeah, you got it off your face. Except..." I took a strand of her hair between my finger and thumb, and it came away green. "You have it in your hair, too."

"I'm a messy painter, I guess. I like to use my hands. At home, I don't even use brushes. But the teachers here want me to try and expand my 'vocabulary as an artist' or some bullshit like that." She put air quotes around the phrase, mocking it. "Mom was the same way."

Something in her eyes and voice when she mentioned her mother, along with the fact that she'd used past tense, had me on alert. "She's a messy painter?" I didn't want to ask, or assume anything.

"Was." Ever turned away from me and focused on her canvas, dabbing her brush into a glop of green on her palette, darkening the shade closer to the green of the pine needles.

"Why 'was'?"

"Because she's dead." She said it calmly, matter-of-factly, but too much so. "Car accident. Not quite a year and a half ago."

"I'm sorry," I said. "I mean…yeah. I'm sorry for your loss." That was a phrase I'd heard before, but it sounded awkward when I said it. Fake and empty.

Ever glanced at me. "Thanks." She wrinkled her nose. "We don't have to talk about it. It happened, and that's it. No point in getting all weepy about it."

I felt like she was putting on a brave face, but I didn't know how to tell her she didn't have to do that. If she wanted a brave face, what business was it of mine to say she shouldn't? I took a few deep breaths and then changed the subject. "I like your painting. It's not quite realistic, but not quite abstract, either."

It was an interesting piece. The trees were thick, blurry, smeared representations of trees, browns and greens that barely seemed like anything at all, but the lake beyond and between them was intensely real-istic, each ripple detailed and perfect, glinting and reflecting the sunlight.

"Thanks," she said. "I wasn't sure it would work when I started, but I think I like it." She stepped back, rubbing the side of her nose with her middle finger, blotting brown on her skin, then realized what she'd done and sighed. "Lemme see yours."

I hated showing people my drawings. I drew because I loved drawing. I drew because it just seemed to come out of me whether I intended to do it or not. I doodled all over my textbooks and notebooks at school, on my desk calendar at home, even on the leg of my jeans sometimes. I didn't draw to impress people. Letting someone see my work was like showing someone a part of me, it felt like. I showed my dad my drawings sometimes, because he was an engineer with a background in drafting and knew what he was talking about. And he was my dad and wouldn't be too harsh or critical.

What if Ever thought I was shitty? I liked her and wanted her to think I was cool, talented.

Before I could rethink the decision, I handed her my sketchpad. To disguise my nerves, I picked up a thick stick from the ground and started peeling the bark off it. Ever stared at my sketch for a long time, looking from it to the lake, and then walked to where I'd been sitting when I drew it. After what felt like a thousand years, she handed it back.

"You kick my ass at drawing. That's really amazing, Caden. It almost looks like a photo."

I shrugged, picking at the bark with my thumb-nail. "Thanks. It's not really all that photorealistic, but...it's not bad for a quick sketch."

She just nodded, and neither of us knew what to say. I wanted to be calm and cool and confident, make casual conversation and impress her with my wit. But that just wasn't me.

I was a bark-picker and a dirt-kicker, words sticking in my chest and tumbling around each other.

"We should draw each other. Just pencils and paper," Ever said, breaking the awkward silence.

"Sure," was all I could say. I flipped the pages of my book to an empty one, then realized she'd only brought her canvas, so I carefully ripped the page out and handed it to her. "You've got a pencil, right?"

Ever lifted her pencil in response, and then sat down cross-legged in the dirt. I sat facing her and tried to pretend that my eyes weren't drawn to her inner thighs, bared and looking softer than I could possibly imagine. I ducked my head and regrouped, then forced my gaze to her face. I started sketching, getting the basic shapes down first. By the time I'd finished the outline of her face and shoulders, I had an idea. I wanted to mimic her own style, mixing realism with abstraction. It flowed easily once I had the concept down. We were companionably silent then, glancing up at each other every now and again, but focused on our work.

Wind blew in the trees around us, and the sun filtered lower and lower, and somewhere voices echoed, laughing and yelling. The scent of pine trees was thick in the air, a smell so pungent it was almost visible. It was the scent of a northern Michigan summer, to me.

I didn't know how long we sat there drawing each other, and I didn't care. I had a sense of complete peace, soul-deep contentment. Our knees were touching, just our kneecaps brushing, and that was enough to make me feel euphoria. Then Ever shifted, and my right knee touched her left shin, pressing close and making my heart skip more beats than could possibly be healthy.

Finally, I knew the drawing was done. I examined it critically, adjusted a few lines and angles, and then nodded. I was pleased. I'd captured her face with as much realism as I possessed, her hair hanging in loose waves around one shoulder, head tilted, eyes downcast. The farther down her torso the drawing went, the more blurred and abstracted it got, so that her feet and knees were charcoal smudges on the paper.

I stood up, leaving the pad on the pine-needle-carpeted ground, and paced, working the blood back into my legs and numb backside. When I returned to my seat in front of Ever, she was holding my sketchbook and staring at it, an oddly emotional expression on her face.

"Is this how you see me?" she asked, not looking up at me.

"I—sort of? I mean, it's just a drawing. I was trying to mimic the way you did that landscape, you know?" I reached for my book, but she held on. "Are you…I mean, you're not mad or anything, are you?"

She shook her head and laughed. "No! Not at all. I was just expecting it to be a profile or something, you know? And this is totally not that. I don't know, Caden. You make me look—I don't know…prettier than I am."

"Not—um…I kind of think it doesn't do you justice. It's not good enough. You're…you're prettier than that."

"You think I'm pretty?"

I was beet red; I could feel it. Once again I wished I could say something debonair like James Bond would say in the old Sean Connery movies Dad watched every weekend. "Yeah."

Nice. Might as well have grunted like a Neanderthal.

Ever blushed and ducked her head, smoothing her hair over her shoulder with one hand. "Thanks." She glanced up at me, and our eyes met, locked. I wanted to look away, but couldn't. Her eyes were mesmerizing, green and almost luminous. "I almost don't want to show you my stupid drawing."

I reached for the drawing, but Ever didn't let go of it. Our fingers touched, and I swore actual physical sparks shot up from where our skin touched. Neither of us pulled away.

After a forever that could have fit into the space of a single breath, she let me take the sheet of paper, and touch became loss.

It was an amazing portrait of me, ultra-realistic. I was sitting cross-legged with my pad of paper, pencil held in my fingers, head down. You could just barely see the upper portion of my face, the frown of concentration.

"It's incredible, Ever," I said. "Really amazing." I was torn between admiration and jealousy. She was *really* good.

"Thanks."

She held my drawing, and I held hers. A cicada sang somewhere, the loud buzzing sound of summer.

"I have an evening composition class," I said. "I should probably go."

"Yeah. I should, too." She stood up, brushing off her backside, an action I tried not to watch, then handed me back my sketchpad. "I had a good time today. Maybe we could do this again. Another day."

I tore my drawing of her free and gave it to her. "Yeah. I'd like that."

"Cool."

"Cool."

She gave an odd, half-circle wave, then looked at her hand as if to question why it had done such an awkward thing. Then, before I could say anything, she gathered her things and left.

I watched her go, wondering what this thing was between us. Friendship? Something else? We'd only hung out twice, but it had felt like more than that. Like we knew each other somehow.

I went to class and then back to my cabin, where I stashed her drawing of me.

I didn't see Ever again until nearly the end of camp, even though I went out of my way to find her. Every time I went by her cabin she was gone, and I never saw her in any classes or workshops, or at dinner. I got a glimpse of her once, swimming with her cabin-mates, laughing and wet and beautiful, but I was with some guys from my own cabin, on the way to shoot hoops in the gym.

It was three days until the end of the camp. Late at night. I was supposed to be in bed, but I couldn't sleep. I had an unsettled feeling in my stomach, a restlessness that had no source or definition, just an anxiousness that I couldn't seem to dispel. I sneaked out of the cabin and went down to one of the docks.

It was a clear night, moonless and dark, lit only by a sky full of stars. The air held a touch of coolness, whispering over my skin. I hadn't bothered to put on a shirt, wearing a pair of gym shorts and sports sandals as I stepped lightly on the creaking wood of the long dock.

I was so wrapped up in my own thoughts that I didn't see or hear her until I was nearly on top of her.

Ever sat on the edge of the dock, feet dangling. I opened my mouth to speak, but then I saw that her shoulders were shaking. She was crying.

I didn't know what to do, what to say. She'd come down here to be alone—I mean, that much was obvious, right? And asking her if she was okay seemed stupid. I hesitated, turned to leave. I didn't know how to even begin comforting her, but I wanted to try. So I sat down next to her, dangling my feet over the black, rippling water.

She wasn't sobbing, just quietly crying. I put my hand on her shoulder and squeezed, a gentle touch that let her know I was there. A short hesitation, and then she turned into me and my arm went around her and held her. I felt wetness touch my shoulder, her tears on my skin. I held her, let her cry, and wondered if I was doing it right. If there was something I was supposed to be saying that would make it okay.

"I miss her, Caden." Her voice was tiny, barely audible. "I miss my mom. I—I miss home. I'm homesick. But most of all, I wish I could go home and see Mom again. Dad doesn't talk about her. Eden doesn't talk about her. I don't talk about her. It's like she died, and now we pretend like she never was."

"You can talk to me." I hoped that didn't sound too cliché.

"I don't know what to say. She's been dead a year and a half, and all I can really say is...I miss her. I miss how she made our family a family." She sniffled and straightened away from my shoulder, although our bodies were still flush against each other, hip to hip. I left my arm around her shoulders, and she didn't seem to mind. "Now it's just each of us by our-selves. Eden and I...we're twins, did I tell you that? We don't even really talk about her, or about missing her, or anything. And we're twins, we almost share a brain sometimes. Like, legit, we can read each other's thoughts sometimes."

"Nothing like that has ever happened in my fam-ily. I don't know how we'd handle it if it did. I know my dad probably wouldn't talk about it. My mom might. I'm like Dad, I think, and I'd have a hard time talking about things. I already do. I'm sure you can tell. I never know what to say." We were quiet for a while. But Ever needed someone to talk to. And I thought about last week, the two of us sitting by the lake, drawing—both of us knew how to speak with our hands and pencils. An idea came to me, and I said it without thinking. "What if we were pen pals?"

God, that sounded stupid.

"Pen pals?" At least, she didn't laugh at me outright.

"I know that sounds dumb, or whatever. But it can be hard to talk on the phone. And we don't really live close to each other, and…I just thought maybe if we wrote letters, we could talk about whatever we wanted, but on our own time." She hadn't said anything, and I was starting to feel intensely self-conscious. "I guess it's dumb."

"No, I…I like the idea. I think it's awesome." She turned and looked up at me. The starlight shone dim silver in her green eyes, and I felt like I could fall into them if I stared long enough. "Like, we'd write actual paper letters? Every month?"

"Yeah, that's what I was thinking. Or it could be more frequently, if we wanted to. Whenever, you know? Whenever we needed to say something." I ran my thumbnail in the grooved grain of the faded wood.

"I really…I think that would be awesome." She rested her head against my bicep.

We sat like that in the silence of a northern Michigan summer midnight, close and touching, but not embracing, not talking, lost in our own thoughts.

I heard voices behind us, turned to see two flashlight beams bobbing toward us. "We've been found," I said.

Just before our respective cabin staffers found us, Ever clutched my hand in hers. "Promise me you'll write?"

"I promise." I squeezed her with my arm, an awkward hug. "Good night, Ever."

"'Night, Caden." She hesitated a beat, and then turned into me, making it a full-fledged hug, bodies pressed against each other.

Totally worth the trouble I got in.

Pickup that Saturday was chaotic, a thousand cars, parents and campers reuniting. I found Dad leaning against the door of his truck, arms crossed. I spotted him from a distance, held up a finger to signal "one minute," then wove through the crowd, duffel bag on my shoulder, looking for black hair and green eyes and a body that had featured in more of my dreams than I cared to admit.

Ever was standing in the open door of a boxy silver Mercedes SUV, looking around almost frantically. She saw me and flew toward me, slamming into me and hugging me. I was so surprised that I didn't react for a moment, and then I dropped my bag and my arms went around her shoulders and I was hugging her back, holding her, smelling the shampoo in her hair and the faint, indefinable scent that made a girl smell like a girl.

When we pulled apart, I handed her a folded slip of paper on which I'd printed my name and address as neatly as I could. The paper she handed me had a heart on it, my name written in a curving, looping script within the heart. Did that mean something? Was the fact that she put my name inside the heart significant? Or was that just something girls did? I wished I knew, and I tried not to read too much into it.

"You'd better write me," she said.

"I will. I promise." I held onto the folded square of paper, not wanting to put it in my pocket in front of her. That would just feel rude somehow.

"Good. And I promise I'll write you back."

"You'd better." I heard her father say something to her sister Eden, and I shuffled back a few steps. "Good luck. You know, with…everything we talked about."

"You, too." She gave me a half-wave, a stiff semi-circle of her arm. Her eyes were on me and her lips were smiling, and it was all I could do to tear myself away, grab my duffel bag, and trot back toward Dad and the truck. My head was spinning, and my heart was doing strange sideways cartwheels.

Dad was waiting for me in the driver's seat, the engine idling, staring off out his window. His expression was pensive, brooding, and dark. I made sure to wipe the goofy grin off my face as I tossed my bag into the bed of the truck and ran the aged black rubber bungee cord through the handle, slipping the hook securely under the lip of the bed rim. I had

Ever's note in my palm, and I slid my hand against my thigh to hide it.

"Got a number, huh, bud?" Dad's voice was amused.

I glanced at him, stifling the urge to roll my eyes. "Sort of."

"How do you 'sort of' get a number?"

"It's not her phone number—it's her address."

"Her *address*?" Dad sounded incredulous. "You must have some serious game, Cade. Where does she live?"

Serious game? My dad was trying to be hip again, apparently. I lifted one shoulder in a shrug, not wanting to tell him about the pen pals idea, but knowing he'd pester me until I did. "I dunno where she lives. I haven't looked at it yet. Somewhere in Bloomfield, I think."

"Bloomfield, huh? The ritzy area. Her pops must be loaded."

I shrugged again, my standby response to pretty much everything. "I guess. I think he works for Chrysler or something. An executive or vice president. Something like that."

Dad huffed in sarcastic laughter. "'Something like that.' How informative. Did you learn anything definite about her?"

"Her name is Ever Eliot. She lives in Bloomfield. She's into painting and sculpture. She has a twin sister named Eden." I wasn't going to mention the fact that her mom had died in a car accident. It seemed like it would be a breach of confidence to tell him. "She's beautiful."

"You like her?"

I shrugged yet again. "I guess."

"You guess." He shook his head in frustration and then turned up the radio as "Springsteen" by Eric Church came on, and we both tuned in to listen. When the song ended, he turned it down again. "So this Ever girl aside, how was Interlochen?"

"It was good."

He waited a few beats, glancing at me expectantly. "Thousands of dollars and three *weeks*, and all I get out of you is 'it was good'?"

Ugh. Adults always wanted more information from me than I ever knew how to give them. "What do you want, Dad, a day-by-day breakdown? I don't know. I learned about all sorts of artistic bullshit. Angles, shading, perspective, composition. I tried my hand at oil painting and watercolor. Even tried clay sculpture, which I suck at. I took a class on drawing anatomy, which was pretty awesome. It was camp. I swam. Played basketball with some of the guys from my cabin."

"And met a pretty girl."

"And that. Yeah."

"Sounds like a great time." He grabbed my shoulder in his iron-hard fist and shook me, which was meant to be affectionate, but ended up feeling rough, like he was trying to be casual, or playful. "Think you'll go back next year?"

I'd been thinking about that a lot the last few days. "Maybe? I don't really know. I'm torn. I did have a good time, and I learned a lot, but...it was like a whole extra summer of school, just for art. Summers at the ranch with Gramps...it's just...different."

Dad nodded. "Well, think about it, I guess. You've got a year. I know Gramps would be happy to have you back next summer, but do what you want for you."

We kept quiet after that, listening to country and classic rock as the miles passed. The closer we got to home, the more pinched and worried Dad's expression became. I opened my mouth several times to ask him what was wrong, but never actually spoke. He'd pass it off, brush it off, say it was nothing for me to worry about. But if he was still acting stressed or worried after three weeks, there was something going on that my parents weren't telling me.

At home, I tried to ignore it, but as the summer days dwindled, bringing me closer to the start of ninth grade and my fifteenth birthday, I couldn't help noticing the whispered conversations while I was watching TV, the increasingly frequent times they left together on mysterious "errands," or the way Mom seemed to be withdrawing into herself. But when I walked into a room or started to ask Mom if she was okay, she pasted a smile on her face and changed the topic to some variation of whether I needed any more school supplies.

When I got home from my absolutely shitty first day of ninth grade, I sat at my desk in my room with the door closed, dug my American literature notebook from my backpack, and sat down to write to Ever for the first time.

Dear Ever,

I guess it kind of took me a while to sit down and write you this first letter. Sorry about that. Just getting ready for school and stuff, you know? I had my first day of school today. Ninth grade sucks so far. I know it's the first day or whatever and first days always suck, but I just have this feeling that high school is gonna blow. I'm not in any classes with any of my friends from last year, and our lunch periods are different, too, so I'm basically starting over. The seniors are assholes, I'll tell you that right now. I thought about trying out for the JV football team, but I'm not sure I want to even bother. I didn't get picked on, like I wasn't stuffed into any lockers like some nerd on TV, but they're just arrogant, pushy, loud douchebags.

How was your first day? I hope it was better than mine.

So I'm sitting here at my desk trying to write this letter, and seriously, I've got nothing. Writing a letter is harder than I thought it would be. It's not like having an actual conversation, you know? I feel like I'm talking to myself, which is dumb 'cause I don't usually do that, but that what it feels like. I'm not sure what to say. Is it childish to ask you questions? I guess I'm nervous this letter is going to come across like a first grader writing a letter to Santa.

So yeah. I guess I'm going to end it now. Not sure what else to say at this point.

Except, good luck with ninth grade.

Sincerely,

Caden Monroe

I folded the letter, stuffed it into an envelope, and mailed it before I could chicken out. My second, third, and fourth days of school were slightly better than the first, but not by much. My house was almost completely silent all the time now, and I was starting to freak out. Something big was going down, either between my parents or to one of them, and they weren't talking to me about it.

When I got back from school on Monday afternoon, a letter from Ever was sitting on the kitchen island. She had neat, bubbly cursive script handwriting, and each line of the front of the envelope was so straight I'd swear she'd used a ruler when she wrote

the address. And the envelope itself smelled funny,
like she'd sprayed it with perfume. Was that normal?
I didn't know. It smelled like Ever, though, and that
was an incredible thing. I might or might not have
sniffed the envelope a few times before opening it.

Dear Caden,

I'm so glad you actually wrote me! I was starting
to think you'd forgotten. I'm glad you didn't. I almost
decided to write you first. I'm not sure why, except it
seemed like you should be the one to go first. Does
that make any sense? Is that too traditional? I guess
maybe. I hope that doesn't bother you.

I'm sorry your first day of school was so bad.
Mine was okay. Eden and I are in only about half of
our classes together, which is fine with me. When we
do too many things together all the time, I start to
get a little claustrophobic. That's not the right word,
though, really. I'm not sure how to put it. It's a twin
thing. It's not claustrophobia exactly, because that's
more about fear of small spaces. This is more about...
identity? If I dress like Eden and look like Eden and
talk like Eden and have all the same classes with Eden
and have all the same friends as Eden, I start to feel
like me myself as Ever is getting lost a little bit, like
I'm just a twin, just one of a pair instead of someone totally unique and myself and not like her at all.

I mean, I am like her, I suppose, in some ways. We are twins after all, and we share, like, all of our DNA and whatever. But inside our heads and stuff? We're totally different. And I hate feeling like I'm stuck inside this twin-bubble even though I love her and couldn't ever live without her.

No, it's not weird for me to use the word "ever" in a sentence. A lot of people ask me that, so I figured I'd give you the answer before you asked.

As for school? Yeah, I know what you mean. The seniors are assholes. I know it's probably different for guys, but senior girls are just as big of assholes as the guys, I'm pretty sure. With senior girls, they're just evil, but they're usually subtle about it. Usually. It's this snipey, snippy attitude. They make fun of your outfit, which is a big deal for girls, if you didn't already know. They make fun of your shoes or your makeup or your purse, simply because you're not them. I'm pretty on top of fashion, I guess, but I just don't care enough to make sure I have the newest style purse or the latest shoes or whatever. It's just stupid. I like to look good, sure, but it's not as important to me as it is some other girls. The popular clique senior girls, it's all they care about. They're so vapid and shallow it makes me sick. They drive their daddy's BMW or Mercedes or Range Rover and act like they earned it. I know my dad has as much money as theirs, and I know that everything I have, all the clothes and whatever, is because of his job, not because of anything I did. These stupid senior girls, the cool, in-crowd ones? Have you ever seen that old movie *Clueless*? Probably not. It's this movie about all these, haha, clueless rich girls at a school in Beverly Hills, and they all act so superior because their daddies are rich. And that's how these idiotic Bloomfield Hills bitches act. Like how much money their daddy has versus mine versus the other girl and whoever is so important, like it's a social ladder, you know? And I just don't care. I don't.

I just want to paint and sculpt and not miss Mom anymore.

And by the way, your letter was totally fine. You sounded just like you, and that's what I wanted. It's fine to ask questions. Friends ask friends questions, right? So ask me anything, and don't ever feel weird about how your letters sound. No one will ever read them except me. Promise.

I guess I've rambled on enough for now, so I'll end here.

Funny, I almost wrote "let you go" like I was talking on the phone.

I hope school gets better for you. I'm looking forward to your next letter.

Sincerely,

Your friend,

Ever

indelible ink inscriptions

Dear Ever,

It's hard to write this letter. I'm not sure what to even say, but I feel like I can tell you things because we're friends, and somehow these letters are almost like a journal. I know you read them, and I read yours.

My mom has cancer. I just found out today. Breast cancer. I guess she's known for about two months, and they never told me. They wanted to wait and see if the chemotherapy would help before telling me, or something. I don't know. But I guess it's not helping, and they don't think anything will.

My dad told me. He used the same kinds of words I'm guessing the doctors used with him, big words, medical terms. All it means, once you cut through all the bullshit, is that Mom is going to die.

Shit. Seeing that in writing is so much different than thinking it.

What do I do?

She's afraid, and my dad is afraid. I'm afraid. But we're not talking about it. They talk about keeping up spirits and thinking positive and fighting to the end, and all that morale-raising shit. They don't believe it. I don't. No one does.

How can you, when each day passes and I can see her getting skinny, like the skeleton inside her is coming out through her skin? Am I supposed to tell myself it'll be okay when it won't?

Shit. I'm not a very good pen pal, I guess. I shouldn't be telling you this stuff. It's depressing.

I'm not even going to bother writing anymore. You don't have to write back, if you don't want to.

I hope you're okay.

Sincerely,

Your friend,

Caden

Caden,

Of course I'd write you back. I'll always write you back. This is what pen pals are for, after all, right? I'm okay. I learned a lot at the arts camp, and I'm using it all in my photography. Maybe next letter I send you I'll include a print of one of my photos. Daddy is thinking of making me a darkroom in the basement so I can do my own developing.

I guess I'm not sure how to talk about your news about your mom. I'm so sorry that's happening. I know "I'm sorry" or "that sucks" doesn't really help, but I don't know what else to write. I wouldn't try to tell you it'll be okay. When someone you love is hurt, or dying, or dies, it's not okay. I know how you feel. I lost my mom, too. She was in a car accident. I think we talked about this at camp. I told you, and I don't tell many people. But I feel like I can trust you. Maybe we understand each other, or something. Like, in some kind of way that words don't really explain. I feel that way. And I know what you mean about these pen-pal letters being like a journal. I write them and send them knowing you're going to read them, but I never feel embarrassed to write things that I wouldn't tell anyone else.

So I'll tell you this: write me as much as you want. I'll write you back every time. I promise. I'm your friend.

I'm sorry you're going through this. No one should have to go through it, but you are, and you have a friend in me. You can talk to me about what you feel.

Be strong, Caden.

Your friend for always,

Ever

I read Ever's letter ten times before I finally folded it back up, slid it carefully into the envelope, and tucked the envelope—which smelled ever so slightly of perfume, like her—in the front of the shoebox that contained the others from her. There were six letters so far, one for every week that had passed since the end of the Interlochen summer arts camp. I picked up the lid to the box, which had once contained the very shoes I was wearing, a pair of Reebok cross-trainers. They were a year old now, and getting too small. I wasn't sure why I had kept the box, but I had. It sat in the bottom of my closet, buried on the left side beneath an old hoodie and a ripped pair of jeans, until I had gotten the first letter from Ever Eliot and needed somewhere safe and private to keep the letter.

Now the blue box with the red Union Jack flag had six letters in it, and it sat under my bed.

I slid the box back under the frame of my bed and moved to my desk. Even though I had a laptop and there was a printer in the living room, I still wrote the letters by hand. I took a long time for each letter, because my handwriting was almost illegibly sloppy most of the time.

I sat staring down at the spiral-bound notebook for a long, long time, the pencil in my fingers, unable to summon the words. I blinked, took a deep breath, clicked the top of the mechanical pencil, and started writing.

Ever,

It feels stupid to write "dear" all the time. So I'll leave that part off, I guess, unless I think of something else to put there.

I'm writing, but I'm not really sure how long this letter will be. Mom is in the hospital full-time now. She stopped the chemo, said no to the surgeries. I guess they said they could do a surgery and it had a 20% chance of working, and it was really dangerous. She said no. They already removed her breasts. She has no hair. She's like a stick covered in paper now. She's my mom, in her eyes, but she's not. I don't know how to put it.

Ever, I'm scared. I'm afraid of losing her, yeah, but I'm afraid for my dad. He's losing his mind. I don't mean that in an exaggeration. I mean it for real. He doesn't leave her side, not even to eat. No one can, or even tries to make him leave.

Will it make me sound selfish if I say I'm afraid of losing him, too? It's like as sick as Mom gets, he's there with her. Going with her. But I'm only 15, and I need my parents. I know Mom is going to die, but does Dad have to go, too? He loves her so much, but what about me?

I hate how whiny that sounds.

Please send me one of your pictures.

Your always friend,

Caden

P.S. I tried something besides "sincerely" because that sounds stupid, too. But I'm not sure if what I put is more stupid.

P.P.S. Is there a difference between saying "photo" and "picture"?

I thought about signing it again, but didn't. Before I could chicken out, I folded the letter carefully and put it in an envelope, stuck a stamp to it, and put in the mailbox. I was home, and Dad was at the hospital. He always made me come home and do my homework before coming to the hospital. Something about "normalcy."

Like any such thing existed anymore.

Sometimes I would just sit at my desk with a pen and paper, like I was going to write a letter to Ever, but I didn't write it and I wouldn't, I knew I wouldn't, because I was delaying. Not going to the hospital. That's what I was doing. I was avoiding going, pretending like I was going to write a letter, when all I was doing was making an excuse not to have to see Mom dying. I knew I should see her, because she'd be gone soon and I wouldn't have a mother anymore, but I just...I didn't *want* to see her. I wanted for her either to be suddenly miraculously fine, or just...to die. To not suffer anymore. I didn't want her to die. Of course not. But that's what it felt like, deep inside me. I never said so, not to anyone, not even to Ever, but it was there inside me, and it was horrible.

So I sat, and tried to just not feel anything. I wasn't even drawing anymore. What was the point?

After putting the envelope in the mailbox, I sat on the front porch and delayed the walk to the bus stop a mile from our house, where the bus would pick me up and take me to the hospital where Mom was a skeleton in a bed, her insides being eaten by some invisible little creature bent on stealing my parents from me.

The distant mumble of the mailman's strange mailman car/van/truck thing echoed off the overhanging oak branches and 1950s brick house walls. Rumble...stop...rumble...stop, closer and closer. I knew he had a letter for me from Ever. I could feel it. I'd started to get a strange buzz in my stomach when the mailman had a letter for me from Ever. It wasn't anything magical or weird. I just...knew.

Finally the mail truck stopped in front of my house, and Jim the mailman poked his salt-and-pepper head out of the open doorway and reached into the mailbox and took my letter, rifled through a stack on his lap and stuffed bills and junk mail and circular ads into the mailbox, and then he held a white envelope in his gnarled fingers and pointed it at me, brown eyes twinkling, winking. I hopped down the three steps from porch to sidewalk and jogged over and took the envelope from him.

"Every week, Caden. You and this girl, one letter every week." His voice cracked a lot, deep as an abandoned mineshaft, broken by decades of cigarette smoke and gruff from yelling in Vietnam, I think. He was missing two fingers on his left hand, and if he wore a short-sleeved uniform shirt in the summer, you could see the shiny twisted skin where he'd been injured somehow. He limped when he had to set a box on the porch.

I nodded. "Yes, sir. One letter a week."

"You sweet on the girl?"

I shrugged. "We're pen pals. Friends."

Jim grinned with one side of his mouth. "Ah. You are. She's pretty, ain't she? Got long legs and soft hands, don't she?"

I hated these conversations adults always wanted to have with me whenever Ever came up. I shrugged and backed away from him. "I guess. She is pretty, yeah. Listen, though, I gotta—"

"Letters ain't no substitute for the real thing."

"We're just pen pals."

He nodded, gnawing thoughtfully on the inside of his mouth. "Gotcha." He waved. "See ya 'round, Cade."

"See ya, Jim." I held the letter balanced on my palm for a moment, watching Jim rumble away, then carried the letter, the sketchpad, and the pencil case to the bus stop, and waited for the bus. Ever's letter was on top of the sketchpad, between the smooth cover of the notebook and my palm. I would open it later, read it later.

Without conscious volition, the sketchpad opened, my fingers flipped pages to a blank white rectangle, and then a pencil, the dark outlining one, began moving over the page. The back of a mail truck appeared, a hand reaching for a mailbox. Details appeared, filled in. The truck itself became blurred, smudged and smeared, out of focus, while the hand and forearm gained clarity and sharpness and detail. The cords of the forearm, the gnarled knuckles, the fine graying hairs on the back of the hand and fingers, disguised shapes of letters clutched in the fingers.

A guttural diesel bellowing announced the arrival of the bus, and I boarded, paying the fare and finding a seat near the middle against the window. The bus resumed forward motion with reckless speed, and I watched the road flit and blur, holding the notebook open to my drawing of Jim's arm.

My heart was a stone in my chest, my stomach a knot pulled tight.

I had to walk half a mile from the bus stop to the
hospital, and my feet dragged. I pushed through the
doors, passed the reception desk to the elevators. As
the doors whooshed open, I had trouble swallowing.
Whenever I blinked, my eyes felt heavy and hard and
damp.

By the time I got to room 405, I couldn't breathe.
Dad was in the chair beside Mom's bed, where he
always was. He was bent over her, face to her knees, one
of her hands clutched in both of his. Her palm rested
against the back of his skull. Her index finger twitched.

I stopped in the doorway, watching a private
moment. I was intruding, I knew I was, but I couldn't
look away.

"Don't go, Jan." I heard Dad's voice, but it wasn't
even a whisper—it was broken shards of sound ripped
from his throat, sorrow made word.

I drew them. It was automatic. I sketched Dad,
his huge broad back hunched over, the bed and the
thin bumps of Mom's skeleton and skin beneath the
blanket, her shoulders and neck tilted against the bed
back, her hand on his head, one finger slightly curled
against his shaved scruff. I stood there in the doorway and drew the same scene over and over and over.
Neither of them saw me, and that was okay with me.

I lost count of how many times I drew them
there, until my pencil went dull and a nurse nudged
me aside with a cold hand on my forearm.

Then Dad sat up and turned around and saw me. His face contorted, twisted, his private grief morphing into the concern of a father.

"Don't...don't cry, Cade." Mom's voice, thin as a single strand of hair.

I hadn't realized I was, but then I looked down and saw that the page I'd been drawing on was dotted with droplet-rounds of wetness, and my face was wet, and the lines of my sketch were wrong, distorted and angular and just...wrong.

"Why?" I wasn't sure what I was asking, or of whom.

Dad only shook his head, and Mom couldn't even do that.

"Show me something...you drew," Mom asked me.

I flipped through the sketches of them, past hands and eyes and doodles of nothing and a bird on a branch and a winter tree like roots in reverse or an anatomical diagram of arteries or bronchioles. I found the duck I'd drawn at Interlochen, the best one, the final one, and I gently tore it out. She was too weak to take it, so I tucked it into her hand, into her fingers, pinching her thumb and forefinger around the middle at the edge. She gazed at it for a long time, like it was fancy piece of art at the Louvre.

"It's beautiful."

"It's a duck, Mom." I was supposed to act normal, I knew. Protest, argue like always, act like a petulant teenager.

"It's…a beautiful duck." She smiled, teasing me with her eyes and her voice. "Quack."

"Quack." I sniffled, a laugh and cry at once. Mom was the only one who could get me to laugh, to be funny when I was always so serious like Dad.

"*Quack*, Aidan. Quack."

Dad frowned at both of us. "Quack?"

I nodded, as if he'd gotten it. "Quack."

Mom laughed, but it turned into a cough, weak and faint. Dad was confused. Mom's hand slid off Dad's head, slumped to his shoulder, and her finger wrapped around my pinky. "I love you, Caden Connor Monroe. Always draw. Art is beautiful. You're beautiful."

I shook my head, hearing the goodbye buried beneath her words. "No, Mom. No. You're beautiful. You're art."

She smiled at me, squeezed my pinky with her index finger, and I squeezed back. Her gaze shifted from me to Dad. She slid her hand from between his paws, and lifted her palm to his face. It was a herculean effort.

She didn't say anything to him, not one word, but I heard it all. It was a poem, the look she gave him. I knew then that I would someday draw that expression in her eyes, and it would be the greatest piece of art I would ever make. But I couldn't do it then. I wasn't capable.

I had Ever's letter in my back pocket, curved and wrinkled from being sat on, a notebook in my hands and a pencil behind my right ear. I felt a sensation of disembodiment. I wasn't me; I wasn't there at all, I was just a point of consciousness without a body, without clothes, without sadness or sorrow, watching my mother's loving gaze lock on my father's desperate wet eyes and fade, fade.

"Jan."

Her eyes went still and vacant, nothing there, not her, not life, not sadness. Her last words were silent, meant for my father. For her husband. I watched as Dad realized she was gone. His shoulders trembled, heavy with muscle yet so frail, so fragile.

And then, like a sudden explosion, he shot up, the chair clanging backward to the floor, and he crossed the room in two long strides, and his fist rocketed out, smashed into the wood of the door post. The door frame crumpled, the wood splintered, the plaster crumbled and cracked, and then he fell against the frame and held on, skin broken and bleeding.

A nurse looked on from the hallway, and she did nothing for a long moment, time like a plateau in the silence.

It wasn't silent, though. We were in a hospital. The monitor blared a monotone signal song of death, a voice echoed incomprehensibly off the walls, and people came and went, oblivious.

I stood where I was, beside the bed. I couldn't move. Dad was on the floor, a proud, strong man weeping in a ball on the floor. That was what uprooted me: Dad, there on the floor. He didn't belong there. I moved to kneel beside him, wrapped two hands around his thick arm and lifted. I felt like a little boy tugging on his bulk. I wasn't, though. I burrowed underneath his chest, set my back to his front, and lifted, bodily heaving him off the floor. He clung to me, weeping silently. I held him up, and he stared past me at Mom, at the corpse that had been her.

I dragged him away. He stumbled beside me, mumbling something I couldn't understand. Someone called my name, Dad's name, but we both ignored the voice.

I found Dad's truck, way in the back of the massive parking garage on the third floor. He was shuffling beside me, as if emptied somehow of his vitality. He always hooked his keys to his belt loop by a thick black carabiner clip, and I unhooked them. I unlocked the doors and had to wrestle Dad into the passenger seat. He slumped against the window, forehead to the glass, staring unseeing.

I climbed into the driver's seat, adjusted the seat and the steering wheel and the mirrors. I'd driven for the first time when I was twelve, on Gramps's ranch, and whenever I was there I'd get to drive by myself. I didn't have a permit or a license, but I didn't care right then. I backed out of the parking spot, slowly and carefully, and navigated out of the garage, out of the hospital campus, onto the main road. I knew the way home, and I drove us there as carefully as I could.

I was numb, felt nothing. Empty.

Dad never said a word, never even moved. Sometimes I wasn't even sure he was breathing, but then the glass would fog from his breath and I would have to look away to drive.

I got us home, helped Dad out and up to his bedroom. He stopped in the doorway, staring at the bed, made carefully, comforter folded back from the plump white pillows. He shook his head, the first sign of life since the hospital. He slewed around, stumped down the stairs slowly, heavily. I followed him, unsure what to do. He went into the kitchen, stood in front of the refrigerator, opened the cupboard above it, and pulled out a bottle of Jack Daniels, full to an inch beneath the neck. He twisted the top off and drank from the bottle, three long glugging pulls. I watched, emotionless. It was expected, some part of me thought. This is what you did when your wife died.

But what was I supposed to do when my mom died?

I took the bottle from him, and he met my eyes. His vacant stare flickered slightly, and I saw some sign of himself, some warring decision, and then he went vacant and distant again, and he released the bottle into my grip.

The whiskey burned my throat, my chest, my stomach. I coughed, hacked, and sputtered. And then drank again, and a third time. By the third time, my gut was roiling, heaving, and heavy. My head spun, and I gave the bottle back to him.

He stumbled past me, into his study. He had a futon in there, and he'd slept there a couple times when he and Mom had had an argument. He fell onto it, whiskey sloshing onto his hand. He drank from the bottle again, then leaned his head back and closed his eyes. I watched a tear fall.

"Jan." It was a sob, and that was when I closed the door.

Such grief was too private to witness.

I was dizzy, drunk for the first time in my life. I went up to my room and sat at my desk. There was only one person I wanted to talk to.

Evr,

shes gone. Watched her die just now. It was just this quiet slipping away. she quacked at me. I showed her the sketch of the duck I did at Interlochen. You remember? I showed her that sketch, and she quacked at me. Like a duck. she told me she loved me.

I still have the letter you sent me in my pocket. Its unopened. I havent read it yet. I might be a little drunk. Is that okay? I didn't know what else to do. Its too much. Too too too much. What the fuck am I supposed to do?

I drove my dad home. From the hospital. I just left her there. But shes not there, is she. Mom is gone. The body in the bed is just meat. But we still just left her there. What happens next? Dad is gone too. Not dead, but just broken. I don't know if he'll ever be fixed. I think he needed Mom too much to live without her, and now he's just meat too. So what about me?

In the last letter I read, from last week, you talked about your dad getting you a darkroom for your photography, but I realized after I'd sent the letter back that I didn't know you were into photography too. Is that new? I know you paint and want to sculpt but I don't remember ever talking about photography. That was just a random thought in my head.

I'm afraid. Will I always be alone? I'm only fifteen. Maybe Dad will just fade away, just stop being alive. Can I stop being alive too? I don't know what to do next. Its like this huge wave has been cresting for weeks and just

now broke and Im drowning. I saw a movie about someone surfing once, and they got rolled by a wave and the
wave kept rolling and rolling and they got sucked under
and spun so they couldn't ever find the air or find the
surface and thats what I feel like, rolled and rolled under
this huge wave that won't let me up and I can't breathe.

I think this is where art is supposed to save me. I'm
supposed to become this amazing artist because I'm
going through tragedy, and that's what births all the
great art, right, is going through something awful and
having art to express it with, but I'm not sure I have that
inside me. I feel like even art is being sucked under. I
drew one of Mom's last moments, though. Dad, beside
her. Waiting. Knowing.

Why didn't they tell me? Why did they act like
nothing was wrong until it was too late? I feel like I got
robbed of goodbye. I would have

I don't know what I would have done. Spent more
time with her. Loved her better. Now there's just nothing.

Just me, and I don't know what to do.

Sorry for the awful letter.

Cade

Spinning walls and tilting ceiling met my gaze.
The words I'd written blurred on the page, twisted
and contorted. I knew it was unfair, but some part

of me, the part responsible for caring about…life, maturity, others, anything…that part was beyond my grip. I shouldn't send this to Ever, but I was going to anyway. I needed these feelings, the things I'd put on the page, to be out there, outside of me. Being able to write letters to someone who couldn't judge me, who would write back and seem sympathetic and friendly, it helped me be me, helped me feel okay.

Now, nothing was okay, and sending this letter to Ever seemed necessary. It would make me okay.

I found the stamps where they always were, in the kitchen, in the junk drawer with scissors and a Phillips screwdriver and a crescent wrench and some tape and mismatched keys on a plastic American flag keychain. There were six stamps left. I had a flash of memory, vivid and hitting me like a hammer, of Mom, just a few weeks ago, digging through this drawer, looking for something—an Allen wrench to fix a wobbly side table, I think—and saying we needed more stamps, that she'd get more next time she went to the post office. Only, that never happened. She got too sick to go to the post office, got too sick to even leave her bed, and that was when Dad took her to the hospital for good. For the end.

And now there were only six stamps left.

I'd never bought stamps before. What would I do when they were gone? I'd have to buy more somehow. What if Dad just stopped living? What if

he totally gave up and I was left to fend for myself?
I was a teenage boy. I was fifteen. I didn't know how
to cook. I didn't know how to do laundry or earn
money. I needed parents.

What I had was six stamps left. A single row of
pastel Benjamin Franklins, one after another. Sweat
broke out on my face, and I stumbled to the side,
dropping my letter on the floor. My stomach pro-
tested as I lurched again, stamps in my fist. I regained
my balance, clutching the counter with my empty
hand, staring at the small white rectangle face down
on the tile. I had to lean over very carefully to pick
up the envelope.

The initial rush of the alcohol had seemed
euphoric and heady, but now it was changing inside
me. Drunk was no longer so much fun. I just felt sick,
and my emotions were rampant and raging through
me without any filters to control them.

It felt like it should be midnight. Death should
only happen at night, in the darkness and the shadows. But it was still light outside. I took one careful
step after another out of the kitchen, through the
living room with the gray microfiber sectional Mom
had been so proud of and the sixty-inch flat-screen
Dad loved so much and out the front door. The heavy
glass storm door slammed back closed before I was
through, bashing me in the shoulder and sending me
stumbling to the side. I caught myself on the railing

of the front porch and stood waiting for the evening world to stop spinning.

It was the golden moment of sundown. The sun was behind the trees and the buildings, but brilliantly shining amber, sending spears of light scattering across the street and the siding and brick and through car windows and house windows and all over everything. It was like a cosmic balloon full of golden light had been popped somewhere beyond the sky and the luminous contents were spilling around me, bathing me with sundeath glory.

I wasn't sure that metaphor made any sense, even as it passed through my head, but it sounded poetic.

A robin's egg–blue Toyota Prius slipped quietly down my street, a lance of golden light slicing across the hood and then the roof, and then the little car was gone, rounding a corner onto Garfield Avenue. The passage of the Prius seemed significant, somehow. Like it meant something in some way I was simply too drunk to comprehend.

I blinked, glanced down at the letter in my hand. I realized I hadn't addressed it. I swore out loud, stumbled around in a full circle before I managed to find the front door. Only instead of going through it, I fell backward into the porch swing, an aged bench with spotted silver chain links that creaked when the swing moved. Oh, god. Oh, god. The swing swept me off my feet, and now I was swinging backward and forward, backward and forward, swinging, sun-light moving and shifting.

The letter. I still had my shading pencil behind my ear. I pinched it between deliberate fingers, set the envelope on the wide, smooth-worn armrest, and wrote my return address in small, shaky, and neat letters. Then, in the center, I wrote her name. *EVER ELIOT.* That was good. Each letter was per-fectly formed, neat and angular. Her street name and number floated through my head, and I focused all my attention on making the pencil do my bid-ding. *17889 Crabtree Road, Bloomfield Hills.* I couldn't remember the zip code, for some reason. I racked my brain, but it wouldn't come. 48073? No, that was Royal Oak. Why did I know the zip code for Royal Oak, but not for Ever in Bloomfield Hills, when I wrote it on her letters every week?

Aha! I lifted my left hip and clumsily fished her letter from my back pocket. 48301, that was it.

I penciled in the zip code and made my way down the three steps to the sidewalk, holding on to the railing and measuring each motion with extreme care. At the bottom of the steps, I fixed my gaze on the mailbox at the end of the driveway; it suddenly looked to be a mile away. I resolved to make it to the mailbox and back without embarrassing myself. It wasn't far, was it? Only twenty feet or so. But when the street and sidewalk and grass were tipping and bucking the way they were, twenty feet might have been a thousand. I left the safety of the railing and took a step, feeling like an astronaut moving away from the protective shelter of a spaceship on a far-away planet. I focused on the mailbox, not counting steps, and trying to act completely normal. Did I look as messed up as I was? I felt like I had a blazing neon sign plastered on my forehead, announcing to the world that I was drunker than anyone had ever been in the history of drunkenness.

I made it to the mailbox after an eternity of carefully placing one foot precisely in front of the other. I opened the black metal front, slid the letter in, closed it, and lifted the red flag. Wait, had I put a stamp on it? I opened the box again and peered blearily at the letter. Yes, old Ben with his idiotic little smirk stared up at me, slightly cockeyed on the envelope.

Now to make it back. No problem at all.

Except for that huge canyon of a crack at the edge of the driveway. When did that get there? And why was it suddenly such a massive problem? It grabbed my toe and sent me sprawling in the grass. Green blades tickled my toes, my cheek, my palms. Even lying down, things spun.

This was not fun.

Mom was still gone, and being drunk didn't help. Well…maybe it did, just a little. The pain was distant. It didn't feel like pain—it felt like something I knew about, like knowing I had a test to take in a few months. It would happen, and it would suck, but I didn't have to think about it right now.

I had to get up. I couldn't stay here on the grass. That would raise suspicion if anyone saw me. People didn't go around lying on their front lawns at six in the evening—or ever, for that matter.

Ever. Ever.

Ever.

I wondered what her latest letter said. Time to get up. I could do it, easy peasy. I climbed to my feet, brushed off my knees and the seat of my jeans. The letter wasn't in my back pocket anymore; where was it? I spun in stumbling circles, scanning the ground. Nothing. Where was it? Panic shot through me. I couldn't lose that letter. It was important. Ever's words to me were important. They were written for me. Meant for me. No one else. It meant she thought about me. That maybe she cared about me.

My gaze landed on the porch, up three steps. There it was, beneath the porch swing. Relief. Up the steps, maybe possibly using both hands on the railing to haul myself up. I landed on the swing, which again swept my feet out from beneath me and swung me in the golden light. I ended up not quite lying down, not quite sitting up.

Finally in possession of the precious letter, and a seat, I held the envelope in both hands and stared at it. The letters of my name and the numbers of my street address faded and blurred and doubled.

I was too drunk to read the damn letter. I fumbled it back into my pocket and tried to calm the dizziness in my skull. I hated this, hated being drunk.

Why did Dad think this would help anything?

I was suddenly exhausted, my eyes heavy and hot. My stomach roiled and twisted, and the swing drifted. The golden haze of sunset was gone, leaving behind an orange-pink fading into gray. I watched the leaves of a tree shake in the breeze, and watched the gray become thicker and darker, and then heaviness overtook me and my head lolled back on the swing.

I woke up sick and disoriented. All was silent and dark around me, blackest night unbroken except by a distant streetlight, the one way down by Eisenhower. None of the houses had porch lights on, no cars passed, there were no stars and no moon. Only darkness, and the sound of my breathing.

Vomit surged in my throat, rising without warning to hit my teeth. I lurched off the swing to lean over the railing and empty my stomach in a hot, acidic flood into Mom's azaleas. Again and again my stomach revolted, eventually leaving me limp against the cold wood, heaving in deep breaths and hoping it was over. I had nothing left to throw up, but still my stomach coiled into knots.

I waited until nothing else came up, and then went inside. Ever's letter was crumpled now. I smoothed it against my thigh, considered opening it and reading it right there in the dim foyer. Not yet. Dad's study was on my right, the door closed. I opened it, peered in. He was on the floor, face down, the bottle under his armpit, empty. His eyes were closed, loud snores coming from him. At least he was alive. I should do something for him. Help him somehow.

I knelt beside him, tugged the empty bottle free, and set it aside. He didn't twitch or respond in any way, just kept snoring.

I shook his shoulder. "Dad. Hey, Dad. Wake up. Get off the floor." Not even a snort. I shook him harder. "Dad!"

He rolled suddenly, knocked me stumbling with his outstretched arm. I heard a retching sound come from him, saw bile trickling from the corner of his mouth. I lunged for him, shoved him onto his side, and a stream of puke glumped from his lips to the carpet. Gagging, I grabbed Dad's arm, dragged him away from the pile of mess. At which point he vomited again.

I let go of his hand and fell backward to my ass, sickness and frustration eliciting a whimper from me. Dad retched again, and again, and then finally groaned as if coming to consciousness. I inhaled deep breaths, trying to calm myself, but the smell of puke overpowered me and I choked, coughed, pushed down my gag reflex, pushed down the tears that boiled just beneath the surface.

Dad sat up groggily, blinking, peered around, saw the mess he'd made, saw me, and then struggled to his feet. He lurched to the futon, his foot slipping in the mess, and collapsed onto his back.

"Jan..." he murmured, the word a broken sob. A tear trickled down his cheek.

I sat with my back to the wall, watching my father weep in his drunken sleep. My proud, strong, father. He'd rarely ever even yelled or raised his voice, even when I'd hit a baseball into the windshield of his truck, or when he and Mom were arguing about something. I'd never seen him sad, or upset beyond irritation and quiet anger. Watching him cry now was simply too much.

Something with sharp, shuddering claws seized my chest and shook me. A sob wracked me, and another.

I clamped my teeth together and cried silently for a full minute, hot tears on my face, refusing to sob out loud. I was hyperventilating, gasping for breath, face buried in my hands, choking on my own tears. I had no thoughts, only sorrow. Confusion. I was alone in this. Dad was alone in this. Shouldn't this bind us closer?

But there I was, alone in my agony.

I forced myself to my feet, wiping at my face with my palms. I found a towel from the hall linen closet and wiped up Dad's mess. It was slimy and hot under the towel. It took four bath towels and half a can of Resolve carpet cleaner. I put the towels into the washing machine. After a few minutes of tinkering, I found the pull-out drawer for detergent, which was clearly marked with "normal" and "max" fill lines, and another cup for fabric softener. I found the corresponding bottles and filled the machine, turned it on, and set it to run on normal.

The first load of laundry I'd ever done on my own.

I felt older than fifteen. I felt ancient. Empty and worn through.

The kitchen was dark and silent and seemed like a foreign place, a strange land I'd never seen before. The green-blue numbers of the microwave clock read 3:32 a.m.

Now what?

I was exhausted, but knew I wouldn't be able to sleep. Already, every time I closed my eyes I saw Mom, saw the way her eyes had gone dead. Her hand going limp. Dad smashing his fist against the door frame. Nurses watching with pointless sympathy. The flatline tone of the monitor.

I refused the sob that trembled inside me, closed my eyes and breathed through it. It passed, and I leaned back against the counter by the sink, listening to it drip, a slow *pit…pit…pit….*

The letter. Ever's letter. I turned on the overhead light and sat down at the kitchen table, placing the crumpled envelope flat on the surface and smoothing it with my palm. I slid my finger under the flap.

Why was I nervous? There was no reason to be. I think I was hoping her letter would provide some kind of comfort.

Caden,

Or I suppose I might actually address the letters "Dear Caden," since you are dear. To me, I mean. Is that weird? Maybe it is. "Dear" means, according to Google, "regarded with deep affection; cherished by someone." I hope that's not too weird for you, but I feel like you and I have a special connection. Do you think so, too?

I'm so, so sorry about your mom getting sicker. I can't imagine going through that. When I lost my mom to the car accident, it was the most horrible thing I've ever experienced. One minute she was there, alive and fine, and then the next Daddy was telling me she was dead. No warning, just…dead. I was home, doing homework, and Daddy came into my room. He was crying. A grown man crying is just…wrong. Grown men don't cry. They just don't. You know? And he was crying, big fat tears on his cheeks and his chin, and he could barely get the words out. Still, I remember the moment as clear as day: "your mom...she was in a car accident, Ev. She's dead. They couldn't save her. On impact, they said." He couldn't say anything else, the words just wouldn't come out. He hasn't been the same since. He just...stopped being himself. Whoever he is now, it's like some part of him died with Mom. You hear about that, right? You read about it in books. I have, at least. But now I see that it's true.

I guess my point is, for me, it was just bam, she's gone. For you...watching it happen? I don't know. I'm just so sorry you're going through it, and I wish I could say something or do something that would help you.

My dad kind of lost it, too. I think I already said that, but it's worth repeating. He's never been the same since. I don't know. I'm fifteen, and I need my parents, but I only have one and he's not really a parent anymore. He goes to work, and he's there all day, and he doesn't really care what we do. He's just...a paycheck, I guess. Which, if I have to be basically an orphan, at least I don't have to worry about starving, right? #alwayslookforthebrightside

Sorry for the hashtag. Everyone at school uses them. Like, ALL THE TIME. It kind of irritates me sometimes, all the text messages and Facebook posts with hashtags in them, but it's become part of the popular method of expression, you know? So I sort of end up using them.

I know I'm rambling. Sorry. I'm supposed to be doing homework, but I'm putting it off. I'd rather spend my time writing you a letter. I know I look forward to your letters, so I guess I'm assuming you look forward to mine, too. I reread your letters, and I have them all saved in a shoebox. Is that weird? It's a box from a pair of Steve Maddens that Daddy bought me the week before Mom died. The shoes don't fit anymore, but the box is awesome, and they were seriously killer shoes.

I guess you don't care about shoes. Guys don't, right?

God, this letter is like four pages long. I'll sign off and do my homework I guess. Write me soon!

Dearly and sincerely,

Your forever friend,

Ever

P.S.: You can start and end your letters however you want. It doesn't matter to me. Nothing will sound stupid to me, I promise.

P.P.S.: No, and yes. A photo is a picture, and a picture can be a photo. But a picture is not always a photo, while a photo is always a picture. LOL. Sounds like an algebra word problem, doesn't it? The point is, you can call it a photo or photograph, or a picture. I tend to use "photo" since that sounds more...professional, I guess. That's just me, though. I didn't have an envelope big enough to send a photo without bending it, so I'll get some big envelopes and include one in the next letter, okay?

I read the letter four times. Especially the "dearly and sincerely" part. And the "Your forever friend" part. I wanted that to mean something, to be deep and personal and meaningful and lasting.

Or I suppose I wanted anything to be all of that, since nothing in my life right then was.

painted by pain

Ever

I dropped Caden's latest letter onto the bed and cried. It was for him that I cried, but also for me. His mom's death reminded me all too poignantly of my own dead mother. I knew there was no comparison in the ways we'd lost our moms, but I also knew pain was pain, always relative to the person feeling it. All I could go by was my own pain, and try to empathize with Caden. He'd lost her in the most horrible way possible: slowly.

His pain bled through the pages of his letter. It was in the way he was clearly drunk while writing it, in the uncharacteristic misspellings, in the things he didn't say. I'd learned to read between the lines of his words to see what he wasn't saying, but was trying to. He was lost and alone and desperate.

I wished I could do something besides write him another letter. But I couldn't. I didn't have a license or a car, and Daddy was at work, probably not due home until nine or ten at night. He stayed at work later and later these days. He'd be at work already by the time I got up for school at six, and he wouldn't be home until eight at the soonest, usually later. Sometimes he wouldn't come home at all. He slept in his office, I supposed.

The only thing I could do was write Caden a letter.

Or…I could paint him a picture and mail it to him.

I left the letter on my bed and went into my studio. There were five bedrooms in our house; Dad slept in one, Eden in one, me in another, and then Eden and I each had our own private studios, me for painting and Eden for playing cello. I put on my painting shirt, an old white long-sleeved button-down of Daddy's. It was huge on me; the sleeves rolled four times still came to my forearms, and the hem fell just above my knees. I liked to paint wearing just the shirt. The free feeling of the soft cotton against my skin let me focus all of my attention on painting. I left my T-shirt and jeans in a pile on the floor, locked the door, and unfolded my painting case.

I stroked the smooth wood of the case's edge, thinking of Mom. The case was the last gift she'd ever given me, a reward for getting straight A's for the first half of the year. I was supposed to have gotten an even bigger gift for a 4.0 at the end of the full year, but she'd died and Daddy hadn't followed through on her promise. Not that it mattered now. If it wasn't *her* giving me the present, it didn't really matter.

Now the case was my most prized possession. I didn't care about anything else. The expensive clothes I'd once been so consumed with, the latest iPhone and jewelry, all that? None of it mattered. Mom had been an artist, and the paint case was all I really had left of her.

Thinking of Mom, and then Caden, I dabbed my brush—a medium-point one, just to start out with—into the blue. Sometimes, if I knew exactly what I was setting out to paint, I would use a pencil and sketch it out first. Other times, like now, when I was letting my instincts take over, I just painted without any planning or forethought. I imagined my mind as a canvas as blank as the one in front of me, and let my hand and wrist take over. It was pure emotion, really. I tapped into my gut, my heart, and my soul.

One stroke began the process. A single diagonal sweep across the lower left corner of the canvas. Another. A curve. Suddenly, it was a lake, rippling and unfocused. More brushes, finer ones, broader ones, melded colors and smeared shades. An image of Caden flashed into my mind, the way I'd drawn him that day beside the lake. I imagined him alone at home, in bed. On his back staring up at the ceiling, tears trickling down the side of his face onto his pillow. He'd cry alone, in his room.

Me? After Mom died, I would burst into tears at the most random times. I couldn't help it. I'd be in math class and then I'd be crying, and people would stare at me because they *knew*. Caden would likely hold it in and wait until he was at home in his room, and then he'd just quietly let go. Or maybe he wouldn't, not ever. He'd hold it in and hold it in, and never let it out, and then someday he'd explode, because he never let it out.

A sun appeared in the sky above the lake, blurred yellow and bright, reflecting on the water. Trees. Bushes. A clearing just beneath the lake, which would be the foreground, the focal point of the piece.

And then Caden. Just the back of him, his hair shaggy and thick and brown like bear fur. Broad shoulders, also like a bear. He'd be big like a grizzly when he was full-grown, I knew. I had an image of him ten years from now, huge and burly, with unkempt but beautifully wild hair, and eyes like burning dark brown orbs in his handsome face. I didn't paint him that way, but I imagined it. I saw his eyes, and in my fantasy he was smiling at me, teeth white as porcelain and even. In the painting, he was facing the lake, one hand at his side, the other, the left, stretched out to the side. He was reaching for something. For some-one. For someone to hold his hand.

I couldn't help it. It was how the painting was meant to be, so I let it happen. I painted myself beside him, my hair loose and tangled in the breeze around my shoulders, nearly to my waist. My right hand was outstretched as well. Reaching for him. Our fingers didn't quite touch. It was painful to paint it that way. Literally, physically painful. I wanted our hands in the painting to touch, to tangle and twine, but they didn't. A breath of wind blew between them, in the space between our fingertips. I could feel the wind, and so I painted the leaves skirling around our feet, autumn reds and yellows and oranges, broad maple leaves.

I stepped back and stared at the painting, head tilted to one side, trying to figure out what it was missing.

Oh.

Two doves, flitting between the trees, almost invisible through the foliage. Two doves, side by side, flying away from Caden and me.

He'd know what that meant. He'd get it.

It was done, then. I took off my paint shirt, washed my hands and face, as I inevitably got paint on myself, then re-dressed and left the piece to dry.

For once, I hated the length of time it took to let oil paint dry; usually I didn't care, as I only painted for myself. I had stacks of paintings in the corner of my studio, dozens and dozens of unframed pieces, with others lying face up on my drop cloth to dry. I left Caden's piece on the easel, knowing I'd want to look at it later, perhaps adjust it or correct it. I preserved my mixed colors and washed my brushes, closed the window, and left the studio.

For the next few days, though, I couldn't get the painting out of my head. The next time I looked at it, I knew it was complete, needing no alterations. I saw it when I closed my eyes to sleep, the way Caden's and my fingers didn't quite meet. It was torture.

What did it mean? Why did I want our paint-selves to hold hands?

I even dreamed of the painting. I was on a bluff overlooking a too-blue lake. Everything was that too-colorful, too-vivid brilliance of dreaming. I felt wind blowing, a stiff, steady breath smelling of pine needles and distant campfire. I wasn't quite standing, either; I was floating a few inches off the ground, just high enough for my toes to point at the leaf-strewn forest floor. It wasn't odd, in my dream, that my feet didn't touch the ground. It was perfectly normal, and I simply noticed and accepted it, the way you do in dreams. And then something changed. The peace of the moment vanished, leached away without warning. I twisted my head, and the motion took a year to complete, the ninety-degree rotation lasting for minutes and minutes, as if I was moving through thickened water.

Caden. He was beside me, floating like me, staring out at the water and the green needle points of the pine trees. He knew I was there. I could sense his awareness. He turned to look at me, and this action, for him, was unfairly normal and quick. His eyes pierced me, deep brown and heavy with sadness.

And then he was several feet away and reaching for me. I reached for him, stretched, seeing the sadness in his eyes and knowing that if I could just take his hand in mine, he would be okay. But I couldn't reach. It was like there was an invisible force field between our hands keeping us apart. As soon as our fingers neared, they would shear off, slide away, unable to quite meet.

I woke up sweating, heart pounding in my chest, sadness washing through me. It was almost like it had been a nightmare, rather than merely the inability to hold someone's hand in a dream.

A thought struck me and I left my bed, tripping over my feet as I rushed down the hallway toward my studio. I flicked on the light switch and stood in front of the easel, staring with my mouth open. Even as I painted it, I hadn't realized what I'd done.

In the painting, neither Caden's nor my feet were touching the ground.

Caden

The funeral was the second worst day of my life. Gramps had called Dad to say he and Gram couldn't make the trip. They couldn't leave the ranch for that long. Uncle Gerry showed up, though, red-eyed and silent and stoic as only a Monroe can be. Grandma and Grandpa Kensington, Mom's parents, had flown in from Miami, red-eyed and looking ancient. They'd never approved of Dad, I'd come to realize. They never came to see us, and we never went to see them. They sent me a card on my birthday and at Christmas, but that was it. When I'd asked about them, at age ten or eleven, I think it was, Mom had simply told me she didn't get along with her parents, that they disagreed on some issues. I let it go then, since I didn't understand how that was possible, or what it meant. But at the funeral, I began to glean some understanding. It was silent anger, their disapproval clear in the way they glared at Dad, in the way they stayed far away from him. I might as well have not even been there.

I sat next to Dad in the church for the service, listening to words by some preacher I'd never met, who clearly didn't know Mom and only spoke in generalities. Then I sat in the passenger seat of Dad's truck, the orange flag waving from his antenna. The radio was off, and his eyes were glazed, staring at the road ahead of him. Twenty minutes from the church to the cemetery, and he never said a word. He hadn't spoken a word to me at all, as a matter of fact, since the day she'd died. Two weeks, and he'd come and gone in silence, trudging as if weighed down by something I couldn't see.

He didn't speak at the burial, either. He stood in his suit, looking uncomfortable in it. He rubbed the twisted, broken knuckles of his hand with his thumb and stared at the casket as the minister spoke yet again.

"...Janice will be missed, this we all know. She was much loved, and was an amazing mother, a wonderful wife, and a loving daughter." The preacher was old, thin gray hair swept back, pale blue eyes that seemed falsely sympathetic and even a little bored. "So now, as we prepare to say goodbye to Janice, let us remember her as she lived—"

I couldn't take it any longer. "Enough! Just stop!" I heard the words burst from me, saw the shocked expression on everyone's faces. Dad just watched me in apathetic disinterest. "You didn't know her, you old asshole. So just—just stop talking. No one else seems to want to say anything, or even admit the truth. She died a shitty death. It was slow, and painful. And...Dad doesn't know how to live without her.

Look at him! I know you're supposed to celebrate a loved one's life instead of mourning their death or whatever, but that's bullshit. She's gone. She was my mom, and she's gone. I'll never get her back. So the rest of you can stand here and act all pious and sad, but I'm…I'm not gonna listen to any more bullshit that doesn't mean anything. It's fucking stupid. I'm going home. I just…I want my mom back, but that's never gonna happen."

Grandpa Kensington stepped forward, rage on his face. "Listen here, young man! I won't have you disrespecting my daughter—"

I stormed past him. "You don't get to talk to me. You weren't here while she was alive, and you weren't there when she died, and you don't get to act like you care now. So just shut up."

No one else moved. The preacher was stunned into silence, Mom's friends and co-workers clearly didn't have any idea how to react, and Dad…he was just staring down at the casket. I kept walking, leaving the cluster of people around the hole in the ground. It was another beautiful day, warm, the sun high and bright, the sky blue. And yet…behind me was a wooden box containing my mother's corpse.

I wanted to go back and clutch the casket, beg for her to come back, to hug me. Beg my dad to hug me. To tell me it would be okay. I wanted to go back and say goodbye. Instead, I kept walking. I walked between the rows of headstones, past concrete angels and white stone crosses. I found the main road and kept walking. Mile after mile, until my feet hurt. I wasn't even sure I was going in the right direction, and it didn't matter. I just kept walking. Eventually I came to an intersection I recognized, and oriented myself homeward. About two miles from home, Dad passed me, pulled into the next driveway, and waited. I climbed into the passenger seat, and he drove me the rest of the way in silence.

I'd been walking for over two and a half hours, I realized, and he was just now heading home?

I smelled the alcohol on him, the stench potent even from a couple feet away. "You're drunk? And you're driving?" He stopped at a stoplight, and I threw the door open. "I'll walk the rest of the way home." I slammed the car door closed.

He didn't answer, just pulled away as the light turned green. When I got home half an hour later, he was in his study already. I passed the closed door, but stopped when I heard the distinctive sound of Mom's favorite song: "Paint It Black" by The Rolling Stones. She used to listen to that song all the time. She would play the album on repeat every Sunday morning as she cleaned the house, blasting it loud enough to hear it throughout the house. Whenever the album would come to "Paint It Black," she would stop what she was doing and sit down and listen to it, turn it back to the start and listen to it through. It was nostalgic, I think. Dad was always listening to either country or classic rock, and I think "Paint It Black" had been a song they'd listened to while they were dating, just getting to know each other. She told me once that it was their song. Hers and Dad's.

Now Dad was listening to it. I leaned against the wall beside the door and listened, too. The song ended, and then began again. I didn't have the stomach to listen to it through a second time. I collapsed on my bed, too heartsick to do anything but sleep.

The box was waiting for me when I got home from school, about two weeks after Mom died. It was a huge box, thin but four feet wide by six feet high, and fairly heavy. It was addressed to me, and it had Ever's address in the upper left-hand corner of the UPS shipping sticker.

I carried it inside, up to my room and leaned it against the bed. I didn't open it yet. I was almost afraid to. I knew what it was: a painting, something by Ever. Her letters lately had been full of rambling chatter, which I actually found soothing. It was a few minutes of randomness in my week, time when I could unfocus from my life and tune in to Ever's.

Her sister was driving her nuts, she told me. Always exercising and dieting and trying to get skinnier, when according to Ever, her twin sister Eden was just simply not built to be skinny and svelte. I didn't know what to say back to her about her sister, so I didn't write anything about it. I had tried to keep my letters fairly upbeat, but I couldn't always manage it. I wasn't doing well. I was lonely. I was scared. Dad was a zombie. He went to work, he came home, and he vanished into his study. I hadn't found him passed out again since that first night, but I knew he was drinking. The kitchen garbage bags clinked when I took them out, and the can that I wheeled to the street every week clinked and clanked as well. I searched his office one day while he was at work, but found nothing. And even if I had found a bottle, what was I supposed to do with it? Throw it away? Dad wasn't stable; there was no telling how he'd react.

I finally opened the box and slid the Styrofoam-padded wooden brace free from the cardboard. Unwrapping the painting took forever, as Ever had packaged it to kingdom come in an effort to keep the piece from getting ruined during shipping. As I finally revealed the painting, I understood why.

It showed Ever and me side by side, facing a lake. We were nearly holding hands, but not quite. There was something achingly sad in the way we both were reaching for each other but not touching. In the upper right-hand corner of the painting, almost lost amidst the trees, were two white birds. Doves.

Our mothers.

I almost started crying all over again.

It wasn't until I'd pounded a nail into a stud over my desk and hung the painting that I noticed neither Ever's nor my feet were touching the ground. There was something significant to that, but I couldn't quite figure out what.

Dear Ever,

I love the painting you sent me. It's really, really amazing. I bet when you're a famous artist, it'll be worth a ton of money. Not that I'd ever sell it, but you know what I mean.

There's a lot going on in that piece, though. I don't even know where to start. The way our hands aren't quite touching, it's like looking at a picture of someone about to fall. Maybe that doesn't make any sense to you, but that's the feeling I get. The only thing I don't understand is why we're floating. I almost didn't notice it.

My dad isn't doing well. He's drinking a lot, I think. I mean, I know he is, but he's hiding it. He was never a drinker before. A few beers on the weekends, maybe a glass of wine with Mom in the evening. Nothing like this. I didn't tell you then, but the night Mom died, Dad drank a whole bottle of whisky by himself. He puked all over his study and I had to clean it up.

I don't know what to do. I'm going to school, I'm making myself breakfast and dinner. I'm cleaning the house and doing the laundry and the dishes and Dad just...ignores me. Growing up, I never doubted he loved me. I knew he did. He's not the type to say it all the time, but he spent time with me. You know? He'd play Legos with me, or throw the football. Take me to a Tigers game every once in a while. Talk to me, give me advice on drawing. Watch a movie with me. He used to watch James Bond movies every weekend. He only watched the Sean Connery ones. He had them all on DVD, and he'd watch one or two every Saturday.

Now he works, drinks, and sleeps. He sleeps in his study, I'm pretty sure. He showers in the bathroom by my room instead of using the one in the master bedroom. I'm pretty sure he hasn't gone back in there since Mom died.

Some days, I think your letters are all that keeps me sane.

Your friend,

Cade

School was just something to do. I went, I attended class, I did my homework. I didn't know what else to do with my life. Dad was in a similar holding pattern. He was still drinking, I think, but he kept it to himself. I never found him passed out, never caught him coming home drunk. He finally closed the door to his and Mom's room. I think he took his clothes out, and I know he switched the old beat-up leather couch in his office for a futon. He worked, paid the bills, and left money on the kitchen island for me. I did the grocery shopping, but I did it the way a fifteen-year-old boy would. I got what I could carry home. That meant Mac 'n Cheese, hot dogs, frozen meals that could be microwaved, burritos and oven pizzas.

I didn't make any friends in high school. People tried to talk to me, but I just couldn't figure out what to say to them. I wanted to go home and draw, read Ever's latest letter, and play *Call of Duty* and *Modern Warfare*.

Time slipped by, fall giving way to winter, winter to spring. In April, I had to find another shoebox to hold all the letters.

My sixteenth birthday had passed almost unnoticed. Dad had left me a card on the island, with *"happy birthday, love dad"* written in sloppy block letters, and the keys to Mom's Jeep Commander. That was it. I'd taken to forging his signature for things, including the practice time for my license. I did practice driving, too, although it was always alone. I'd go around the block in my neighborhood a few times, and then once I got comfortable with that, I'd go a bit farther, a few blocks around, always within my subdivision. It was two months after my birthday that I finally got the courage to venture two miles down Nine Mile Road before turning around in a Burger King parking lot and going home. I paid for, took, and passed the level two test on my own.

Ever's letters were still the highlight of every week. I got a letter from her on the day school let out for the summer.

Cade,

We never talked about when our birthdays were, so I don't expect you to know that I turned sixteen yesterday. Daddy took me to a BMW dealership and bought me a car. It was kind of stupid, since I just barely got my restricted license. Going to get the car was the most time we'd spent together in months, and it was awkward at best. He didn't know what to say to me, and I'm just mad at him for shutting down when I needed him, and now I don't need him, really. Now that I've got a car of my own and my license, I'll be pretty much completely on my own, I think.

You had a birthday too, didn't you? I mean, of course you did, but I just don't know when it was, or will be. Regardless, happy birthday. I hope it's a good day for you.

What are you doing for the summer? I'm not going back to Interlochen this summer. It was fun, but it's not something I want to do again. I'd rather stay home and paint and wander around taking pictures. That's what I did today, actually. I kind of skipped the last day of school and drove myself (yay!) down to Birmingham with my camera. I spent most of the day downtown taking pictures of pretty much everything. I'll probably paint using a couple of the photos I took. I don't know for sure yet, though.

In good news, Eden is eating normally again, finally, after spending most of the year eating no carbs and counting calories and drinking shakes and exercising. She went kind of nuts, honestly. Hours every week with Michael, the personal trainer Dad had hired after Eden pestered him about it for a month last spring. Thank God for that. It's not a weight thing. I've told you about this before, I know, but it's a big issue between Eden and me. It's the only thing we actually fight about. We're sisters and we bicker like you'd expect, but we never really actually fight-fight about things, except Eden and her insecurity. I want her to be happy, you know? But I think she feels like she's not as good as me or something. I hate that SO MUCH. I can't even tell you. I'm just me, nothing special. I've got friends at school and I guess I'm kind of popular or whatever, but it's not like I'm trying. And I always make sure Eden is part of everything.

I'll miss not seeing you at camp this year, but maybe now that we both are sixteen we can meet somewhere? Maybe not. I don't know.

Anyway, write back soon, and remember, you can always tell me anything.

Always your friend,

Ever

I felt shitty that I hadn't even thought of her birthday. I pulled out a sheet of blank paper and started sketching a birthday cake. I colored it pink and white, drew in the candles so they looked like they'd just been blown out, and wrote "Happy Birthday" above it and "Make a wish!" beneath it.

Ever,

I'm sorry I didn't know about your birthday. Mine was a few weeks ago. June 3rd. Yours is June 12th? Happy birthday! I drew you a picture of a birthday cake. Kind of stupid, I guess, but happy birthday anyway. Mine was pretty lame. Dad gave me Mom's car, but I didn't even see him. He just put the keys on a birthday card, and that was it. I'm used to it, though. Nothing strange. I actually taught myself to drive. Although I think I mentioned that

I drive on Gramps's farm a lot, but it's different when I'm completely alone, when I could get pulled over. No one cares on the farm. Gramps has like several thousand acres, and I can't really get arrested or get in a wreck out there, you know?

I'm glad to hear about your sister. Is it okay if I just leave that topic there? I think as a guy anything I say would be either wrong or stupid, so I just won't say anything. Except, you ARE something special. You really are.

I'm going to Gramps's farm this summer. I need it. I need to get away from Michigan, away from Dad, away from the house where Mom should be but isn't. I need to be exhausted and sore and out in the open. I don't know if you get that, but I just need it. So I'll miss you, too. Maybe we can meet before school starts. I'll still write you from Wyoming, and after you get that letter you can write me there. I don't know the address off the top of my head. I know Dad has it written down somewhere, but I stay out of his study. I'm not sure how I'm getting to Wyoming, honestly. Usually Dad flies out there with me and stays a few days, then goes back home, but somehow I don't think he's going this year. Maybe I'll just drive myself out there. I have Gramps's phone number, so I could call him and get directions. I think Dad has a GPS system in his truck I could borrow.

Driving all the way to Wyoming by myself sounds scary, but I'm not sure how else to do it. I don't think

I can get a plane ticket on my own. I guess I could ask Dad for help, but I just don't want to. I'd rather do it myself. He's checked out of my life, basically, and I don't see the point of even trying to involve him. So I get what you said at the beginning of your last letter about being mad at your dad. If I was to spend time with Dad, I'd be mad, too. Now, I'm just...trying to make it one day at a time on my own.

Would you draw me a picture? It doesn't have to be paint, 'cause it takes forever for paint to dry. Just anything. So I have something of yours with me in Wyoming.

Cade

I mailed the letter, then sat down to plan. I found Gramps's phone number and address. I would need a detailed map with directions, plus some food and water and some money for gas. I had no idea how long it would take to drive from Michigan to Wyoming, or how much gas I would use, or how much money it would take. The more I thought about everything involved in this crazy road trip, the more scared I got. I wasn't even supposed to drive between ten at night and five in the morning, but I knew I'd end up doing so anyway.

Maybe I should just ask Dad to buy me a plane ticket.

I packed my clothes, everything I could think of needing except money. And then I waited for Dad to get home. It was after nine, and I was waiting for him in the kitchen. He looked…old, frail, and tired. His skin sagged around his eyes, under his chin. He'd always been huge and strong and vital, and suddenly he'd aged a century. He shuffled through the side door, letting the screen slam behind him. He dropped his briefcase onto the kitchen counter and sagged back against the sink, fingers pinching the bridge of his nose.

I don't think he'd seen me yet. I was sitting at the table sketching an abstract map of the U.S., no state or country borders shown, only the interstates and U.S. highways; the idea had been inspired by having studied a road atlas to get an idea of how to get from home to Gramps's Wyoming ranch.

"Dad?"

He visibly started. "Oh, hey, bud. Didn't see you there." He tried to straighten from his hunched, defeated posture, but couldn't quite manage it. "What's up?"

"I'm going to the ranch this summer."

He squeezed his eyes shut and sighed. "I'm not sure I can make the trip this year, son. I'm—"

"I know, Dad. I was gonna drive. I just need some money for gas and food. I've got the route all mapped out and written down turn by turn."

He stared at me, perplexed. "You're going to drive from Michigan to Wyoming by yourself?" He rubbed the side of his face. "That's a fifteen-hundred-mile trip, Cade. You're sixteen."

Some hot, insistent emotion in me bubbled up and out. Anger, maybe? "I'm not a kid anymore, Dad. I taught myself to drive. I grocery shop on my own. I saved for, studied for, and took the road test by myself. I went to school and got all A's and B's, and did the laundry and cleaned the house by myself all year long. I don't—I'm not blaming you. I'm just telling you, I'm not a kid. I'm going to the ranch. I just need a couple hundred bucks for gas and food."

Dad seemed to crumple even further. "Cade, god…I've been a real shitty father, haven't I? You've—"

"Jesus, Dad. I'm not trying to lay a guilt trip on you. I swear I'm not." I stood up and circled around the table, stopped three feet from him. My father, who had once seemed almost super-human to me, looked afraid and empty. "I can do this, Dad. I am doing this. I need to."

He waved a hand. "Fine. I think I've got some cash in the safe. Hang on." He left the kitchen, heading toward his study. Each step clearly required effort. When he came back five minutes later, he had an envelope thick with cash and a cell phone still in the box. "This is over a grand. Should hold you for the summer. Plus, Gramps'll spot you if you need it." He handed me the cell phone, a brand-new iPhone. "This was going to be Mom's gift to you for good grades at the end of the school year. I guess you earned it, and you'll need it regardless. Download a GPS app. I'll write down all the phone numbers you'll need: mine, Gramps's, Gram's, and Uncle Gerry's."

"Is the phone connected?" I asked.

He nodded twice, slowly. "Yeah. Your own line. You know how to use it, I imagine?"

I shrugged. "Sure. I can figure it out." A long, awkward silence extended between us. Finally, I stepped forward and gave him a one-armed hug. "Thanks, Dad."

He was stone-still for a beat, and then he wrapped me up in both arms, held on to me so tight I lost my breath. "I'm sorry, Cade. I'm sorry. Jesus, I'm so sorry, I just—I can't…"

He sniffed, and I couldn't bear to pull away to see if he was crying. "She was all I had. All I've ever known. I've been with her my entire life. She was the first friend I ever made in Detroit. She was… everything. I—I—" He stuttered to a stop, and his shoulders shook. "I'm just sorry I'm not—I can't…"

"Dad, stop. Please. It's fine."

"It's not. You lost your mom, and all I can think of is my own—"

I jerked away. "Stop! Fuck! Just stop! I don't want to have this conversation with you. She's gone, and we both just have to deal with that as best we can. I'm not holding anything against you. I promise. Just…don't you go and die on me too, okay?" I tried to make it sound like a joke, but it wasn't.

He laughed, but it was mostly devoid of humor. "I'm doing my best, kiddo." I don't think he was exaggerating any more than I was.

Another tense silence rose up, and the moment became too much. I stuck the envelope in my back pocket and left the kitchen, holding up the cell phone box in a gesture of thanks or farewell or both. "I'll probably leave first thing tomorrow, so…'bye."

"'Bye, Cade. Drive safe. Call if you need to."

I nodded, but I wouldn't call him unless it was an emergency.

He left. I sat at my desk in my room, trying not to think as I put some of the cash in my wallet and the rest in my backpack, which held my sketchbooks and pencil cases, toiletries, maps, directions, and some snacks. I fell asleep wondering what it meant that Dad so easily let a sixteen-year-old kid—his only child—drive by himself to Wyoming. *Nothing good* was the only conclusion that I could come to.

I was halfway to Chicago before I realized I'd never talked to Gramps about the fact that I was coming to spend the summer with him. The problem was, I knew Gramps would lose his shit if he knew I was driving there alone. I had to tell him, though. Gramps hated nothing more than surprises.

I pulled off onto the shoulder of I-94 and scrolled through my short list of contacts until I found the entry for Gramps's cell phone. Taking a deep breath, I hit the "CALL" button.

It rang four times, and then Gramps's deep, gruff, solid voice answered. "Hello? Who is this?"

"Hi, Gramps. It's Caden."

"Caden? Your Pops finally give you a cell phone, did he?"

I laughed nervously. "Yeah. Good grades this year, you know." I cleared my throat. "So, I'm coming to the ranch this summer."

"Oh, yeah? Had enough of that artsy-fartsy camper bullshit, did you?"

"Gramps. It was an exclusive program for the most talented kids my age in the country. It was an honor to go last year."

"But you ain't goin' back, though." I could almost see his eyes narrowing as he said this.

"Yeah, you're right. I had enough artsy-fartsy bullshit. I'm still an artist, though. So don't get your hopes up." He liked to joke that someday I'd come to my senses and decide to move to Wyoming and let him groom me to take over the ranch.

"Well, shit. Got me all excited there for a minute, grandson."

"Sorry, Gramps."

He cleared his throat, a signal that jokes were over. "So, when's your flight get into Cheyenne?"

I hesitated. "Well, that's the thing, Gramps. I—I'm driving myself this year."

For once, Gramps was speechless. It took several moments for him to respond. "Bullshit," he grunted. "You're barely sixteen. Ain't no way your Pops will allow that."

"I left already. I'm halfway to Chicago."

"The fuck is your dad thinking?" Gramps tried not to curse around me too much when I was younger, but like Dad, the older I got, the less he censored himself.

I wasn't sure what to say, since I didn't know what Dad was thinking. "He's...he's been working a lot."

"You didn't run away, did you?"

"No!" I winced as a semi roared past, rocking the car as it went. "Dad knows."

Gramps was silent for a long time, but I knew him well enough to know he was thinking it over. "Guess I can't do much from here. I want you to call me every four hours, Caden. You got it? Every four hours, precise. Means you have to stop and pull over to call me, you got it? No texting or talking while

you drive. Keep the music down. Watch your blind
spots. You hear me?"

"Yes, sir."

"This is the dumbest goddamn thing I've ever
heard of. Sixteen years old and driving damn near
thirty hours by your own damn self. I should call
Aidan and have a word with him is what I should do."

"Don't, Gramps. He's…just don't call him. I'll be
fine. I swear."

"He ain't dealin' well with losin' your mom, is
he?"

"No sir, he ain't." I felt a pang of loss hit me. I
always came back from the ranch talking like Gramps,
with a twang and saying "ain't." Mom would have a
fit every year, whacking my shoulder whenever I said
"ain't" or "don't got" or anything like that. There'd
be no one to care this year.

"It's a damn shame, Caden. She was a good
woman, too good for him, I always said. I know losin'
her is the hardest thing that could happen, but it ain't
no excuse for lettin' a kid your age go off on a road
trip alone."

"I know, Gramps. But I'm not a kid anymore.
Okay? I've been taking care of myself for a long time
now."

"You're a good kid, Cade. You'll be one hell of a
man, too. But you're still a kid. You need your Pops
to be a father to you." He grunted. "Four hours. I

better hear from you on the dot. You stop anytime you're tired, you hear? There ain't no rush. Just get here safe."

"I will."

"'Kay, then. Love you, boy."

"Love you too, Gramps." I hung up and set the phone in the cup holder, wiping my face with both hands.

For a moment I was struck by disorientation, doubt, fear. What was I doing? I couldn't do this. I wasn't ready. Another semi rushed past, buffeting the Jeep. I took a deep breath, let it out slowly. Another. I pushed away the emotions, the doubts. I recited the route to Wyoming instead.

I-94 west, then take I-294/I-80 west toward Iowa. I-80 all the way to Cheyenne. I-25 north toward Casper. Take the 220 past the fairgrounds, then SW Wyoming Boulevard toward Casper Mountain. The M-Line Ranch would be about twenty miles down an unnamed dirt road off Wyoming Boulevard, deep in the wilderness south of Casper, Wyoming.

I could do this. I could do this. I pictured the ranch, hundreds of square miles, thousands of acres of rolling hills and knee-high grass and foothills spiking the sky in the distance, waiting to be crossed and begging to be climbed.

I put the Jeep in drive and checked my mirrors, waited for traffic to clear, and then accelerated down the shoulder until I was at speed and pulled into the right-most lane. I waited a few minutes before I turned the radio on, settling into a comfortable seventy-five miles per hour. Mom's Jeep—now my Jeep—had satellite radio, which was probably the most awesome thing I could ever imagine. I scanned the stations until I caught something with a good groove to it. Chugging guitars and distinctive vocals met me; the information readout told me it was Volbeat playing "The Sinner Is You," a song I'd never heard before. The lyrics swept me away from the very beginning: "What's life without a little pain…"

It was a philosophy I wanted to hold on to. But I'd take life without so much pain, if I could. I'd heard all the bullshit, of course: what doesn't kill you makes you stronger, and how the hard times make you appreciate the good times more. I didn't buy it. Hard times were hard, and no amount of thinking about the good times supposedly to come would make them suck any less. What good could come from losing my mom to breast cancer? What was I supposed to appreciate about that? I'd survive it, and be stronger for it? Well…I wasn't going to curl up and die, so yeah, I'd survive it. But I also knew I'd never be the same. I felt the scars on my heart and in my mind. I'd been cut deep, and the wounds would never really heal. You didn't watch your mother die and your father simply give up without being changed for the worse.

I'd been painted by pain. Several coats of it, a deep, thick varnish that wouldn't ever fade.

Miles passed, hours passed. I slipped south of Chicago, cutting around the metropolis through the industrial forest of smokestacks and gouting pyres of flame. I was somewhere between Joliet and Davenport, Illinois, when I stopped for Burger King and to call Gramps. Another four hours saw me between Des Moines, Iowa, and Omaha, Nebraska. There were hours that passed slower than a lecture on economics, and others that zipped by so fast I couldn't believe how far I'd gone. Iowa and Nebraska were endless and flat, and only the constant blare of music kept me from going insane from boredom. I would feel myself getting drowsy, and I'd roll all the windows down, turn the music up so loud it hurt my ears, and sing along at the top of my lungs.

The road never ended. It was always unfurling just beyond my hood, always another mile to go, another hour more. Just another hour. Another hour. I talked to myself. I talked to Ever. I talked to Mom.

I didn't talk to Dad.

Sunset found me parked underneath a light in a rest stop outside of Lincoln, the doors locked as I slept fitfully. I'd driven twelve hours straight, stopping only for food, gas, and to call Gramps every four hours. When I woke up, I was hit by fear. It was pitch black beyond the pale orange circle of light underneath which I was parked. There were semis idling at the far edge of the rest stop, and a faint white glow of fluorescent lights from the rest stop building itself. I exited my car, locked it behind me, and used the restroom. Graffiti stained the walls and the dividers, gouged and scribbled swear words, names, and other randomness.

I bought a Coke from the vending machine, checked in with Gramps, and hit the road again, driving through the drowsing, heavy darkness. Nothing lay beyond the span of my headlights except blackness and the high silver moon, nothing existed but music and the yellow center line and the blacktop and the white road-edge borderline and the occasional pair of headlights whipping past.

I wondered often who that was in the car approaching, what their life was like, what problems they'd lived through, faced down, and survived. Did they have friends, or were they lonely like me? Maybe next year I'd do better. Hang out with someone at school, a guy who shared interests with me. Or maybe even a girl. A girlfriend.

Yeah, right.

I passed Kearney, Lexington, and North Platte. Empty fields lit by gray. Cows in scattered clumps, horses browsing and nosing and shaking manes.

Sidney. I stopped at McDonald's, ate, and called Gramps. Those calls became my goals on the trip. Make it four hours, call Gramps. It meant a break, a chance to breathe, to stop and realize how far I'd driven.

It was well past midnight on the second day of travel when I passed under the sign announcing that I'd arrived at M-Line Ranch. My tires crunched over the half-mile-long, ruler-straight driveway leading up to the sprawling, three-story log home. The house— the log exterior, at least—was older than some of the states, Gramps liked to say, having been built in 1843. The interior had been remodeled extensively over the last few decades, so that it was open-plan and modern, with a huge two-story living room with massive windows, a kitchen with miles of granite counters and gleaming stainless steel appliances. I loved Gram's and Gramps's house. It was huge and luxurious and fun. As a kid, they'd let me run in the hallways and skid in my socks on the hardwood floors, and Uncle Gerry could often be persuaded to toss me the football from across the living room, lobbing it up to the top of the twenty-five-foot-high ceiling.

I shoved the shifter into park, shut off the engine, and just sat in silence. There was only one light on in the main house and no other light for miles. I slid out of the car and closed the door quietly, then leaned against the vehicle and craned my neck back to stare up at the sky. The stars were infinite, numberless and beyond counting, sparkling and twinkling and scattered and spattered across the inky black, a universe of silver light. The moon stood at the center of it all, a thin crescent amid the wash of stars. A falling star streaked across the horizon, slanting down in a slash toward the ground before vanishing.

I didn't make a wish.

I heard the side door off the kitchen squeak slightly and click closed, and then Gramps's slow and steady tread clomped in my direction. I kept my gaze starward; I picked a tiny square of stars near the moon and tried to count them as Gramps approached. He stopped a couple feet away from me, body angled partly toward me. I heard the rustle of cardboard, and then a metallic grinding accompanied by a sparking flame. Gramps lit his cigarette, inhaled deeply, and blew the smoke skyward. He smoked four cigarettes a day, no more, no less. It was his one vice, carefully chosen. He didn't drink, didn't take days off, didn't sleep in. He drank a pot of coffee every day, and smoked his four cigarettes. One in the morning with his first cup of coffee, one after lunch, one after dinner, and one late at night right before bed. The smell was nostalgic, for me. It made me think of Gramps, of late night conversations and early mornings on the range with a thermos of coffee and the smell of smoke trailing from Gramps as we brought the herd of green-broke quarterhorses out to the north pasture.

"Long drive, huh?" Gramps asked around a long exhale.

I nodded. "Yeah. I stopped to sleep just past Omaha, but only for about two or three hours. I'm beat."

"Those miles from Iowa into Wyoming are the worst, if you ask me. Nothing but nothing for as far as you can see."

I laughed. "Iowa to Wyoming is most of the trip."

"Exactly. I'm proud of you for doin' it, even if I don't rightly approve of you tryin' it so young."

"Didn't have much choice, Gramps. I was losin' my fucking mind in Michigan."

"Watch your fuckin' mouth, boy," Gramps growled, but chuckled as he said it. "When'd you start talkin' that way?"

"No one to make me stop cursing anymore, I guess," I said, and heard my voice catch. There was a sudden lump in my throat, hot and hard and rising.

"You're here now, and you know Grams'll wash your mouth out if she hears you talk like that."

I nodded, but the gravel at my feet was blurry. I'd driven 1,458 miles in twenty-six hours. I was just tired from the drive, that's all.

Except the burning in my eyes was getting worse, and then something dripped onto the top of my shoe.

I was gathered into a rough embrace. Gramps smelled like cigarettes and cologne and wood smoke and something else indefinable, something uniquely Gramps. My shoulders heaved, and I tried to push away, tried to push it down. Gramps held me in place.

"No shame in it, boy. Let it out." He held me tight against his thin cotton T-shirt. Even at seventy-eight years old, Gramps was still hard as iron. "You're allowed to feel it, son. Ain't no one gonna think less of you. Least of all me."

I shuddered, shivered, and then felt it overwhelm me in a hot flood. It all came out, sobs wracking me, shaking me. Gramps just held me and kept silent, comforting simply with his presence and his thick hard arms holding me upright.

"I miss her, Gramps. I miss her so damn bad it doesn't seem possible. And I miss Dad." My fingers clawed at his shirt as I forced myself upright. "He's gone, even though he's still alive, still living in that house. He's there, but he's not. And I needed him, but he…he just quit. I'm lonely. I'm so alone. I'm sick of it. I'm sick of myself. And I'm so tired. Tired of hurting. Tired of missing her."

"I know, Cade. I know. I got nothin' to say will make it better. Just keep on through, 's all you can do. Saw men die, you know that. I never talked about it much, but…. Good men, friends, guys I trained, fought beside, and loved like brothers. Never hurts less. You just get up every day and do what you gotta do and eventually…well…the hurt is replaced by other things. Other hurt. Good things, too. Met your Gram when I finally left the Army, after my third tour in Vietnam. Served for ten years, most of that in combat zones. Saw some shit you can't never imagine, and I hope to God you don't see it yourself. I was fucked up, is what I'm tryin' to say. Met your Gram, and that was the good what replaced all the bad I seen." He paused to suck on his cigarette and exhale the smoke away. "If I was to lose my Beth, well…I can't honestly say I'd be in any better shape than it seems Aiden is in. Until you know that kind of love, Caden, you can't imagine how it gets—I don't even know how to put it. I ain't no good with words. It gets all hooked up inside'a who you are. Like vines wrapped around a sapling, growing together until you cain't tell the tree from the vine. If you lose that, it'd tear you up but good. Tear you up forever. Wouldn't be nothin' left'a me, were I to lose Beth. That's what I'm tryin' to say. So don't be too hard on your ol' Pops."

"I'm trying, Gramps. I get all that, at least as good as I can. But I'm…I'm just a kid. I'm trying not to be. I know I've gotta grow up. But…I don't want to, sometimes."

"No harm in that, son. I was barely a kid myself when I joined up for Korea. Barely a week over eighteen. I had to go, I knew I did. All the guys I grew up with, we was all acting gung-ho and eager and excited, but inside, deep down where you keep all those secret feelings you don't know how to deal with, we was scared. Plumb terrified. Most of us had never left Wyoming. I hadn't. My best buddy Hank hadn't neither. We joined up together, got our draft notices the same day. Went through basic and got assigned to the same unit. Some luck, we thought."

Gramps lifted his boot to rest on his knee, brushed the cherry off his cigarette and stuck the butt in the breast pocket of his T-shirt. "Hank…. Goddamn. That boy was a fuckin' lunatic. Absolutely fearless. Heroic. Problem was…heroic and fearless is what gets a man killed, and that's what happened to Hank. Our whole unit was pinned down on this hillside. A machine gun emplacement had us dialed in to the inch. If any of us moved a single inch, we got popped. Dozens of guys bought it that way. Fuck, that was nasty. Well, Hank, he gets it into his head that he can get us out of it. Says, 'Cover me,' like we could do jack-diddly shit to cover him. We tried, though. Tossed some grenades, laid down some lead as cover. Crazy-ass Hank jumps up and starts running hell for leather, dodging like nuts. Bullets was whizzing past 'im, missing by a gnat's whisker. He gets up to within a fuckin' inch of that emplacement, tosses some 'nades, one in each hand, slings his rifle down and starts blasting. And goddamn if he didn't take the entire emplacement out his own self.

"But...he caught one in the gut. Didn't stop him none, not till every last fucker in that emplacement was dead. Then Hank just falls over. I watched 'im fall. Bullet to the belly is an ugly thing, Cade. Ugly fuckin' way to die. Took him days. We was out in the field, days out from HQ. No one but Kyle the medic for miles. And Kyle couldn't do shit to save him. He died screaming. Took...days. Fuck—fuckin' *days* for him to finally go.

"And me? I cried like a baby, Cade. That's the whole point of this story I shouldn't be tellin' you. I fuckin' bawled my eyes out when he finally gave up his ghost. I didn't want to grow up. I was nineteen when I lost Hank. I was growin' up quick, sure enough, but that? Losin' my best buddy? Grew me up all the way. Sometimes life just makes you grow up. You can't fight it, son. You just have to wipe your eyes and keep puttin' one foot in front of the other and do what you gotta do."

I nodded, and stared up at the numberless stars, and Gramps stood beside me, smoking in silence and each of us lost in our own thoughts.

billy harper, warm rain at a funeral

Ever

It was the summer between my sophomore and junior years that I met someone who was able to pull my attention away from my paints and my photographs.

His name was Billy. I knew of him, of course. He was the guy at school who was just effortlessly cool. Didn't have to try, didn't seem snotty about being the cool kid. He just…made you like him without having to try. He was the type to have tons of acquaintances, "hangers-on," the old books would call them.

I met him by accident, in the parking lot of the high school. I'd been using the school art room to frame a piece I'd done, since they had the space and tools to do it properly, especially since the piece I was framing was eight feet by six. It was an abstract piece, my most abstract yet, I think, but my best as well. All swirls of color streaking across from top left to bottom right, curving and arcing in almost arabesques, Arabic spires of blue and minarets of yellow. It seemed almost like a Middle Eastern landscape, but it wasn't, quite.

I'd borrowed Dad's SUV for the day so I could cart the piece there and home. Only, I hadn't anticipated how much heavier the painting would be after I'd framed it, and I was having trouble getting it into the car. I'd nearly dropped it several times, and was struggling to hold it up, to keep it from sliding out of my grip and to the ground. I had the front end in, but not enough of it. I was stuck, perfectly trapped, unable to lift it any higher, unable to lower it without dropping it and ruining the frame I'd just spent four hours making in the woodshop.

I was near to tears, sweating, struggling, whimpering. Then I felt the weight miraculously lessen, and a pair of tanned arms slid around me, hands on the frame to either side of my hands, lifting, pushing, hefting the front end over the tire well that had been stopping it.

I turned around, and there he was. Tall, with blond hair perfectly spiked above ice-blue eyes and carved cheekbones. Billy Harper. He had his trumpet case dangling at his side from a strap, and his body was inches from mine as he pushed the painting into Dad's Mercedes.

"Thanks," I mumbled, feeling startled at his sudden presence, as well as the surprising reaction I was having to his proximity.

My heartbeat was ramping up, and my breath was fluttering in my chest. I felt like the description of a southern belle in the old romances, all atwitter, flustered.

"No problem." His voice was low and calm, like the surface of a mirror-still lake. He lifted up on his toes and glanced at the painting. "It's an awesome picture."

"Painting." I couldn't help the correction from popping out of my mouth.

"What?" He seemed genuinely puzzled.

"It's not a picture, it's a painting."

"Oh. Right. Yeah." He shrugged a sculpted shoulder. "Anyway, it's great. Looks kinda like…the desert. You know? Or a city in the desert. But it's not, though. It's just…lines. It's cool."

"Thanks. That's kind of what it's supposed to be. Not quite one thing, not quite another, but nearly both."

He grinned, and my stomach flopped. "That's cool." He stuck out his hand. "I'm B—Will. Call me Will."

"Will? I thought—"

"Yeah, everyone calls me Billy, I know. But it's a nickname I've had since I was a kid, and I hate it. I always introduce myself as William, or Will, but everyone always hears others call me Billy, and it just sticks."

I shook his hand, and my palm tingled at the heat of his palm. "Ever."

"Yeah. I've seen you around. You have a sister, a twin sister, right?"

I shrugged. "Yeah. Eden."

He just nodded, and an awkward silence descended. He gave a funny, nervous little laugh, and then waved at my car. "So. Taking that painting home, huh?"

I wanted to roll my eyes at the completely pointless statement. "Yeah. I wanna hang it in my room."

"Need help?"

I did, actually, so I shrugged and nodded at the same time. "Sure, yeah."

Will followed me home, and carted the ladder in from the garage. He also knew how to use Dad's stud finder and hung the painting over the couch along the far wall of my room, opposite my bed. "So. That's hung. Um…you want to grab some dinner, maybe?"

And that's how it started. Innocent enough, at first. Dinner at Eddie Merlot's, an exceptionally expensive restaurant. His sleek black BMW valeted, the keys left casually in the ignition. A table in a quiet corner, despite the crowd of people waiting and the fact that he'd clearly not planned the date. He was a wonderful conversationalist. He could talk about anything, from music and movies to politics and philosophy. But…there was something niggling at the back of my head. He could talk without end, and did, saying lots of great-sounding things, well-structured sentences and funny stories of skiing in Switzerland and getting into trouble with aristocratic Europeans. But something was missing, and I couldn't identify what it was.

Yet my hormones, my body, something inside me that I didn't quite have complete control over, reacted to him. On a visceral level. He leaned forward while he spoke, the sleeves of his thin, cloud-soft cashmere sweater pushed up to his elbows, his eyes intent on mine, and he told me his funny stories and his nearness seemed to set some secret inner part of me on fire, and I couldn't quite help it and didn't know if I wanted to, even though I felt the tiny worm of something not quite right wriggling in the back of my head.

After sharing a thick, decadent slice of cheese-cake drizzled with raspberry sauce, he helped me into his car, holding my palm in his while the valet waited behind the door. I slid into the seat, the leather cool against my legs through the fabric of my skirt. He drove me around slowly, Sigúr Rose playing "Hoppipolla" in the background, soft rolling strains of exotic music rising to a symphonic and almost alien rolling blend of triumphant sound and song and falsetto voice and horns. Fat droplets of rain pattered against the windshield as we cruised the winding Bloomfield roads, and I felt like I was lost in some fairy tale, some movie where I was the starlet and Will was the star, falling in love in perfectly choreographed splendor.

I felt the pounding of my heart and the sizzle of my skin as he casually rested his right hand on the armrest between us and slid his fingers through mine. I felt the ache of trembling fear and the pulsing of anticipation as we sat in the parking lot of a closed park, in the shadows a few spaces down from the streetlamp, faint slow romantic jazz, a trumpet playing delicate notes in the silence between us as our faces neared and....

He tasted like cinnamon gum, his lips soft and warm and wet. His hand traced up my arm, across my shoulder, curled around the back of my neck and pulled me into the kiss, and my entire being shuddered, and I lost myself in it, in the purely perfect teenaged wonder of the moment.

A strange awareness kept ahold of me, however, as Will kissed me with practiced passion. A kind of poised, tensed knowledge that this was a moment that I was indulging in, allowing to happen, and that despite the fervor of my body's reaction and the heat of my skin in my clothes, a part of me was kept back. Held in check, for some reason I couldn't fathom.

I wanted to let go of that part. I didn't like it being held back. It meant…it meant that there was something empty and false in this moment, this perfect first kiss with Will Harper.

He didn't push the moment. He didn't grope me or take the kiss too far. He pulled back, assessed that I needed a moment, and let it fade.

I touched my lips and stared at Will, at his carved cheekbones and smooth hands on the steering wheel and his calm, glacier-blue eyes. "Who…who is this, playing?" I asked, to cover the confusion I felt.

Will seemed puzzled, then blinked several times. "This…um. It's Miles. Miles Davis. 'Sketches of Spain.'" He twisted the knob to turn the volume up slightly so I could hear the Latin-infused trumpet. "Miles…man, he was a god on the trumpet. Just amazing. Listen to the way he plays it. You can't ever mistake Miles for anyone else. There's some amazing trumpet players out there, but Miles? He's the best there ever will be." Passion infused Will's voice and his eyes.

That settled my confusion a bit. If he was passionate about music, what could be wrong? He was gloriously handsome. Not just hot, that was too commonplace a word for William Harper. He was truly handsome. And so, so polished. He took my hand and chattered about jazz as he drove me home, talking about "Birdland," whatever that was. How jazz was real, true, proper music, the kind you jam to and improvise, or craft this architectural masterpiece all from merely a piece of metal and your breath. He was eloquent about jazz, and that was hard to resist, that passion, that knowledge of something he loved, the ability to woo me with words and make me want to love music I'd always thought was boring. Listening to Miles Davis in Will's car was magical somehow, a continuation of the strangely perfect date we'd had.

Except for the moment of doubt after he'd kissed me, but I'd all but forgotten that by the time he'd pulled up to my house and dropped me off.

As I slid out of the warm cocoon of his BMW, he turned the music down and called my name. "You want to have dinner again? Friday?"

I smiled, feeling excited. "Yeah!" I smiled at him. "Sounds great."

"Cool. I'll pick you up at seven." He waved, and I closed the door.

Eden gave me a strange look as I passed her studio. She was lying on the floor, sheet music held above her head and a pencil in her mouth. Her windows were all wide open, letting in cool evening air and the scent of rain and the sound of raindrops against the roof. Her studio and bedroom were at the front of the house, giving her a view of the driveway.

"Who was that?" she asked, taking the pencil from her lips. "And why were you out so late with him?"

I glanced at my phone, saw that it was nearly two in the morning. "That was Will Harper. And... we were on a date."

Eden sat up, shock causing her to let the pencil drop onto her thigh. "A date? With Billy Harper?"

"Will." I didn't know why I corrected her.

"Will." She tucked her feet under her and stood up. "Why were you on a date with... *Will* Harper?"

I shrugged. "Because...he asked me. He helped me get my painting into the car, and then helped me hang it, and we went on a date. He's...nice."

Eden took a hesitant step toward me. "Ever...he's Billy Harper. He's the hottest and most unavailable guy at school. I know girls from other schools that know who Billy Harper is, and wish they could get a date with him. His dad is famous or something, and he grew up all over the world. He goes to parties with movie stars, Ever. And you just...went on a date with him? Just like that?"

I'd heard all those stories about Billy Harper, of course. The rumor mill at school was insane, full of half truths and lies and jealousy. I'd assumed most of the stories about him were just that, stories. But now, having spent time with him...I could almost believe it. He had the kind of poise and confidence about him that made me think he'd be as comfortable at an A-list party as he was playing his trumpet in the courtyard.

I wasn't sure what to say to Eden. "I don't know, Edie. He was...really nice. I had a really good time."

She stared at me for several moments, and then her expression cleared and turned excited. "Did... did he kiss you?"

I felt myself blush. "Yeah, a little."

"A little? A *little*?" She closed in, grabbed my arm, and shook me. "Was it amazing? What was it like?"

"It was a kiss." I shrugged, and then giggled with her. "Yeah, it was amazing. He had this jazz playing in the background, and it was raining outside, and I don't really like jazz, but he makes it seem cool, you know? And he kissed me, but he wasn't crazy about it, you know? He kissed me, but didn't, like, try to make it anything else."

"God, like that would have been a bad thing."

"Well, on the first date?"

Eden made a dismissive gesture with her hand. "It's Billy Harper. I should be so lucky. If he tried to feel me up on the first date, I'd let him."

I shrieked and slapped her arm. "You would not, Eden Eliot, and you know it."

She backed away, and I sensed that the joke had soured. "Yeah, maybe not. But I wouldn't know, since I've never been asked out." She turned away and knelt to pick up her sheet music. "We're turning seventeen this summer, and I haven't even been on a date, much less been kissed. You're way ahead of me. First kiss… with Billy Harper, no less. *So* not fair." I just shrugged and fiddled with one of my brushes, smoothing the bristles between my fingers and thumb. Eden realized I wasn't taking the bait and huffed in irritation. "Fine. Don't tell me anything else. I didn't want to know anyway."

"There's nothing else to tell. We went to Eddie Merlot's. We drove around in his car and ended up in the parking lot of a park somewhere, I'm not sure where, and we ended up kissing. I didn't know it was going to happen, and I didn't plan it. It just… happened."

"He took you to Eddie Merlot's? That place is impossible to get a table at, and expensive as hell."

I wondered how she knew that. "I know…he just walked in and they gave us a table."

Eden's eyes were about to pop out of her head. "Was it his first kiss, too, do you think? I mean, I can't imagine it was."

I shook my head. "No way. He was a really good kisser. Too good at it for it to be his first time. I mean, it was my first time, so I'm not sure, like, one hundred percent sure, but it felt like he knew what he was doing."

"Are you gonna go out with him again?"

"Friday. He's picking me up at eight. No, it was seven. He said seven."

Eden huffed again, flipping idly through the stacks of painted canvases in one corner, glancing at each one for a few seconds before flipping to the next. "I'm so freaking jealous of you right now, you don't even know."

I sighed wryly. "I can feel it coming off you in waves. I'm not sure what you want me to do about it, though. Not go, because you haven't been asked out yet? How is that fair to me?"

She shrugged, which was both of our signature move when we didn't know what to say. "No. You have to go. It's Billy fucking Harper. Of course you can't not go just 'cause I'm lame."

I groaned in frustration. "*God*, Eden. You're *not* lame. Why does everything have to be a competition between us? You don't have to keep up with me or anything like that. That's stupid. When you meet a guy you like, just…make sure he asks you out. Make sure he knows you're interested in him, and get him to ask you out. If that doesn't work, *you* ask *him* out. I don't know. Just be you. You're hot, Eden. We *are* twins, after all. It's not like you're some ugly stepsister just because you don't wear the same dress size as me. God."

"I'm not trying to compete with you…I'm just—"

"Then why can't you let me have this without being jealous?"

She seemed to wilt, deflate. "Sorry, Ev. I'm happy for you. I am, for real." She said it flat, monotone.

I laughed. "Yeah, you really sound like it." I stepped up behind her and wrapped my arms around her middle, rested my cheek against the back of her head. "Eden. Sis. Listen…I'm not saying you have to be, like, all giddy for me. Just…I don't know—"

"You're my twin, Ev. I want you to be happy. I really am happy you had a good time with Billy today. For real. It's just…all the good stuff happens to you."

"Good stuff will happen to you, too, Edie. It will, I promise. Just you watch."

"'Kay." She turned in place and hugged me, then pushed past me. "I have to play through this movement once more before bed. 'Night."

"'Night." I watched her go, feeling more confused than ever.

A few minutes later, the sounds of a complex piece of music filled the air, long high notes and low tones and skirling swirling melodies overlapping and weaving a spell around me. Eden's talent with the cello never ceased to amaze me, even though I heard her play every single day.

I went to my room and undressed, then sat at my vanity in my underwear, brushing my hair and thinking about the day I'd had. As I thought and brushed, my eyes wandered to the stationery set, the colorful, perfumed paper and the refillable faux-quill pen. The set had been a gift from Daddy a few years ago.

I hadn't written Caden in a long time, and I hadn't heard from him in two weeks, since the letter with the picture of a birthday cake included. Well, that wasn't true; he'd sent me a note with his Gramps's address in it, but it was literally three sentences and the address, so it barely counted. I'd laughed so hard at that picture of the birthday cake, and it had made my heart flop at his cute thoughtfulness. I wondered what was happening with him, how he was doing. Maybe if I wrote him a letter, it would help me sort out my own feelings?

I pulled the pad of paper in front of me, slipped the bleed-through backing under a new sheet, and wrote Caden's name across the top line, adding a curl to the tail of the "N," letting my thoughts and feelings coalesce inside me and flow down toward my pen.

Caden,

Sorry for taking so long to write you back, I've just been so busy, you know? I've been shooting several rolls of film every day, developing them myself, and I've also been experimenting with large-format paint-ing, like six-, seven-, and eight-foot-tall canvases and stuff. It's really fun working on that scale. Every stroke is huge and broad, but you still have to find the details, the fine strokes, you know?

So anyway, I hate asking, but...how are you? For real? How's your gramps's farm? I can't believe you drove all the way to Wyoming by yourself. You did, right? You said you were going to. I don't think I could do that. I'd be too scared. I'd probably get lost and end up in Montana by accident or something.

Eden for real is driving me insane. I love her so much, she's my best friend and all that, but her sense of competition makes me crazy. I went on a date yes-terday, with a guy from my school. Eden got super crazy jealous. I don't get it. Just because she hasn't been on a date yet doesn't mean she needs to go and be all jealous of me. We're twins, but we're not the same person. It's like...it's like she thinks everything we do has to be equal. If I go on a date and have my first kiss, then she feels like she has to do the same thing. But I'm not her, and she's not me. You know? God, that sounds so selfish, but it's just true. Growing up, we were always dressed the same, had the same things. We either had to share, or we each had a copy of the same thing. If I got a CD, so did she. If she went to the mall, so did I. Same clothes, same haircuts. All the way up until we were...

Well, honestly, it was that way up until Mom died. The twin-same thing was Mom's gig, I guess. I never really thought about this until now, but it's true. It wasn't until Mom died that Eden and I started really figuring out who we were apart from the other. I mean, I was always more into arts and crafts and stuff, and Eden was very obviously musically talented from the time she was, like, four. She picked up Dad's guitar, the thing was literally bigger than she was, but she sat down with it on her lap and started playing with the strings. It wasn't like she started playing Brahms or anything, but it was obvious she had musical talent. But that was really the end of our individuality until Mom died. Everything else we did had to be exactly the same.

And now I think I'm swinging in the opposite direction, you know? I just want my OWN things, just for me. Things that are only for me, only mine. I want to be unique. I know every person feels that way, wanting to be unique, but when you're a twin and someone else looks identical to you and shares your every facial expression, your verbal tics and mannerisms, uniqueness becomes even more of a big deal.

This thing with Will could really be a problem between us, but I just don't know what to do about it. I don't think she wants Billy for herself, but he's kind of like one of those guys at school that every girl has a crush on and he doesn't seem to realize it. Or if he does, he acts like he doesn't know, and he's just a great actor. I don't know. I honestly think he doesn't realize it, personally. He's not at all arrogant, especially considering how rich he is and the fact that his dad is some famous movie producer or something. I'm not sure. I don't follow that shit, but everyone at school makes a big deal about his dad. He was really cool with me. He didn't act like he was arrogant or cocky or whatever. He was just cool.

It was my first date. It kind of happened by accident, though.

Is it weird for me to tell you about this stuff? I won't if it bugs you.

I hope you have a good summer at your gramps's farm.

Write back soon.

Your friend,

Ever

Caden

It was almost two in the morning, and I was about to faint from exhaustion. Gramps, Uncle Gerry, and two of the other ranch hands and I had spent the last twenty hours on horseback. A section of fence had been damaged in a storm and several hundred head of Gramps's best breeding stock had gotten loose, scattering apart over the space of several miles. It had taken us three days to catch them all, herd them back into a fenced-in pasture, and fix the broken fence, and we'd been out checking the rest of the perimeter for breaks since then.

Finally back at the stables, I slid off Jersey's back and led her to her stall. All I wanted to do was collapse into bed, but you didn't quit until the job was done, and you always, *always* took care of your horse before yourself. So, despite the fact that I was so tired I could have slept in the pile of hay in the corner of Jersey's stall, I removed her saddle and blanket, hung them up in the tack room, and set about currying and brushing the tall dun's coat. She whiskered and murmured as I made her coat shine, and when I finished she nuzzled me with her warm nose, nibbling at my shirt with her flexible lips, hunting for a treat.

I patted her neck. "I'll bring you some apples tomorrow, girl, okay?" I scratched her ear, and she whiskered again, bobbing her head as if she'd understood what I said.

I made sure she had feed and a full water tank before latching her stall and dragging my sore carcass out of the barn and up to the big house, where Gram had coffee and hot, fresh stew waiting. Gramps and the others were still in the stables, so it was just me and Grams in the kitchen.

I slurped at the coffee in between shoveling bites of stew into my face. Gram slid into the chair beside me, sipping from a tiny porcelain mug filled with tea, the string and tag of the tea bag draped over the edge of the mug and wrapped around the handle. She watched me eat for a moment, her gaze thoughtful.

"What?" I asked. "Something wrong?"

She shook her head and smiled, her gray-brown hair tied into a neat bun at the base of her head. "No, sweetie. Just glad you're here this summer."

There was still something in her eyes, though, a spark of something. "What is it, Grams? For real. You've got something on your mind, and I know it."

She laughed and reached into the pocket of her robe. "This came for you today. It's from an Ever Eliot." She smirked at me, her eyes sharp and knowing as she handed me the purple envelope. "It's scented stationery, Cade. Pretty fancy." Grams had married a rancher and she'd lived her entire life here, but she'd come from a wealthy West Coast family. She was educated and perceptive, wise, and unfailingly polite.

I took the letter, blushing. "It's not like that. She's just a friend."

Grams continued to smirk at me. "Friends don't send friends letters in scented stationery."

"Ever and I have been pen pals since camp last summer. The perfumey letters are just her thing, I think. I don't know. We're friends."

"Pen pals, huh?" Gram sipped her tea, then reached out a finger and tugged the letter across the table and examined it. "This is expensive stationery, you know. Engraved and personalized, scented. The paper is basically linen, it's such high quality."

I'd never noticed any of that. "Huh. Never really realized that. All I know is she sprays perfume on it before she mails 'em to me."

Grams laughed, covering her mouth with her hand. "Oh, god, you're such a typical man, Caden Monroe. She doesn't spray it with perfume, honey—the paper is scented. Made to smell that way by the manufacturer. It's actually hard to find these days." She smiled lovingly at me. "I think it's wonderful that you two are pen pals, real, honest-to-goodness pen pals."

"Oh. That makes more sense, I guess. I thought it was weird. It's still weird, just less weird." I rose to dish up a second bowl of stew. "She lost her mom about two years ago, and I—" My throat closed, and I had to redirect. "We just have some things in common, is all."

The sounds of Gramps, Uncle Gerry, Ben, and Miguel laughing as they approached the house floated through the cracked window. Grams gestured at the letter. "You'd best put that in your pocket. If the others see that, they'll never let you hear the end of it."

I stuffed the envelope into my back pocket and tugged the tail of my T-shirt down over it, waving at the guys as I trudged upstairs to my room. I closed the door, locked it, and collapsed onto my bed with the letter on my chest. I opened it, read it. I had to read it through twice before the contents really sank in.

Billy Harper. Date. First kiss.

I felt dizzy.

Billy Harper. Date. First kiss.

I'd told Grams that Ever and I were just friends, just pen pals. I knew that's all it was. We spent some time together at an arts camp a year ago. We'd traded a few letters. So why did I feel betrayed somehow? Why did I feel like I'd lost something, knowing Ever had gone on a date, had kissed a guy?

I shouldn't feel that way. I had no right to feel that way, and I knew it. But knowing I shouldn't feel it didn't change the fact that I did. I read the letter through again, and again. I wanted to write back, to tell her how I felt, even if I wasn't even sure exactly how I was feeling. Off-kilter, like suddenly I was off-balance.

I had a sketchbook on my nightstand. I reached out and snagged it, opened it to a blank page, and started writing. I didn't think it through—I just wrote.

Ever,

It sounds like your sis has some recurring self-esteem issues. Do you think it's connected to losing your mom? I wish I could help you with that. I just don't know. We all have to find contentment in who we are as individuals. I don't know much, but I know that. She can't be you, and you can't be her. She has to live her life and be who she's supposed to be.

I don't have any siblings, but I'd imagine jealousy like you described in your letter seems like it might be pretty common? If she's got self-esteem issues, then that may be showing up in this thing with that guy in the form of jealousy. Maybe she doesn't feel like she'll ever have what you have, because she's not comfortable with how she looks, or whatever? I'm just a guy, okay? I'm not a psychologist, obviously, and you two are girls, and no guy ever really understands any girl. But that's my two cents on the subject.

I got to Wyoming just fine. I had to get away from Dad. He's...not doing well. It's hard for me to watch that, and I needed to get away from it. Honestly, the longer I'm here, the more I don't want to leave. And you know, there's not much keeping me in Detroit, except school, and I can transfer. There's a high school in Casper. Maybe I'll just stay here. I love it here. It's peaceful. Gramps respects me as a worker, and is giving me more and more responsibility, and Uncle Gerry is pretty cool, too. Grams is…Grams. Steady, solid, and always baking cookies or pies. Always has coffee and hot food ready when we come back from the range. She knows things, too. She knows when I'm upset in a way even Gramps doesn't.

As far as your discussion of identity goes, I think you have a pretty unique view of the topic. I've never had the problem you do, obviously, since I'm an only child. But…do I know who I am? I don't know how to answer that. Am I defined by who my parents are? Or were, since Mom is dead, and Dad is…absent. I mean, they raised me, they infused me with their beliefs and morals, gave me their DNA and the genetics that make up my talents and what I look like. But I'm also a product of society, right? I mean, our society is different now than when our parents were kids, and the structure and fabric of our society is a huge factor in creating who we are, right? But none of that says who I am. I'm Caden Connor Monroe, son of Aidan and Janice. I'm an artist. I guess I'm also kind of a cowboy, too. But who else am I? What else am I? I don't know, and I don't even know how to start answering that question.

I'm not a kid here. In Wyoming, I mean. I don't think I'm a kid at all. Mom dying grew me up. Driving to Wyoming did, too, in a way. I mean, it was just a road trip, but somehow, the process of making that decision and carrying it out on my own eradicated the last bit of my childhood. I'm expected to get up at dawn with Gramps and Uncle Gerry and Ben, Miguel, Riley, and all the other ranch hands. I'm expected to pull my weight, and as Gramps's grandson, as I get older and learn more, I'm also given more responsibility. I work from sunup to sundown, seven days a week. Before sunup and after sundown some days. I actually just got back from a twenty-hour nonstop ride around the entire perimeter of Gramps's fence line, fixing breaks and collecting some horses that had gotten out. I mean that literally when I say twenty hours nonstop. We started at 4 a.m., and it's past 2 a.m. now, and we just got in. I'm still in my boots as I write this, but I'm literally so tired the words are swimming on the page. I'm surprised it's legible at all, honestly. I don't mind the work, to be honest. It keeps me busy, keeps my mind occupied so I can't get stuck thinking about Mom and Dad.

Anyway, I'm gonna pass out now. Talk to you soon.

Caden

I didn't mention Billy Harper, or the date, or the kiss. I never would. Not my business. My business was breaking horses, foaling, herding. My business

would be school. Art. Surviving. My business was *not*
Ever Eliot and who she went out with or who she
kissed. She was just my pen pal.

I put the letter in an envelope and sealed it, then
passed out.

The next few weeks went quickly. I got a letter back from Ever, but it was short and kind of
empty. She talked about her latest painting project,
an attempt to re-create a Monet piece stroke for
stroke, color for color. I wrote back describing what
an average day as a ranch hand on a working horse
ranch was like. She didn't mention Billy Harper
again, and I didn't ask.

Weeks turned into months, and then the start of
the school year was approaching, and I had to decide
whether to go back to Michigan.

"You're goin' back, Cade," Gramps said, when
I asked him what he thought. "You ain't quittin'
school, that's for fuckin' sure."

"No, Gramps. I mean I'd finish the last two years
in Casper. Then I'd be here in the early mornings and
evenings to help out, not just the summer months."

"Oh. Well, I guess you'd best discuss that with
your Pops. You know you're welcome here, and I'd
honestly be glad for the year-round help, as long as
you finish school."

"Dad won't care."

Gramps frowned. "He's still your father, Caden Connor Monroe, and you ain't an adult yet. You still owe him the respect of askin' him, tell him what you're thinking."

I sighed. "I know. I just…I don't want to go back. I'm…I'm worried he's worse. He hasn't even called once. Hasn't texted. Nothing. Years past, he'd call a couple times a week to check in."

Gramps shook his head. "I know, son, I know. But you gotta make the effort. I'll fly you there, and if you decide to come back, I'll help you move. I can spare about two weeks, most. We'll rent a truck and drive you out here, if it comes to that."

"Gramps, I don't have nothin' to move. Nothin' at that house means anything to me. It's just a bed and an empty dresser. I brought everything that was really mine that I cared about with me."

Gramps bought me a one-way ticket to Michigan. I called Dad from the tarmac as the plane was taxiing, and he agreed to pick me up. He sounded like he had before: apathetic, absent. When he showed up an hour and a half later, he looked thinner than I'd ever seen him. His eyes were haggard, tired-looking. His skin was wrinkled, sagging. He hadn't shaved, and even his scalp, which he was normally fastidious about keeping egg-smooth, was stubbled with receding gray stubble.

I tried not to stare at him as he drove us home— back to his house. I wasn't sure where home was anymore. Home used to be this house, the one in Farmington where I'd grown up. But now...the ranch seemed more like home.

When we pulled into the driveway, he switched the car off but didn't move to get out. He just sat with his hands on the wheel, staring out the windshield, focused on nothing. Seeing something I couldn't see, maybe.

"Dad?"

He started, glanced at me. "Yeah?"

"Are you okay?"

He didn't answer right away. "I'm tired, Cade. Haven't been sleeping well. Not for a long time. Don't sleep much at all. Can't eat much, either."

"You're not sick, are you?"

"Don't think so. Just...I'm tired. I just don't have any energy."

I had no response for that. I waited for something to say, something to do, but came up empty. Eventually, I simply left him there in the truck and grabbed my single overnight bag from the bed and waited on the porch. It wasn't until we were inside and Dad was halfheartedly stirring and adding spices to some chili he'd left simmering while he came to pick me up that realization struck him.

"You only brought one bag." His voice was thin and sandpapery, a drastic change from the gruff and stentorian boom I'd grown up hearing.

I shrugged. "Yeah."

"Care to explain?"

I twirled my shading pencil around my middle finger, a trick I'd worked to perfect during long boring hours in history and math classes. "I'm—I guess I'm pretty set on moving out to Wyoming permanently for the rest of high school."

Dad didn't answer for a very long time. I almost started wondering if he'd heard me. "Oh, really?" He set the lid back on the chili and rubbed his scalp with his palm. "What makes you say that?"

"I like it there. I…well, I don't really have any friends here, and—I'd just rather be there."

"I see." He turned away from me, snatching a paper towel from the roll and wiping the counter. "Just like that, huh?"

"Look, Dad, I—all there is here for me is you and school. There, I'm working, and I can draw at school and stuff, and I—"

"I get it." He was scrubbing vigorously at a spot on the counter, although I didn't see anything on the counter that needed cleaning. "You need me to sign off on the transfer?"

"I guess I was thinking maybe you could emancipate me."

His eyes registered shock, hurt, and I winced to think I'd hurt him. "Why?"

"Just because it would be easiest. I'm basically on my own anyway. Gramps will be paying me ranch hand wage, and—"

"No. There's no need for that. You're sixteen. I'm fine with you moving to Wyoming, as long as Gramps is okay with it. But I'm alive, and I'm available. I get that you want your space and don't need me anymore, but I'm not going to emancipate you."

"It's not that, Dad." I didn't want to say what I was thinking, why I'd even considered emancipation.

"Then what is it?"

"It's just..." I couldn't bring myself to say that I was worried for him, for his health. For his... longevity.

"Move to Gramps's ranch. Fine. I'll sign off on that. But that's it."

I nodded. "Okay, then." I wasn't going to push the issue.

He sighed and went sort of limp, leaning on the counter and staring out the window listlessly. "Why'd you come back, then? Why'd you come back at all?"

God, he sounded so...lost. And lonely. I didn't know what to say to him, what wouldn't hurt him further. "I—it just seemed like the right way to do it, I guess."

"Meaning it was Gramps's idea." He pushed away from the counter, heading toward his study. "Stay as long as you like. You know where things are." And then he was gone, closing the study door behind him.

The kitchen echoed with his absence. The chili smelled good, but I knew it wasn't done yet. Dad always ate at seven, and it wasn't quite six. I heard the faint strains of music emanating from his office, and I recognized "House of the Rising Sun" by the Animals. Sunlight poured in from the west-facing window, golden and brilliant. A bird chirped.

My stomach twisted, and something inside me ached, for no reason at all.

And then I heard a *thump* from the study, and I knew.

Eighteen steps from kitchen to study door. Half a twist of the wrist, vision blurring, the door sliding open slowly on silent hinges.

Well, it's one foot on the platform/And the other on the train…

He lay on the floor on his side, curled up into a fetal position. His right hand clawed at the left side of his chest, and his eyes were wide and calm, tinged only a little by fear. He wasn't breathing, but struggling for it, or struggling perhaps against the instinct to fight for breath.

I collapsed to my hands and knees beside him, fumbling my phone out of my pocket. "Dad…no. Please, no." I unlocked the phone, tapped the icon to make a call, and had the nine and the one dialed when I felt his hand, heavy and urgent, on mine.

"No…Cade. Too—too late."

"No, it's not, Dad. They can get here and you'll be fine. Just fight, okay? Please? Just hold on. Don't— oh, god, oh, god—" I heard myself sobbing. "Don't die on me, Dad. Not you, too."

He gazed at me with soft, calm eyes. "I died with—with Jan. I'm just—just catching up to her." He paused to wheeze, wince, and the light in his eyes faded.

"No, Dad. No. I'm sorry. I didn't mean what I said about leaving. I love you."

"No sorry. Don't. Live. Love." He squeezed my hand with his, sudden frantic strength crushing my bones, but I didn't pull away. I squeezed back and cried like a baby. "Love you, Cade. Always."

And then the light faded, faded, and was gone. The bruising strength in his huge hand vanished, sluiced away. I couldn't breathe.

"Dad?" I shook him. "No!" I screamed. "No!"

There was nothing after that. Only a hand going cold, and my voice going hoarse, giving out.

I woke up in my childhood bed, the smell of cigarette smoke touching my nose.

Gramps.

I sat up. Gramps was at my desk, flipping through one of my old sketchbooks. Anyone else and I would've lost my temper a little, but it was Gramps, and I couldn't do that with him. My window was open, and as he flipped pages, he sucked a drag on the cigarette, blew it out the window, ashing into an empty beer can every once in a while. Gramps would flip, flip, flip, then pause to examine a sketch, flip again, drag in and blow out, ash, flip, flip, flip.

"Can't remember what movie it is, but there's a line in a movie," he said, his voice thick and scratchy. "'No parent should have to bury their child,' the line is."

"That's from *The Lord of the Rings. The Two Towers.* Theoden, King of Rohan says it." I'd gone through a phase, the year before art camp at Interlochen, where I'd watched those movies one after another for months on end. I could quote all three movies backward and forward.

"Ah. Yeah. So it is. You brought them with you to the ranch a few years back."

"How'd you get here? When, I mean?"

"Your Grams had a feeling. I caught the flight after yours. Found you in there, with him. I think you'd been there a while. Not sure how long, but he was...he'd been gone a while." Gramps shut the book and came to sit on the bed near my feet, the bed creaking under his weight. "You got shit luck, Cade."

I started to sob. "I know. God, I know. I watched…I watched him die. Just like Mom. He… he said he'd died with Mom, that he was just catching up to her."

"Sh-shit." Gramps rubbed at his face, thumbed the corner of his eye. "Your dad and I had our differences, but…he was still my son. And I loved him. I was proud of him, you know. I don't think…I don't think I ever told him, but I was. He'd made good for himself, goin' his own way, doin' his own thing. Made good, for damn sure."

"What now?" I whispered.

Gramps wiped at his face again, huffing in a deep breath, letting it out, broad, hard shoulders spreading and curling back in. "I don't know, Cade. I don't know. Carry on, one day at a time. S'all you can do, I think." Carry on, one day at a time. I wasn't sure how to do even that. Gramps clapped me on the shoulder as he stood up. "Take your time, Cade. I'll handle things."

Take my time? To do what? I wasn't sure what I was supposed to do. I was empty inside, and wished I could go to sleep and stay that way. But my eyes were open, and I knew I wouldn't sleep anytime soon.

I ended up at my desk, drawing. I don't even know what I drew. Only that sunlight shifted through the window, rising and falling as daylight streamed past me. I remember lines, arcs, and whorls, abstractions of the sorrow inside me. Heavy shading, shadows cast by nothing. I remember a raven, stark black on the white page. Wings furled, shown in profile, beady eye glinting and reflecting something hidden. A pocket watch hung by a chain from the raven's mouth, the hands stopped at 6:35.

Then a lined sheet of paper, slightly angled to the left on the desk.

Ever,

That summer we met, Interlochen. The lake. Drawing all day. Sitting on the dock together. It was the last of my childhood, I think. The last happy days of my life.

Dad died yesterday. Heart attack. Or a broken heart, if you want to get truthful about it. I don't think he could handle life without Mom. He just gave up, and his heart gave out. He wasn't even fifty.

I'm not sure why you and I are even doing these letters anymore. You've got your own life to live, and I'm just. I don't know. Cursed, maybe? Just living. Breathing, one day at a time. I miss back when things were simple, you know?

I hope things go well with Billy Harper. Hope he treats you well.

I'm rambling. I know I am. I'm lost. But...I drew until my hand ached, and I still have all this inside me. Where does it go? What do I do? Who am I? Too many questions. No answers. And you're with Billy Harper.

I understand your sister's jealousy. I feel the same way, a little. Jealous. Of you. Of Billy Harper. I haven't been on a date, or had a first kiss. First anything.

But that's whatever. Fine. I'm moving to Wyoming. Permanently, maybe. I don't know. I'm sure at some point in my life a girl will take pity on a cowboy orphan. Not angling for pity, FYI. Just...venting. Rambling. Sorry.

Cade

I signed it and sealed it and sent it without thinking about the repercussions. I didn't care. If she wanted to date Billy fucking Harper, that was fine with me. Why should I care?

I attended another funeral. Dressed in black, my eyes damp with tears that wouldn't shed. It rained this time. Appropriately enough, to my thinking. Warm rain, hissing on the awning as the dark wood casket was lowered into the ground. Gramps's hand on my shoulder.

Wyoming became home, permanently. I had an inheritance from Dad, savings plus life insurance.

Enough that I would be fine for a while. Enough for college, if I went. I didn't want the money, though. I went to school in Casper, rode the range, and didn't even try to meet anyone, or make friends.

And that, of course, is how I met Luisa Alvarez.

first love, dreams like memory

Ever

The letter had a place in my purse, folded in half and tucked into an inside pocket, nestled between maxi pads and a pack of Trident gum. I didn't want to open it. I had a bad feeling about it.

Instead, I left it there and refused to open it and waited for "the right time" to read Cade's latest missive. It was a selfish thing. The letter was…I didn't even know why, but I felt like just touching the envelope made me sad. As if I knew somehow, maybe psychologically or emotionally, maybe psychically, that it contained more tragedy. And I didn't want to have to feel that.

Dates with Will were amazing things. He was amazing. He took me to interesting places. Concerts at the Joe Louis Arena, plays at the Meadowbrook. Long drives late at night, listening to jazz. Talking until dawn.

Kissing in the darkness. It started easily, just a kiss goodnight that lasted for an hour. Sneaking away during lunch hour to make out in his car at the far corner of the school parking lot.

His hands didn't begin to wander until we'd been dating and making out for two weeks. I'd started to wonder, honestly. The idea of horny teenage boys was imprinted firmly in my head, strengthened by the stories I'd heard from girls at school. A phrase I heard all too frequently was "I wanted to, just not as soon as he did." I knew what that meant. Of course I did. But with Will, it was different.

So I was more than ready for it when his palm touched my knee. We were in his car, as usual. Jazz played in the background, something quick and jaunty and almost aggressive in its frenetic energy. My body was buzzing, high on Will's lips, drunk with his proximity. He made me aware of myself. Aware of my body. Of my hands and my thighs and my breasts and my clothes and my own desires. I *wanted* him to touch me, just a little. That was it, just…a little exploration.

So when his palm touched my knee, hesitated, and slid up my leg to my thigh, I didn't demur. My hands were on his shoulders, touching but not holding, embracing but not pulling. When his hand went up to my thigh, I let my fingers graze down his shirt to caress his chest, touching the muscles there. His lips parted and his tongue slid into my mouth, and I tasted it, felt it, was shocked pleasantly by it, by the heat of his hand on my thigh. I touched his tongue with mine, gasping at the tang of tongue touching tongue and the way my entire being buzzed and hummed.

Now his hand was on my waist, and I waited, breathless, kissing him, to see what he'd do next. A fingertip under the hem of my Lumineers T-shirt, touching bare skin. Oh, my god. I couldn't breathe if I wanted to. My palms skated around his arms to his back and down the soft cotton, and now I was touching the heat of his skin as well, and together we explored flesh, upward, upward. I didn't dare even think of what was happening, of the fact that Will's hand was under my shirt and skirting across my ribcage, not even an inch beneath the underwire of my lacy red bra. Lacy red bra, that I'd put on for this date. Not because I thought he'd see it, but because some part of me I didn't dare examine too closely wanted him to.

We paused for breath, foreheads touching, exploration halted.

"Ever…" Will breathed, "is this okay?"

I nodded. "Yes."

"Are you sure?"

I kissed him to cover the fact that I wasn't quite sure, not entirely. A thought skittered in the back of my head that maybe this was all happening too fast, but I knew, from the girls at school, that for most of them two weeks was an eternity to wait, that for many of them, I was being strangely careful. That being a virgin at sixteen put me in the minority of the girls I knew. That I was just now getting to this point, to second base, as I supposed the boys thought of it, was unusual.

But I didn't want to think of that. I just wanted to kiss Will and let him touch me and feel his skin under my hands. It felt nice. I felt wanted. I felt liked. I felt like someone other than Ever Eliot. I wasn't drawing or painting or taking photos or going to class. I was with a boy.

An image of strong, sure hands and dark serious eyes flashed through my mind: Cade's hands, Cade's eyes.

I blinked, and met Will's eyes, blue eyes blazing with heat. Saw his hands on my waist, strong hands, yes, but clean, soft hands. Cade's had been roughened by work, callused.

Why did that matter? It was Will's hands on me, not Cade's. And that was fine, right? Cade was my pen pal, Will was my boyfriend. End of discussion.

I pushed the niggling wondering doubt from my mind and closed my eyes and touched my lips to Will's. Sparks flew, heat billowed. My skin tightened and my mind whirled and my stomach flipped. The kiss deepened, and Will's hands slid up my sides and skated across my ribs beneath my bra, tempting and tantalizing. My own fingers were dancing up his back and across his chest and over his shoulders, touching bare skin beneath his shirt. I couldn't breathe and didn't care. This was exciting, a daring adventure I flung myself into willingly. I arched my spine and sucked in a breath, swelling my breasts, and now Will's palms were brushing the round of my bra. I felt my nipple harden, felt his touch stutter and stop so the bottom edge of his palm rested on the hard nub, dragged back across. Lightning sizzled inside me, threatening to arc and bolt if only he touched more, touched skin.

I almost made a noise of disappointment when he slid his palm away and up my chest to my shoulder, but oh, yes, okay, he was brushing the strap down, freeing the weight of my left breast, and now his fingers were tugging the edge of the cup away and our kiss was a fiery maelstrom of lips and tongues and I felt so adult, so alive, so energized by the knowledge of what we were doing that I couldn't contain it all.

Now the other strap was sagging around my bicep and he was pushing the cups down and my boobs were free and his palms were slipping over skin and I was on fire, gasping into his mouth as his fingers touched a nipple and brought it to diamond hardness.

My T-shirt was still loose and draping over his hands, shielding me from view, mine and his. What if I took my shirt off? I thought about it, and the notion made me dizzy. It would be a huge step. Letting him touch me was one thing, somehow, but intentionally taking my shirt off to show him my body was another.

Before I could second-guess myself, I broke the kiss and stripped the shirt off. Will sucked in a deep, sharp breath as my pale flesh was bared to the moonlight streaming in through the sunroof of his car. He grinned at me and peeled his own shirt off, and now it was my turn to gasp at the sight of his rippling, sculpted abs, and the elastic band of his Calvin Klein underwear peeking out above his Hugo Boss jeans. I ran my hands over his chest, let my fingers trace the lines of his abs, and he just watched me touch him. And then his thumb dragged slowly across my nipple, sending a bolt of pure arousal through me.

I arched my spine and tipped my head back, and his palm closed over my boob and lifted the weight, cupping it, gentle and knowledgeable. I knew he'd done this before, that much was clear in the way he touched me, especially when he reached behind me and unclasped my bra with one hand in a single, deft motion.

He met my eyes as he brought the lace and silk away, and I held his gaze steadily, telling him silently that it was fine, even though my pulse was a wild tribal drumbeat in my chest and I wanted desperately to cover myself, but I didn't, because Will's gaze was frankly appreciative, taking in my skin and my breasts with greedy hunger.

And then he rolled toward me, leaning over the console between us and kissing me, hovering over me so his chest brushed the tips of my boobs. With one hand he fumbled for the seat controls and leaned my seat backward so I was lying down and he was above me, and his fingers were tracing lines on my belly, stopping at the button of my jeans, and I knew what he was asking.

"Not yet," I whispered. "Not that far, not yet."

He kissed my neck. "Sure thing, Ever. Maybe I could just…touch you a little, though? I know ways to make you feel really good."

I knew what he was referring to. I might have been a virgin, but I wasn't ignorant. I'd touched myself, of course. Discovered the various ways to make myself come, and I could imagine how good that would feel when someone else was doing it to me. But…that would be as good as admitting I was willing to have sex with Will. I knew that's where it was going, of course I did. I knew that's what he wanted. And a part of me wanted it, too. But there was also another part of me that wasn't sure. Both about whether I was ready at all, and whether Will was the right person to have my first time with.

Will. I intentionally thought of him as Will, but in the back of my head, he was always Billy. In my private thoughts, he was Billy. And I'd written to Cade and referred to him as Billy. What was the significance? I didn't know, but there was a significance. I just wished I could figure out what it meant.

All these thoughts raced through me, and all the while Will was kissing my shoulder and my throat and my clavicle and my breastbone and between my boobs, and I was frozen by the heat of his lips on my skin, and by the fact that now he was kissing the slope of my breast and closer, closer, and now I did gasp aloud, almost a moan, as his lips closed over my nipple and drew a bolt of lightning from me.

My body betrayed me. My body refused to do anything except respond to Will's touch. My hand wouldn't stop him as he unbuttoned my jeans and drew down the zipper and slid his fingers under the elastic and found me waiting for him, hot and wet, and my voice wouldn't rise from my throat to tell him to stop because my body liked it, even though the doubts still raced through my brain and my heart was unsure where it was or what it wanted, but my body didn't care because my body was in control; or rather, my body was under the spell of Will's touch, and I was letting it happen.

His fingers found the perfect place, and now my hips were bucking and I was moaning and he was doing something else to me between my legs with his hands, something I'd never done, and now everything inside me blew up, just detonated, and I couldn't help the noises coming from me.

Will chuckled. "God, Ever, you're noisy, aren't you?"

"S-sorry," I breathed.

"No, it's cute. It's…hot."

Now that adrenaline and arousal and post-orgasm chemicals were blasting through me and leaving me, something like shame hit me. I pushed his hand away and sat up, shaky fingers hunting for the control to bring the seat upright. Had I really just let Will finger me? Oh, god. Did that make me easy? Did he think I was going to be an easy conquest? What if he just wanted my cherry, and then he'd not want me anymore? Ellie Myers had had that happen to her. A hot, popular guy had acted all interested in her and dated her and lured her step by step into sex, kiss by kiss and touch by touch, and then after he finally got her to sleep with him, he'd dumped her, and she'd been devastated. She'd just wanted Brian to like her, because Brian was a basketball star and a senior with college prospects and hot as hell, and we all knew how it was going to end, because that was just how Brian Washington was and everyone knew it but Ellie.

Was Billy that way? There weren't any rumors about him, not like with Brian. I'd never heard anybody at school talk about getting with him. He didn't have the reputation Brian did. Billy was mysterious, seeming uninterested in the popularity game, but he was all the more popular for all that, especially because he clearly came from big money and was hot and talented. But was he a player?

I just didn't know.

I was pulling my clothes on while all this bubbled up in my head.

"Hey, are you okay?" Billy—Will—dragged a hand through his spiky blond hair and peered at me in concern. "Did I...did I rush you?"

I shook my head and shrugged as I tugged my T-shirt over my head. "No, I let you do it. Now I'm just not sure...I don't know....I don't even know what I'm saying. You didn't rush me, and you gave me plenty of opportunity to stop you, and I didn't. But now I'm—I don't know."

Will found his shirt and pulled it on. "I get it. That's how I felt my first time, too. During, it was great. Afterward, I was all mixed up."

"That wasn't even my first time, not really. Not—not all the way."

Will shrugged, fiddling with a loose thread on one of his belt loops. "No, but I was just saying I know how you're feeling. To some degree, anyway."

I decided to just go for it, tell him what I was feeling and see how he reacted. I could sense a lie pretty well, I thought. "I'm just wondering…have you done this a lot? With a lot of different people?"

He rubbed the back of his neck. "Yes and no. It's complicated. See, number one, I'm seventeen. I missed a year of school. Well, I didn't miss it, I was just out of the country getting tutored privately, and the U.S. school system wouldn't count some of what I did, so I had take junior year all over again, even though I should be a senior, age-wise and according to what I've studied. And…while I was over there, in Germany, with my parents, I had a girlfriend. We… were together for almost a year and a half, and we did…well, it was like with you and me. She was my first, but I wasn't hers. She was older than me. Eighteen when we met, and I wasn't quite sixteen. And Elsa…she taught me a lot. So I've done it a lot, but not with a lot of different people."

"Were you around when everything happened with Ellie Myers and Brian Washington?" I asked.

Will nodded. "Yeah. That was shitty. He's a douchebag. I heard him talking about her the day before I guess she actually slept with him. He was just…bragging. About how she was following along like a little puppy. Telling the guys in detail what she looked like naked, how he'd gotten her clothes off, how he'd gotten her to go down on him, and all that. How she was a brown-bagger."

"A what?"

He didn't answer right away. "The kind of girl you put a bag over her head when you're banging her. It's a shitty-ass phrase, and I hate it. I'm not like that, Ever. I swear."

"I guess I just don't want to be like her. Everyone knew his rep, knew that's what he did. Even I knew he was a player, and that he was playing her. But… with you, I don't know. You don't have that same kind of rep, but—"

"Look, Ever, I like you. I really do. I'm not gonna tell you I love you to get you sleep with me. I'm not in love with you, not—not in a forever kind of way. Just honestly. I'm attracted to you, and I like you, and I like spending time with you. If you want this with me, great, awesome, but if you don't, tell me. And don't think that just because you're not ready that I'm gonna ditch you. If you need time, that's fine. I'm not rushing you or pushing you. At least, I'm not try-ing to." He turned to look at me, and I saw nothing but honesty in his features."

"So then what is this, between us?"

"I don't know. We're dating? We're just...I don't know. Does it have to be something defined? Does it have to be one true love to do what we want to do together? If we both want it, and we both agree, what's the problem?"

"Nothing, I guess." I watched clouds drift across the face of the moon. "I just never thought about it, but now I am. I don't know what I want. When we're...making out and whatever, I'm all into it. I like it, and don't want to stop. But then after, I wonder if it should mean something. I mean, like you said, I like you, and I'd definitely attracted to you, but am I *in love* with you? I don't know. I don't think so. Should I be? Or what if, like you said, we just do what we want to do, because it feels good? It does, too. But shouldn't it mean something?"

Will took my hand, twined our fingers. "But— why doesn't it mean something, just because we're not, like, star-crossed lovers or whatever? We don't have to be in love for it to mean something. Right?" He squeezed my hand and gazed at me intently. "And we don't have to do anything. I like going out with you. I have fun with you. Just...it's up to you, okay?"

I nodded, and Will put the car in drive, pulled out of the parking lot of the park that had become our usual spot, and drove me home. We didn't talk on the way, just listened to fun. and held hands and watched the Bloomfield Hills mansions whisk past us in the midnight darkness.

After he dropped me off, I tiptoed past Eden's studio door, not wanting to explain what I'd been doing, knowing she'd sense it on me, and closed my bedroom door behind me. I stripped off my clothes and stared at my naked body in the full-length mirror in my walk-in closet. What did I want? Should I go all the way with Will?

No answer came to me from the mirror, from my reflection. Only my pale white skin and heavy breasts with their wide, dark areolae and thick pink nipples. My privates. I touched myself, remembering how Will's fingers had felt.

I took a shower, dried off, put my hair into curlers for the next day. I got into bed and found myself unable to fall asleep. I kept going over what I'd done with Will, how it had felt, what we'd talked about. When I finally drifted into the twilight of almost-sleep, I dreamed of hands touching me, lips on my skin.

In the dream, even though my eyes were closed and I couldn't see, I knew I was naked. I was bare to the air, to his touch, his kiss. I knew, too, that he was naked as well. In the dream, I was nervous. I was going to make love to him. With him. But somehow I knew it wasn't my first time, or his. It was dream-knowledge, there without source or memory.

Yet we were both still nervous, scared, trembling together. His touch wasn't sure and knowledgeable and skilled. He was hesitant, hungry and needy but seeking, wondering. Wondrous. As was my touch, my hands on his body, my lips on his skin.

In the dream, darkness faded. Eyesight returned, as if floating upward from the bottom of a pool, no, from the deepest depths of a fathomless ocean, and I saw him beside me. Not above or beneath, but beside. Touching, kissing, holding, together.

And it wasn't Billy. Awareness hit, the strange way it does in dreams. Before I was able to make out his features, I knew, instinctively, inside myself, that it wasn't Billy—and my dream-brain thought of him as Billy, not Will.

It was Caden in my dream.

There were no doubts with us, only tender needing aching dreaming perfect wonder. And meaning. Deep significance in each touch, each kiss.

His eyes were blazing bright and clearest sunlit amber, fixed on mine, serious and sad, yet hot with desire and need. His mouth opened and his lips moved, and he said my name in a whisper that echoed throughout time, out of sync with the motion of his lips.

"EVER..."

The dream faded, and I was left aching with emptiness. I wanted to hold on to the dream, to the comforting swell of belonging I'd felt in Caden's dream-arms.

Caden

Henry was restless. He was a huge young stallion, over seventeen hands high, black with three white socks and a thick mane. Powerful, spirited, and eager to please, Henry was often difficult to keep under rein because he simply wanted to run, *run* until sky met land in a permanently unrolling horizon. Gramps hadn't been sure I was ready to ride Henry—whose full name was Henry V, an homage by Grams to Shakespeare—but I'd convinced him to let me try. So over the last few weeks I'd been learning to ride Henry and to make him understand that I was boss. I'd been thrown twice, and nearly broke my arm the last time, but now he was finally getting the picture.

I'd finished moving the herd of green-broke mares to the hilly pastures at the northern edge of the property, near the river, when I saw her. She was sitting by the bank with an open book on her lap and a sleek dun gelding I recognized as belonging to Miguel tethered to a stake not far away.

I let the herd drift and reined Henry to a stop, wondering who she was. Thick black hair loose around her shoulders, fluttering in the slow breeze, dark-tanned arms bare, wearing a sleeveless white shirt printed with purple flowers and a pair of faded jeans, well-worn feminine cowboy boots crossed at the ankles.

I swung off Henry and held his reins in my fist as I approached her. She turned the page of her book, and then after a moment stuck a ribbon in her place and shut it. When she turned to face me, I recognized her. Or rather, I saw the immediate resemblance to Miguel and figured she had to be his daughter.

She was beautiful, and I was tongue-tied.

"*Hola*—I mean, hello." She was soft-spoken, with a thick Hispanic accent.

"Hi." I stood a few feet away from her, holding on to Henry's lead, letting him browse the grass.

"You are Caden, *sí?*" She stood up and brushed off the seat of her jeans. "Mister Monroe's *nieto?* Son of his son? I do not know the word."

"Grandson. Yeah. You're Miguel's daughter?"

She shook her head. "No, not daughter. He is my *tio*. Uncle? My name is Luisa."

"Oh, okay." I held out my hand, and she took it. Her hand was tiny, soft, and warm. "Nice to meet you, Luisa."

"Nice to meet you." She said the phrase as if repeating what I'd said.

"So, did you move up here, then? Or…"

Luisa nodded. "I come here to live with *Tio* Miguel. To go to school in America." She pulled up

the tethering stake and we walked along the river-
bank together, leading our horses.

"So how long have you been here?"

She gazed out at the hills, and the herd of mares
nosing at the green grass. "Um…since two weeks.
Your *abuelo*, he will hire my papa in the spring, *tio*
says. Until then, I live with *tio*."

I nodded. "Yeah, I heard Gramps talking about
hiring some hands for foaling season."

"Foaling…season?" Luisa glanced at me in confusion, her expression asking for clarification.

"When mama horses have their babies. It's usually between February and April."

"Oh. This. Yes." She nodded as if familiar.

"You ride a lot? Back home?"

Luisa shrugged. "Oh, *sí*. My family, Miguel, Papa,
my *abuelo*, we work on the same rancho for many
generaciones. I grow up there, ride the *caballos*, bring
the *potros*, the baby horses. Foals, you say it?"

"Yeah, foals. Baby horses. So you know horse
ranches, then?"

She nodded. "All of my living, *sí*. This is much
like my home in Mexico."

We'd walked quite a ways as we talked, and I realized I had to get back to where my herd was. "Ride
with me? I've got to go back thataway." I jerked my
thumb toward the cluster of horses.

Luisa swung gracefully into the saddle, and I followed suit. Together, we kept the herd bunched as they grazed, and talked about horses, and riding, and life on a ranch. I told her about having just moved to Casper full-time, which of course led to telling her about my mom and dad dying.

Luisa's gaze went sad as I spoke, and when I was finished, she toyed with the reins, not looking at me. "My mama was from Mexico City. Met my papa when he was there for a holiday. They fall in love, and she come pregnant with me. She only very young. Mama and Papa marry, and go together back to where Papa live, to *el rancho*. Only, she never want to live there, so far from the city. From all the people and the...busy-ness. When I am only five years old, she run away. Back to Mexico City. Find another man. Send Papa the papers for breaking the marriage, for the *divorcio*. I no see her again, after then. Papa, he sad. All the time, so sad. She is not dead, like your mama, but she is gone."

"That sucks."

Luisa laughed, suddenly brightening. "Sucks? I hear this before, but...I do not understand. What is sucking?"

I furrowed my brow, realizing I had no idea how to explain the phrase, since I wasn't sure what it really meant in any literal sense, or where the phrase had come from. "Um...I guess it just means...like, 'wow, that's horrible.' I guess I don't really know how to explain what it means. It's not, like, sucking on a straw, you know? More, just…some people say 'sucks ass,' if that helps you any."

"That is gross. But I think I understand."

We rode some more, and I found myself talking easily, laughing, even, for the first time in months. I was so caught up in conversation with Luisa that I didn't notice the clouds coming in until it was too late. By the time I realized that the sunlight had been replaced by heavy gray thunderheads, the first drops were pattering on our heads.

"Uh-oh," I said, "We're gonna get rained on."

"Is only rain. It will not hurt us."

At that moment thunder growled overhead and a bolt of lightning flashed, striking a few miles away. "No, the rain won't," I said, pointing at the second flash of lightning that struck closer to where we were, "but the lightning will. We're out in the open, and we're liable to get struck."

The rain picked up, going from a few scattered drops on our head to a steady downpour. By the time we'd gotten the horses heading back toward the north paddocks, we were both soaked the skin, and the rain was only getting harder. I tried to keep my gaze on the horses around us, on Henry's bobbing head, on the sky and the lightning, but it was hard. Luisa was wearing a white shirt, thin cotton that went completely see-through, sticking to her skin. If she noticed my gaze being constantly drawn to her chest, she didn't let on. I really did try not to stare. It was nearly impossible, though. She wasn't wearing a bra, and her small, high breasts were outlined in perfect detail, the dark circles surrounding her hardened nipples showing clearly.

I thought about offering her my shirt, which was just as wet but was black and so would cover her, but then realized that to do so might make it obvious I'd been staring at her boobs. So instead I kept quiet and did my best to not be too blatant about stealing glances.

Except once I glanced over at her and simply couldn't look away. She had her spine arched and her face tipped up to the sky, catching raindrops on her outstretched tongue. Her shirt was simply plastered to her skin, delineating the curve of her spine and the dimpling of her ribs and the perky roundness of her boobs, which bounced with the trotting gait of her horse. I was entranced, hypnotized.

And then she opened her eyes and looked right at me. My mouth might have been open, a little. She grinned at me, and then let her gaze rake down my body. My own shirt was sticking to my abs and biceps, and I supposed Luisa liked what she saw, since her expression was appreciative.

The air was charged between us then, rife with tension. Luisa brought her mount closer to mine so we were riding close enough that our legs touched. Thunder boomed directly above our heads, cracking so loud that the air shivered and our horses both tossed their manes and whickered, nervous, sidestepping and bobbing and shaking. The hair on my arms stood on end, prickling, a thickness in the air choking me, tangy and acidic. We were passing a stand of trees just then, a small clump of short ash trees of some kind. I heard thunder clap twice more, and saw bright flashes to my left, just out of my peripheral vision.

Henry whinnied, reared, and danced backward on his hind legs. I clung to his neck, leaning against him to keep my balance. Luisa's horse was rearing as well, and even as I struggled to calm Henry, I couldn't help but appreciate how skillfully she handled her frightened mount.

Time seemed to slow then, as a blinding explosion of white light struck a tree a few feet away from us. The air itself seemed to detonate, billowing outward with hurricane force. I felt myself thrown from Henry's back. Even as I hurtled through the air, I heard horses screaming and Luisa shrieking and hooves pounding, and then I hit the ground, painfully hard. I couldn't breathe, and my feet were cold. I stared up at the gray-black sky, watching the rain fall, twisting and windblown, shreds of low clouds skirling, flashes of lightning bouncing from cloud to cloud, arcing down to strike the trees again. I watched a thick pinkish-white bolt hit the tallest tree, and smaller curls of electricity sizzled down the fractured and smoking trunk and danced across the ground. I still couldn't breathe, and my chest ached, my lungs burned.

Why were my feet cold?

I glanced down at my feet and realized my boots were gone. My breath slowly returned, and I struggled to my feet, dizzy and wobbly. Henry was several yards away, shaking his head and dancing away from Luisa, who was trying to calm him enough so she could grab his dangling reins. One of my boots was stuck in the stirrup, while the other was standing upright on the ground, as if I'd taken it off and left it there. My hat was several feet away, tumbling in the wind.

Luisa managed to snag Henry's lead, and tugged him back toward me. She saw me standing up and rushed toward me, pulling both horses with her, transferring the reins of both horses to one hand as she reached me. "Caden, *estás herido?*"

"Huh?" I didn't know a lick of Spanish, and I didn't think my brain was working on all cylinders just yet anyway.

"*Herido*…hurt? Are you okay?" She looked me over, saw my now-soaked white sock feet. "Your boots, where they go?"

"I think I'm okay. It didn't hit me directly, I don't think. Close, though." I grabbed for the boot wedged in Henry's stirrup but couldn't get it free. The rubber was fried to the metal of the stirrup, and I saw that Henry's coat was singed where the stirrup had been touching. "I think the bolt hit the tree and then arced at the stirrup. It's melted, see?"

Luisa examined the boot and stirrup, wiggled the boot, and finally got it free. "You are very lucky, I think."

"No shit," I agreed. "Lucky as hell. Are you okay?" I stuck the boot back onto my foot, grimacing. It had been blasted out of shape, but it was better than being essentially barefoot. The other boot was intact, and I put that on, too.

Luisa nodded. "Oh yes, *estoy bien.*"

We were standing face to face, the thunderhead having moved on, leaving us in a torrential downpour, the kind you can only get from a freak Wyoming storm. The horses whickered, Henry nosing Luisa's gelding. The herd had kept moving, I thought, but wasn't sure. I'd have to find them and get them back to the north paddock, but at the moment all I could think of was Luisa, standing inches away from me. Her face was turned up to mine, and she seemed to be getting closer, closer. I felt the cold wet touch of her shirt against mine, and then softness pressing against my chest.

Every cell in my body was attuned to her in that moment. I didn't even know her last name, but I knew what was happening. I knew I wanted it. I wanted to feel her lips against mine. I hadn't thought of Mom or Dad since I'd seen her, and I hadn't thought of the empty hollow ache in my heart, in my soul. I wasn't lonely. I was Caden and she was Luisa, and that was all that mattered.

I could feel the hard nubs of her nipples against my chest, and somehow my hands were on her waist and she was pressing the length of her body against mine. Her eyes were so brown, so wide. Long lashes fluttered in the rain, hair like ink curled in wet strands against her cheek and forehead and down her neck. I felt her hands on my shoulders, and her breath on my face.

"*Bésame…*"

"What? I don't—I don't speak Spanish." I thought I might have an inkling as to what she was saying, though. "Can I kiss you?"

She just smiled and moved even closer. "*Sí*. This is what I said."

Her lips were warm, a counterpoint to the cold rain. I felt like lightning was still sizzling inside me, striking me at every point of contact where her body touched mine. She arched into the kiss, pressed her mouth to mine, and clawed her fingers into my shoulder blades.

The kiss lasted an eternity. Neither of us broke free first; we both pulled away at the same moment, gasping. Luisa's eyes searched mine. "I have…been kiss before, but not like this." She put her hand to the back of my head and pulled me to her, pulled my lower lip into her mouth, and something inside me went nova. "I wish it was not raining."

I pulled back and gave her a quizzical look. "Why?"

"So the kiss does not have to end." Something in her steady, hot gaze told me she meant more than merely kissing.

I felt my cheeks heating up as I realized what she meant. She seemed so quiet, so contained. As we'd talked, she always spoke calmly, evenly, never swore or used vulgar expressions. She moved with poise and grace, and this…this forwardness was unexpected.

She must have noticed my blush, because her lips quirked up in an amused and almost predatory smile. "*Eres virgen?*" I caught that last word, sure enough. I nodded, eyes on my feet. She touched her lips to mine once more, briefly, and then backed away and handed me Henry's reins. "Come, we should go. This rain will not stop *para muchas horas.*"

The herd had scattered, and it took us more than an hour to get them bunched and back to the paddock, where Gramps was waiting, his expression equal parts concern and anger. "Where you been, Cade?"

I lifted my boot and showed him the melted sole, and the scorched bit of Henry's hair. I'd checked him out before mounting, and he wasn't hurt, only the hair of his coat slightly charred. "Got caught in the storm, Gramps. Nearly got struck."

Luisa spoke up. "He was hit, *Señor* Monroe. He was knocked from his seat."

Gramps narrowed his eyes. "You okay, son?"

I nodded. "Sure. Wasn't a direct hit. Struck a tree and arced to the stirrup. Knocked me off, but I'm fine. Need new boots, though."

Gramps's eyes moved to Luisa, and then quickly away. Luisa glanced down and then crossed her arms over her chest. "Give the girl your shirt, Cade. She needs covering."

I peeled my shirt off and handed it to her, but instead of trying to put on the sopping-wet shirt, she pressed it against her front, glancing at Gramps after she was covered. "*Lo siento,*" she mumbled.

"*Que está bien.*" Gramps's Spanish accent was nearly perfect, which kind of surprised me. But then I realized Miguel had worked for Gramps since before I was born, and he usually hired friends or relatives of Miguel's for the busiest seasons. Gramps waved at Luisa. "*Vete a casa, niña.*"

"*Sí, señor.*" She glanced at me and gave me a small smile. "Thank you for riding with me, Cade. Perhaps we can ride together again?"

"I'd like that," I said.

"Me too. *Adiós.*" She wheeled her horse around and was gone.

Gramps was leaning against the railing of the paddock, his gaze thoughtful. Rain dripped from the brim of his Stetson. "So. You met Luisa, huh?"

"Yeah, guess so." I wasn't sure where he was going with it, so I figured it was best to stay neutral.

"Nice girl."

"Yeah."

"And pretty."

"She's beautiful, yeah." I slid off Henry and scratched between his eyes.

Gramps seemed to be hunting for the right words. "Ain't up to me to say why she moved out this'a way, but...look, she's Miguel's niece, and he feels responsible for her. So just...be careful, all right?"

"She said she was moving up here to go to school."

Gramps shrugged, an uncharacteristically noncommittal gesture. "More than that to it, but like I said, ain't my story."

"Was she in trouble or something?"

"Dinner soon," Gramps said by way of not answering, "so best get Henry put up and some dry clothes on you."

Midnight saw me still awake, exhausted but unable to sleep. I'd worked since five that morning, and had to be up at five again the next morning; yet sleep eluded me. I wondered what Gramps had been alluding to regarding Luisa. It sounded like he'd meant she'd been sent here for more than just school. Maybe it had something to do with how…open… she'd been about kissing me, and wanting more.

I finally drifted off, floating just above the blackness of true sleep, tilting and falling in the weightless space of not-asleep, not-awake. I dreamed of hands on my chest, skin against skin. I knew the silk-soft texture of breast in my hand, even though I'd never experienced that before. I knew the taste of lips on mine, and knew that she was mine, I was hers, and this was *right*. Perfect and true, everything we'd ever wanted and ever needed, the fullness of desire made flesh, and nothing existed, nothing mattered. Nothing but *her*.

Darkness lightened to the haze of moonlight, or a candlelit bedroom.

I saw, not dusky Latin skin and brown eyes, but porcelain flesh and jade-green eyes. Ever's eyes. It was her body I saw, too, generous curves, heavy breasts, not Luisa's small and delicate frame. She was naked like me, flesh against flesh, and her lips met mine and I knew heaven in that dreaming kiss, bliss like nothing I'd ever felt. In the dream, there was nothing to forget, nothing to be distracted from, because she was everything.

It didn't feel like a dream. It felt like something I'd lived, love I'd known. It felt like a memory.

When the dream ended, I felt as if I was missing a piece of my soul, like the memory was all that was left of a love I'd had and lost.

interstice

Ever

Caden,

I don't know who else to turn to. I've never been so mixed up in my life. It's about Will. I know this kind of goes beyond what we usually talk about, and maybe it's kind of weird. I don't know. I'm just messed up in my head, in my heart. He's...amazing. He's this talented jazz musician, which is just cool by itself. He's not a rock star, although he has that same kind of presence and magnetism, but he just wants to be in a jazz band, like Miles Davis or John Coltrane. He's been teaching me about jazz, which I never thought I'd like, but I do. It's different and cool.

And he treats me well. He's not like the other guys at school, you know? I know if I was dating any other guy, he'd be all over me, pressuring me to sleep with him. Most of the girls I'm friends with have already done it with their boyfriends, and I've heard how a lot of them felt pushed into it. Like the boys wanted it, and they felt like they had to go along with it to prove something to their boyfriends, or to themselves. Not everybody, of course. I know Irene Oliver basically seduced her boyfriend because she was ready to get rid of her V-card, as she put it. I don't want it to be that way. And Will understands that, which is so cool.

But I know he wants it. He says he's willing to be patient and wait for me to be ready. But what if I'm never ready? How do I know I'm ready? I mean, when we're making out, I can't think of anything else, and it feels like I could just do anything and it would be amazing. I'd be lying if I said I didn't feel pressure from people at school to lose my virginity. But I don't want it to just happen, you know?

Do you know?

I don't want to wait forever. I want it. I do. And I think if I'm going to do it with anyone, Will would be perfect. But...I'm just confused. Do I wait for a sign? I mean, I don't think I'm in love with him, you know? He and I even talked about that. But is love like it seems in the movies? Does it just hit you and make you go crazy? Do you just know, know in your soul that you're in love?

I had a dream of you. It was...weird. Intense. We were...together. Is that weird to you? I don't know what it means, if it means anything, but it was...it was like... god, how do I put it? It was remembering something that had already happened. Does that make sense?

How's Wyoming? Are you a full-time cowboy now? That's kinda hot, actually.

Always yours,

Ever

Ever,

I'm a little unsure what to say, to be honest. I don't know the answer. I'm feeling something similar, actually. With a girl that lives on the ranch, niece of one Gramps's best hands. She's Mexican. Luisa. I don't know a lot about her, but there's just this...tension between us. This electricity. We've only kissed once, but I know if we had the chance, it'd go farther. And I want to, but I don't. I'm a little afraid that it would be a mistake, or that it would change things. I mean, I know it would change things. For me, and for whatever Luisa and I would have. But like you said, I don't think I'm in love with her. In love? I feel like that's something you can't miss.

I guess you just have to take things one step at a time and make the best decision you can. That's all you ever can do, I think, in life in general.

I have to be honest. It is a little weird talking about this with you. I mean, I know we're pen pals, and friends, and I love that. These letters are often all that get me through week to week. Even if it's just random stuff, nothing important, they're important to me. Gramps is great, and I love working on the ranch. But...I'm lonely. I feel disconnected, like I'm no one, like I don't belong anywhere. Like I'm just here until something else happens. I don't even know what I want with my future. I used to think I'd go to art school, find a career using drawing, but now? Maybe I'll just be a cowboy forever. And your letters, they make me feel connected to something, to someone.

But hearing about you dating Will or Billy or whatever his name is, hearing about you thinking about having sex with him? It's...kind of hard.

I had a crush on you when we first met. I thought you were beautiful. So beautiful. It was hard to think of anything else. Then camp ended and we never got together, and now all I have of you is these letters.

Shit. I just told you I have a crush on you. HAD. Had a crush. Not sure what it is anymore. A letter-crush? A literary love? That's stupid. Sorry. I just have this rule with myself that I never throw away what I write and I always send it, so hopefully this doesn't weird you out too much.

Did you get my last letter? You didn't respond to anything I wrote, so I was just wondering.

I had a dream about you, too. Same kind of thing. Us, in the darkness, together. Just us. And it was like you said, a memory turned into a dream, but a memory of something that's never happened, but in the dream it felt so real, and it was more, I don't even know, more RIGHT than anything I've ever felt, in life or in dreams. I wonder what it means that we both had the same dream about each other. Maybe nothing, maybe everything. You tell me.

Cade

As I finished the last line, I realized with a bolt of horror that I'd never read Cade's last letter. Everything with Will had pushed it straight out of my head. My brain was spinning, my heart whirling in mad, confused circles. Cade had a crush on me? Literary love? He'd dismissed the phrase as stupid, but to me, it was raw poetry. It meant something. Literary love. I'd only spent a few hours with Cade at the camp, but I knew so much about him.

I dug through my purse until I found his previous letter, ripped it open, and read it. By the end, I was sobbing. He'd lost his dad, too? How much could one person endure?

And then I'd sent him this selfish, rambling letter about how I was confused about having sex with my boyfriend. He must think I was such an asshole. Yet, he'd told me my letters were important to him. Were they still?

He thought I was beautiful. He thought I was beautiful?

Did Will? He hadn't said so. He acted like he wanted me, but was that different from thinking I was beautiful.

Cade,

I'm so sorry about your dad. I can't even begin to put into words how sad I am for you. You've lost so much in your life. No one should have to go through what you have. I actually put that letter in my purse to read later and then got sidetracked and forgot. That's a shitty explanation, I know. I'm sorry. I treasure your letters, too. I really do. I cried so hard when I read that letter.

I know my letter about Billy must've seemed especially inconsiderate and self-centered in light of that. I won't write about him anymore.

Regarding your feelings for me, god, that really complicates things. I felt the same way. You were so different from everyone I'd ever met, ever seen. You're handsome, but that's not the right word. It's not enough. You're...god, "rugged" is the only word

I can think of. Is that stupid? It's better than cute, which just doesn't apply, in a good sort of way. And I really did have a crush on you. When you came out to the dock right at the end of camp, the way you put your arms around me and just held me, I've never felt so comforted in all my life. I know I said I wouldn't talk about Will, but he's a part of this discussion. He and I are dating. It's just a fact. But then I have this relationship with you. I feel like I know you, like we're connected in some way, like our souls are cut from the same cloth. Does that make sense? So it almost feels like cheating to have this with you, but it's not. We're pen pals. Maybe that's all we'll ever be. I don't know. If we met IRL (in real life, in case you're not familiar with the term) what would happen? What would we be? And just FYI, the term you used, a literary love? It was beautiful. So beautiful. That term means something, between us now. We are literary loves. Lovers? I do love you, in some strange way. Knowing about you, in these letters, knowing your hurt and your joys, it means something so important to me that I just can't describe. If that's unfair or unfaithful to Will, I don't care. Maybe that's horrible of me, but it's the truth, and it's a truth only you know. There are things, if I'm being honest, that only you know. Like for instance, I've never told anyone, ever, how I feel about Eden. How I love her with all my heart and soul and could never live without her, but sometimes just...just can't stand her. Hate her. She's so impossible sometimes. No one knows that but you. No one knows how mixed up I am about Will, either, except you, and to some degree him. No one knows how fucked up I am about missing Mom. How all my art is an attempt to find her inside me, to feel like I've found her. Like she's here with me. That's why I paint, why I take photos and draw and sculpt. I have to do it. I'm an artist, so on some level I simply have to make art because that's who and what I am and what I do, but Mom, missing her, needing her, that's why I am what I am, who I am. Because she was an artist and I need her back, and I keep hoping on some bizarre metaphysical level that I'll find her through my art. That's stupid, I know. It'll never happen. Her ghost won't ever suddenly appear in my paint, and I won't ever suddenly have some life-changing epiphany about Mom because I'm an artist. But that doesn't stop me from trying on some unconscious level.

Related, but different: don't give up on your life, or your art. You lost your parents, but you didn't lose yourself. You're alive. Be alive, Cade. Don't give up. Please? For me, if nothing else. Because I need your art and your letters and your literary love. If we never have anything else between us, I need this. I do. Maybe this letter will only complicate things, but like you I have a rule that I never throw away what I've written and I always send it, no matter what I write.

Your literary love,

Ever

Ever,

Don't be sad for me, Ever. I'll be okay. One day at a time, I'll be fine. Some days I don't know how I'll manage, and other days I'm just me and I'm fine, content and happy enough to be on horseback in the rolling wilds of Wyoming.

I was thinking, though. When you sent me that letter about being mixed up about Will/Billy, you said at the beginning that you didn't know who else to turn to. And I completely understand. I don't really, either, when it comes to things with Luisa. So how about this: we keep on confiding in each other, even when it's hard? Even when I might feel jealous or hurt or confused because I do still have some kind of feelings for you, even though I know we'll probably never meet again, you tell me what's going in your life, no matter what. We've always told each other everything in these letters. We said at the very beginning of this epistolary relationship (I learned that word in history class. My teacher, Mr. Boyd, is reading us John Adams' letters to his wife Abigail, and they're so beautiful. You should read them.

I've learned a lot from those letters), that these are like journal entries that we send out. And we get responses on those journal entries, and we understand each other. So don't stop. And I won't, either.

In light of that, I'll share this with you: I went on a ride with Luisa. Horse ride, I mean. We had a picnic and rode out into the middle of nowhere, no one for miles. And...we nearly did it. I guess I chickened out at the last second. Not quite ready. She is, though, and she's not shy about telling me. Gramps hinted that she came to Wyoming from Mexico because she'd gotten in trouble back home, so I just flat out asked her, and she told me the truth. She'd gotten kicked out of her last school for being...promiscuous. Had a pregnancy scare, I guess, and her parents decided she needed a change of pace, or scenery or something. And now she's trying to hook up with me, and I'm mixed up about it. If she's up here to make better decisions, is being with me a bad idea? I want it, though. I can't think of anything else when we're together, in the moment, you know? I know you get it—you said as much in your letter about Will/ Billy. I don't know what's right or wrong anymore, and sometimes I just don't care. She makes me feel good. She likes me for who I am, and she wants me. Feeling desired, wanted, is addicting. I can't help it, can't help wanting more. And, good or bad, I don't think I'm going to try and resist that. It's going to happen with us, and soon, and I know it, and I'm not fighting it. I deserve some happiness, right? I'll be careful, though. You too, okay?

Cade

Caden's letter sparked in me a weird kind of jealousy, displaced and confused. I couldn't stop it, didn't quite understand it, and didn't know how to deal with it. Especially since I'd had a very similar experience with Will. In his car again. We went farther than before. I touched him. Made him come with my hands. Got so close to doing it, but didn't quite. And like Cade had, I'd just chickened out. It would happen soon. I knew it, Will knew it. We hadn't discussed it, except that I told him if and when we did have sex, I didn't want it to be in his car. He said he'd figure something out.

Weeks passed, letters went back and forth. I explained the Will/Billy name issue to Cade, how I vacillated back and forth in how I thought of him and how that difference seemed significant but in a way I didn't understand. Just after Thanksgiving, I learned, via a short but intensely uncomfortable letter, that Cade had had sex with Luisa. He said it was amazing, but not what he'd expected: *It didn't last as long as I thought it would, and I don't think Luisa was too happy with how quickly it was over, but she was great and didn't make me feel bad about it. I can definitely see what the big deal is, though. You feel like…like you've grown up, afterward. Everything is different, in some way I can't quite explain, after you're no longer a virgin.*

Christmas break, Will's house. His parents were gone, having left for vacation to Europe, and since he'd been so many times, Will opted to stay home with me. I knew why, and when he invited me over the day after Christmas to open our presents to each other, my heart pounded. We opened presents, had eggnog spiked with his dad's rum, and watched *Elf*.

And then, casually, Will asked if I'd like to see his room.

Caden

Dear Caden,

We did it. Will and I. In his room, yesterday. His parents are in Switzerland for the rest of the break, and we have the house to ourselves. Like you said, I feel totally different now. I see why it's the subject that seems to make the world keep spinning, you know? My lit of the ancient world teacher—who is also the history teacher—once said that kingdoms and empires have been torn apart by sex. That for a woman, rivers of blood have been shed. I get it, I do. It's life-changing. But not what I thought it would be.

Maybe this is TMI, even for us, but I didn't come. He's made me before. But during actual sex, I didn't. And the most horrible part? Will asked me if I did, and I lied. I said I had. I'm not sure why. I guess I knew he'd be upset if he knew I hadn't, and didn't want to make him feel like he'd done something wrong. He hadn't. It felt good, really good, but I just didn't get there before he was done. Lying about it made me feel worse than anything, though. I thought for sure that I would, but I didn't, and I actually sort of felt like I'd been the one to do something wrong, you know? Like there was something wrong with me that I couldn't.

Sorry, Cade, I know that's probably way, way too much information, but I HAD to tell someone, and it couldn't be Eden. I don't think I'll ever tell Will, to be totally honest. I'm worried he'll be mad at me. And I'm also hoping the next time will be different. Better, somehow.

Always your own,

Ever

I wanted to throw up after I read the letter. I'd told her about my experience with Luisa, and I'd been pretty blunt, too, so I couldn't be upset. And we'd agreed to be totally honest with each other no matter what, but I still felt sick hearing she'd had sex with Will. I knew, for myself, that Luisa hadn't come while we were together. She'd said it still felt good, and I believed her. I told her not to fake it, or lie, just to tell me or show me how to make her enjoy it more. So she did. The more time we spent together that way, the more I learned how to make Luisa respond.

I guess that was part of what upset me about the letter from Ever. I thought, deep down inside where I didn't dare admit things even to myself, that I could be better for Ever than Will. I'd know she hadn't come, and I'd make sure she did. I'd make sure she felt good. That was the point, right? Not just for him, but for both of them to feel good.

That was a truth that I didn't dare tell Ever. Some secrets are best kept locked deep down in the silent places of one's soul.

As junior year raced away, turned to summer, and from there into senior year, there were three constants in my life: riding, roping, and breaking horses; Luisa; and letters to and from Ever. Miguel knew Luisa and I were together, and seemed okay with it as long as she stayed in school, passed her classes, and didn't get in any trouble, especially of the out-of-wedlock maternity kind. Against which eventuality we'd been very careful, Luisa with pills and me with protection every time. Ever confided in one letter that she and Will were being careful, too, after I'd directly asked her about it.

Our letters, Ever's and mine, hadn't changed in terms of personal details, or the strange kind of faux-lover intimacy, but as we got closer and closer to graduation, they'd become less frequent. Once a week became once a month, and then, by the time I'd walked the aisle and gotten my diploma, the letters were sporadic at best. I still told her everything, and she told me everything, too, I think, but we just didn't have time to write as frequently. I was busy with the ranch and Luisa, and Ever had been just as busy with Will and an apprenticeship program at Cranbrook Academy of Art that was earning her college credits in preparation for attending Cranbrook's collegiate program after she graduated.

I'd not mentioned, to her or anyone else, that I'd decided to stay in Wyoming, working the ranch. Ever had asked more than once what my plan was, but I'd avoided the discussion.

Gramps had asked, too, but I'd said I was still thinking.

It was a week after graduation, and I was sitting in the pre-dawn darkness sipping coffee. Gramps came in, poured himself a mug, and sat down across from me, taking a long drink of his black, scalding-hot coffee. "So, grandson. Tell me your plans. No more evading, no more bullshit. You've graduated. Now what? Where are you going to college?"

I took a sip, and met his steady gaze. "I'm not. I'm staying here."

Gramps let out a long breath. "No, Cade." He leaned forward, wrapping one hand around the mug. "Listen, son. It's true, my heart wants you to stay here, but…you're too talented an artist for that. You're a damn fine ranch hand, and I've been lucky to have you. But you have to go to college. You have to follow your own dreams."

I shook my head. "Gramps…I've changed. This is my dream now."

"Bullshit." Gramps slammed his palm on the table. "You've given up. You're here because it's easy. It's what you know. I accepted that when you were sixteen. I knew you needed family and something familiar to give you a solid footing after you lost Jan and Aidan so close together. But now, you've settled. And I won't have it. You hear me? I won't fucking have it. You've got your mom in you, and Aidan. They were both intelligent, driven, artistic people. You are, too. But losing your parents, it's taken something from you. You're responsible, and you're steady. But…you've got more life to live than simply staying here in Casper fucking Wyoming, breaking horses and making babies. There's more in store for you than that, boy, and I'm not gonna be the one to stand aside and let you wallow in apathy."

"I'm not apathetic, Gramps. I like it here. I don't have a plan, not for art. I don't know what I'd do. Plus…Luisa is here."

Gramps pinched the bridge of his nose. "Cade, son. Tell me. What do you love about Luisa?"

I hunted for what to say. "She's beautiful. She's smart. She gets me."

He didn't answer right away. When he did, his words were slow and careful and measured. "Your Grams completes me. Every moment I spend with her makes me a better man. It's not just because I'm attracted to her that I love her. She was—and is, as much as ever—a knockout, to me. When I met her after the war, she was this sweet, sassy, independent, sexy little thing, and I didn't have a chance of resisting her. I met her in a café in San Francisco, before I moved back here. I knew from the moment I saw her that I had to make her mine. And I did. She made my world, Cade. She still does. I've spent every single moment of my life for the last forty-plus years with her. I've not left her side once, not once, since the day we met. And I'm not ever going to. I love her mind, her heart. I love that she takes care of my boys, the hands. She's taken you in like her own and loved you. She puts up with my cranky, moody ass." He leveled a sharp gaze at me. "That's what I love about my wife. Now, what do you love about Luisa?"

"Gramps, you've had forty years to figure all that out—"

"If you'd asked me that question the day we married, when I asked her to marry me, or while we were dating, after I knew I loved her, I would have said much the same. I get what you're saying, that I've had a lifetime with her to learn how to put it like that. But my point is, you're not in love with Luisa. And you know what? I think you know it. You're settling. There's nothing wrong with Luisa. You've been good for her, and her for you. She brought you out of your shell a little, and you settled her down some. But do I think that you should not go to college, not finish your education and find a career worthy of your talent, because she's here? Hell, no. Have you talked to her about your plans? About hers?" He sighed again, rubbing his face. "I love you, Caden. You're my only grandchild. I want the best for you, and I've said my piece. You're eighteen and an adult. You make your own decisions. But if you stay here, my forecast is that you'll end up bitter and lonely. There's something missing in you. I can see it. I may be nothin' but an old soldier and a cowboy, but I can see well enough. You're incomplete. And you ain't gonna find what you need here."

I sat in place long after he'd left, ruminating on his words. Luisa found me there and sat across from me, a brooding expression on her face.

"You're leaving, aren't you." It wasn't a question, and her eyes seemed resigned, but not exactly sad.

"I haven't decided yet. I was gonna stay, but Gramps doesn't think I should."

"Well, I think you should do what you want. Not me and not your *abuelo*."

"That's the problem. I don't know what I want." I looked up at her, met her eyes directly, searched her. "Do you love me, Luisa?"

She took a deep breath, let it out, ran her fingers through her hair, a nervous gesture of hers. "I…I think—I think no, Caden. I wish I could say I do, but that would be a lie. I care for you, very much. But do I love you, deep and with all of my heart? I cannot say yes without any doubt, so I think it must be no." She tilted her head to one side. "And you? Do you love me?"

"I…god. I think it's the same answer. No. I thought I did, but like you said, I care about you, I've really enjoyed the time we've spent together. But… is that forever love? No." I reached for her hand, but she pulled hers back and folded them on her lap. I sighed. "What are your plans, Luisa?"

"I think maybe I will go to Mexico City. Attend university there. I have applied and been accepted.

I would also like to find *mi madré.*" She was silent for a long moment, and then she looked at me with an expression I couldn't decipher. "You know, I've always known about your letters to your friend. This Ever Eliot. It was not a secret for you. But what you do not know is I once, while you were sleeping... after...I read two of these letters. One from you to her, the other hers to you. Here is a truth, *y tal vez usted no conoce esta,* but you love her, and she loves you." I'd learned enough Spanish simply being with her and around Miguel that I understood the phrase she'd used. "I am not jealous, though, am not now, and was not then. And that is another reason to know that we are not in love, you and I."

"She's got her own life."

"And so do you. But that does not mean you shouldn't find her, Caden. You never will know what will be possible if you do not give it a try." She stood up, circled the table, and took my hands, pulled me to my feet. "Come. Ride with me one more time. As we so often do. I will be leaving for Mexico City next week, I think. So this will be our last time together."

We rode far, out into the rolling wilds where we'd spent so many long afternoons and starlit nights together. It was slow and delicate, and neither of us cried, although we knew it was goodbye, a forever farewell.

a breath of time

"Hey. You must be Cade."

This was punctuated by the metallic scraping of a transparent yellow plastic Bic lighter, flame spurting, lighting something in a colorful glass pipe, the lit contents crackling as the speaker inhaled deeply. A long moment passed as I watched him hold the smoke in his lungs and then spew it out in a tiny, controlled stream. He coughed, acrid, sickly sweet smoke billowing from his nose and mouth, and then set the pipe down on the scratched wooden coffee table.

"I'm Alex." He was tall and thin, with just enough muscle to not quite qualify as gangly. He had long brown hair tied back at the nape of his neck, the ponytail thick and bushy and falling between his shoulder blades, and the kind of scruff on his chin, upper lip, and cheeks that comes from someone who can't really grow a beard.

I shook his hand, trying to unobtrusively lean away from the stench of pot smoke, which was a futile endeavor since the whole open-plan living room and kitchen were hazed with smoke. "Yeah, I'm Caden. Nice to meet you."

"You too, bro. Have a seat. That all you brought with you?" He gestured at the duffel bag I'd dropped at my feet when I closed the door behind me.

I shrugged. "Yeah, pretty much. I've got some other shit in the truck, but this is it, basically." I sat down uneasily on the edge of the couch, at the opposite end from Alex.

"Cool." He took another long, hard hit from the pipe, then handed it along with the lighter to me. I took it, held it, stared at it. "You cool?"

"Am I cool?" I knew I was missing something, some subtext or meaning in the way he asked the question.

He jerked his chin at me. "The bowl. You cool? You smoke?"

"Do I smoke?"

Alex laughed. "Yeah, bro. Do you partake in the sweet embrace of Lady Mary Jane? Do you, in a word, get high?"

"That's more of phrase than a word, actually."

Alex laughed again, pulling his hair free from the ponytail, smoothing it back, and retying it. "Shit, yeah, you're right. But whatever, man. So. Are you cool? I mean, it's kinda late now, if you're not, since you've already, like, moved in and shit."

I'd rented a room sight-unseen in a high-rise apartment in downtown Detroit. The ad on the board in the registration office of the College for Creative Studies had merely read, "Looking for a roommate. Pay your half of the bills and don't steal my stuff. For more information call 313-555-2468." I'd called, spoken to Alex for about ten minutes, agreed to take the room, and that was that. Of course, he wouldn't mention the pot smoking over the phone, I supposed, but still, it would have been nice to know.

I held the blue-red-orange-purple glass pipe, which Alex had called a bowl, in my hand, thinking. I'd never known anyone who did pot. It was an unknown variable. It was illegal, but so was underage drinking, and I'd done my share of that, usually under the watchful tutelage of the other ranch hands, late at night around a campfire, passing around a bottle of whiskey. Did I have a problem with the pot? The smell, now that I was getting used to it, wasn't so bad. I was catching a bit of a contact high, I was pretty sure, and it wasn't unpleasant. Loose, floating. Worry and sadness eased their grip. Missing Luisa faded.

Missing Grams and Gramps and Wyoming seemed a bit further away.

I stared down at the bowl, at the charred bits and clumps of green. "I guess I'm cool. Never tried it before."

"Well, then, give it a hit. See what you think."

I toyed with the wheel of the lighter. "Will I get addicted? Like cocaine or whatever?"

Alex laughed, shaking his head. "No, man. Technically, realistically, honestly speaking, you can get, like, psychologically addicted. Emotionally addicted, too, in a way. Your body won't *need* it, not like you get with coke or meth. It's…it's hard to explain. I've been smoking for a long time, since I was thirteen, and I suppose I probably am mentally addicted to the lifestyle, but I'm okay with that. I accept it as a part of who I am. I'm Alex Hines, charcoal artist extraordinaire, professional bassist, and stoner. Will you turn into a stoner from one hit? No, man. You won't. Guaranteed."

I'd been in Detroit for two days. The first day I'd spent at the college, sorting out my schedule and getting a map and all that. I'd stayed at a hotel, spent $14.99 on an in-room viewing of *Man of Steel*. I'd met three people aside from the office staff. A girl with purple dreadlocks smoking a cigarette in the parking garage, who had asked me if I had any cigarettes, since clearly the one she was smoking wasn't going to be enough. Then I'd met a homeless man after eating dinner at Lafeyette Coney Island. His name was Jimmy, and he was a Vietnam vet, disabled, homeless for twenty years, and he stank of equal parts cheap beer and body odor. Now there was Alex, and he was offering me marijuana.

I put the mouthpiece to my lips, flicked the lighter so the flame cracked into life, turned the yellow plastic sideways until the flame touched the pot, and inhaled. Acidic heat blasted my throat, hit my lungs, and I doubled over, hacking until I was lightheaded. Alex laughed until he was crying, wiping his eyes.

"Classic, man! Classic!" Alex took the pipe from me. "You're doing it like a newb, dude. Don't inhale directly into your lungs. You gotta pull it into your mouth, and then inhale it slowly." He put the bowl to his mouth, lit it, and pulled so his cheeks hollowed, and then lowered the bowl and inhaled deeply. "See? Like this. Then you hold it in. Get a better buzz that way." He said this last part in a strange voice, strained from talking while still holding the smoke in.

I took the pipe from him, feeling a voice ask me if I was sure I wanted to do this. I wasn't, but I did it anyway. Just trying it, I reasoned. New life, new experiences. And what did I have to lose? I did it like Alex had demonstrated, and this time managed to get a lungful without coughing my head off. And when I did blow out the smoke, coughing slightly, I felt...

away. I couldn't find the word. I was up, but lodged in the couch. I sat back, feeling the tattered fabric take hold of me, gather me in. My eyes were heavy, but I wasn't sleepy. Not at all. Just...loose. Not happy, just disconnected in a pleasant way. I watched Alex take a hit, and then I took another without sitting forward. This time, I didn't cough at all. I felt like a pro at it, now.

There was nothing, suddenly. Nothing to the world, just me, and the coffee table, and Alex, my new friend, and the sketchpad open to a blank page with a charcoal pencil. I hadn't noticed those until just then. I picked up the pad and pencil, and let my right hand do what it wanted. It drew a circle first. I watched with interest as my hand drew without consulting my brain. The circle became ovular, taking up most of the page. Then the line down the center and the slightly curved cross-line near the top of the oval. I was drawing a face, then. Hmm. I felt like maybe Alex was watching, which was fine. Everything was fine.

Or no, it wasn't, really; I knew that, but I simply didn't care. I was drawing, and it was really great. I hadn't drawn in forever. Since...since before Luisa and I had our break-up sex.

Eyes, a delicate nose. Not Luisa's nose, and not her mouth. Who was I drawing?

It was when the hair appeared, curving across her eye and left cheekbone, that I knew. Ever. I was drawing Ever. But…it wasn't Ever from my memories of camp. It was the Ever from the dream, that crazy dream she and I had shared. The differences were subtle, but I saw them. A sharpening of the gaze, sadness in the eyes. A tilt to her mouth that spoke of laughter and a willing smile and something else in her eyes, something kind of dark and hot and needy. It was all there in the sketch, and I couldn't take it. I had to look away, but my hand had other ideas, so I continued to draw her, the lovely features becoming more and more detailed and more and more haunting with every line.

I was done suddenly. My hand stopped moving, and there was Ever, staring up at me from the page.

"Dude. You're…fucking amazing. That's fucking photorealistic shit there, man. Who is she? And why the fuck is she so sad?"

"She's…someone I met a long time ago, and she's…important. To me. She's sad because…well, that's not my story to tell. And I'm also not entirely sure why."

"Enlightening," Alex deadpanned.

I shrugged. "I didn't mean to draw it. My hand just…took over. She's kind of a private thing, I guess."

"I can't honestly say I have any people in my life that qualify as 'private things,'" Alex made air quotes around the phrase, "but I guess I can respect that.

She's got a lot going on in her eyes, though, that's for fucking sure."

"You say 'fuck' a lot."

"Happens when I'm high, which is most of the time, so yeah, I guess I do. That bug you?"

"Nah." I tore the page free, carefully, and set it facedown on my thigh. I couldn't handle Ever's charcoal gaze, not while this sky-wheeling, earth-spinning feeling was coursing through me.

"The closest thing to a person who's a private thing would probably be Amy. She's my fuck-buddy."

"Can't be that private, if you're telling me about her," I said, leaning my head back against the couch cushion, staring at the ceiling and feeling the rotation of the earth around the sun and the tilt of the streets and the glint of the stars.

"Well, you're my roommate. You've smoked my pot. That makes us bros. It's not really anything crazy, though. We just meet a couple times a week and fuck."

"Just sex? You don't talk or anything? Or hang out?"

"We usually smoke a bowl, fuck, eat some snacks, and then go home. Here, or her place, just across town. She goes to Wayne. Lit major. Crazy hot, but also just crazy. I mean, just loony. Talks in these metaphors that don't make any sense and goes on and on about how she's gonna write this book someday. Has it all planned out and does research and writes notes, but never actually writes it. But she's obsessed with it. I get her stoned so she'll shut the fuck up about it." Alex shot to his feet and lurched into the kitchen, came back with two cans of Bud Light, tossed me one. "It's actually annoying as fuck. Like, write the damn book or shut up. Jesus. Character this and plot point that and subplots and arcs and motivations, but I've never seen her writing it or heard her say she made any progress. Nothing. Just talk. But she knows books, that's for damn sure. Read more books than I've ever heard of. Fucks like a goddess, though, and that's all I care about. She knows it, I know it, we talked about it."

I couldn't wrap my head around that, for some reason. I mean, sure, I wasn't in love with Luisa, and I never had been, but I cared about her. She meant something to me. We'd shared almost two years of our lives together. But it was never just sex. It was companionship. It was never fucking, even if it wasn't exactly making love. There wasn't a word for it, I decided.

"If it's not making love, 'cause you're not in love, but it's more than fucking, what would it be called, do you think?" I asked Alex.

He didn't blink an eye at the randomness. "Shit. Not sure. That's a damn good question. Fucking is… it's hot. It's hard. It's dirty. It's about the act, the feeling.

That's it. Making love…that's about your heart. It's about sharing shit. Y'know? I had that. Before Amy. She broke my goddamn heart, that bitch. Lisa. Lisa Eileen Miller. I loved the shit out of that bitch. Five years. Tenth grade until a year ago, and then she went and fucked my my best friend. Had his baby, married him. Left me without a backward glance. Fuck him, fuck her, and fuck the both of 'em." He glanced at me, seemed surprised. "Shit. Sorry, kinda vented there, huh? I'm a chronic over-sharer. Pot kinda severs the filter inside me, you know? So yeah, I don't know what that would be. Emotionally relevant sex? Meaningful fucking? I don't know."

"How do you do it? Have sex without getting attached at all?"

Alex picked up the pipe from where it had been sitting unattended on the coffee table, hit it, passed it to me. "It's all about picking the right chick, I think. I got lucky, you could say. I met Amy at a bar. We talked about our exes, talked about how we both wanted sex without the emotional strings, and that was that. We both agreed that's all it was, and if it ever started to be more for one of us, we'd say so. I guess you just don't think about it too much. Don't make it personal."

"I don't know if I could do that."

"You had a girl you loved?" Alex took the sketchpad and pencil and made a haphazard line across the page. Then another, and then an arc, and then a series of jagged angles, and suddenly there was aesthetic meaning taking shape.

I shrugged. "That's why I asked. She wasn't... we both agreed it had never been love. But it wasn't nothing, either. Somewhere in between. Filling a need, but in our life. We were together for almost two years."

"The girl in the picture?"

I blew out a stream of smoke as I shook my head. "No. She's...something else."

I was feeling like the inside of my mind had expanded, like the walls of my brain were rocketing away on all sides, like my body was losing reality, losing meaning, losing relevance. Like my soul was a point of light in the universe and I could simply float wherever I wished and simply see, not interact. I felt at once heavy as a planet and light as a mote of dust. I felt, without feeling.

I could see the appeal of being high.

Alex stood up. "I got an assignment to finish, man. Your room's in there. You can help yourself to whatever if you get the munchies." He went into a room, his bedroom, I figured, and shut the door, leaving the bowl on the coffee table.

I couldn't understand how he could stand up or talk or think about an assignment. I was nothing, no one, only a mote of dust. Just dust in the wind. I hated that song.

My eyes seemed too heavy to hold up, so I closed them, staring at the inside of my eyelids, discovering fascinating whorls of light upon them.

Darkness woke me. I'd been dreaming of Ever. Of her face, drawn in charcoal, speaking to me. Her words were lost when I woke, but her expression, heated need and sadness, haunted me.

I tried to fall back asleep, even went into the bedroom, but discovered that I had no bed, and the room was completely empty. I found a blanket in a closet by the bathroom, lay on the couch, and stared at the ceiling, wishing I could find the reason for dreaming of Ever, wishing I could write her but realizing I wasn't sure what to say.

Ever

I watched Will sleep. His hair was long, brushing his shoulders. He'd let it grow the past year and a half, and he'd been cultivating a carefully trimmed goatee. I didn't like it, but didn't hate it. He was still hot as hell, just in a different way. We were in my room, in my one-room apartment in Birmingham. He was attending U of M on a music scholarship, double majoring in music and business. He came to see me on the weekends, and we filled Friday evening, Saturday, and

Sunday with dinner at expensive restaurants, concerts, long walks through downtown Birmingham, and sex. It was…idyllic, on those days.

Then, when he left to go back to Ann Arbor, I wondered. About everything. About Will. About our relationship. About myself. About the secret stash of paintings I had in my closet, hidden from Will and from myself.

He'd found my letters from Cade a few months ago. He'd freaked the hell out, said it wasn't fair. Yelled, shouted, scared me pale as snow. He hadn't listened to a word I'd said, hadn't given me an opportunity to even speak. He had no secrets, he said. He hadn't come down the next weekend, hadn't responded to texts or calls, but he'd shown up the following Tuesday with a bouquet of silver roses and a bottle of champagne that I'd imagined was insanely expensive. He'd spent an hour apologizing, then got me drunk and cooked me an effortlessly perfect chicken cordon bleu and made love to me on the sofa, slow and sorrowfully apologetic, whispering that it was fine, he forgave me, we were fine.

I'd never apologized. I'd also never forgiven him.

I'd held on to his shoulders as he moved above me and watched the way his hair fell across his face and wondered if I really dared call it making love, if I loved him, if he loved me. I'd come quietly, shallowly, slowly. Drunkenly. Sloppily.

Now I watched Will sleep and wondered what he would do if I showed him the packet of letters, now thicker by three (only three in the last six months, how sad, how strange, how remote my dear Caden was, and I wondered but didn't dare ask him why he seemed so far away) and I wondered what Will would do if I got up right then, still nude, and pulled the twenty-six paintings from the walk-in closet where they hid beneath my pile of old coats and a ragged Harvard stadium blanket that had belonged to my great-grandfather.

Twenty-six paintings, ranging in size from four inches by six to six feet by six feet. All of them were of the same thing. Various takes, colors, poses, lights, stages of realism. Caden. All faces of Caden. Serious, thoughtful, sad, laughing, looking away, looking directly at me. In one of them, he was gazing at me in a soulful and seductive way, as if he was beside me in bed staring at me with afterglow eyes.

I couldn't seem to help painting Caden's face. When I was stuck on a particular piece, or stressed out by a paper or a deadline for an assignment or by Will's increasingly jealous and possessive behavior, I would find myself painting Caden. It would start out with his eyes, always. The expression in his eyes and eyebrows and then his mouth, and the rest would fall into place. It helped me stabilize emotionally.

Will turned in place, rolling to face me. His eyelashes were full and dark against his cheeks. His sculpted arm was draped across my hip, and his mouth was open slightly. He was handsome, oh, yes, he was. My breath still caught sometimes, just looking at him, like I'd gotten caught in a daydream. Sex with him was a dream. Dates with him were a fantasy, each one a textbook example of Hollywood perfection romance.

Yet…I was discontented. Unhappy. Off balance and confused.

He would call me at random times to see what I was doing. He would demand to know my schedule, hour by hour, day by day. Once he even asked me for a written schedule of what I was doing and when. If I deviated from what I told him I was doing, he would act as if I'd betrayed him.

I would sometimes catch him sending surreptitious text messages, after which he would tuck his phone in his pocket and act nonchalant. "Plans for Monday," he'd claim, eyes shifting away.

He was lying to me. Oh, yes. I knew it. I painted my conviction of his dishonesty once. It was a dark piece, floorboards stretching into the distance, a door standing ajar. A distorted likeness of Will stood partially out the door, looking back at the viewer, lit by a streetlamp on the other side of the door, out of sight. His eyes were haunted, in the painting. If you looked closely, you could see he was clutching his cell phone in his right hand.

Why would he lie to me? Cheat on me? What had I done wrong? I'd devoted all the time and energy to him that I could. He didn't make me happy; I didn't love him. But I cared for him, I enjoyed him. He was my friend. He was my only real companion. Except Eden, of course, who had her own apartment a few blocks from mine, and she went to Cranbrook as well. For now, at least. She'd mentioned Julliard and the Boston Conservatory and other exclusive musical academies and conservatories. We had lunch every day and often would watch movies together at night at my place or hers, eating too much ice cream and being giggly girls.

But Will? He didn't make any sense to me. I lay beside him, watching him sleep, feeling some indefinable ache in my chest erupt and grow and spill out until I couldn't lie still anymore.

I crawled out from beneath Will's arm, wrapped my purple fleece robe around myself, went into the kitchen. I set a pot of water on to boil, stared out the window at the orange glow of a streetlight, watched a black Mercedes slide into the pool of light and out of it, vanish. When the pot whistled, I dunked two bags of peppermint tea in it, and tiptoed back into my bedroom. Will was sprawled out across the entire bed, snoring gently. I stopped in place, watching him.

I saw his pants on the floor, a pair of artfully faded
and ripped True Religion jeans. I searched the pockets; no cell phone. He rolled over on the bed, onto
my side. I checked under the pillow. Yes, there it was.
A black iPhone 5 in a black protective case. I held the
phone in my fist, watching Will, waiting for him to
wake up. Nothing.

I left the bedroom, closing the door with a
near-silent *snick* behind me, and poured a mug of
tea. Steam curled, and I tapped the "home" button. A
photograph of Will with Wynton Marsalis appeared,
taken in New York City when Will was seventeen.
Will had performed at Lincoln Center and met
Wynton, who was one of his heroes. I slid my finger
from left to right. I knew his code; I'd watched him
type it in enough: 1-3-9-5, his birthday.

I found the green icon with the white quotation
balloon symbol in the top row of apps, second from
the right, next to Instagram. The list of text message threads dizzied me: Aimee, Jay, Dolly, Jake, Ben,
Julie, Mackenzie…and, at the very top? "Sweetheart."
I assumed the thread under the name "Sweetheart"
was me. Only, when I opened it up, it wasn't a conversation with me:

*OMG Billy I can't wait for you get back here and fuck
me I want your cock inside me. If you come home right now
I'll blow you so hard you won't be able to see straight.*

jesus Kelly, youre gonna get me in trouble if she catches me with a hardon she'l know somthing is up.

I don't care. Let her find out.

Not yet.

Why?

I'm not ready to get rid of her yet.

You promised Billy. By Thanksgiving. You promised you'd come back to Arlington with me and meet my Dad.

It's not that simple. You wouldn't understand. She's...delicate.

WTF is that supposed to mean? And am I supposed to care?

She called him Billy. She wanted him to meet her dad? She knew about me, and wanted *Billy* to dump me. He thought I was delicate. Delicate?

She gave him blowjobs. He'd asked me once, and I'd refused. He'd been upset, irritated. I had wanted...other things. He'd...not quite begged, but nearly. I didn't want to, I'd said, not right then, maybe another time. He'd gotten up and left the room, and he'd never asked again. And I'd never offered.

Maybe that was part of why he'd gone to her, because she did that for him when I didn't.

Something else about the thread niggled at me, but it took me half a cup of tea worth of rereading to figure it out. *If you come home right now...* the message said.

Home.

Where she was, was home to him, and her.

When he came here, he brought a backpack with a change of clothes rolled up tight. Jeans, boxers, a T-shirt, socks. Cologne, a toothbrush and toothpaste, hair paste, and deodorant, all kept in a leather Armani Collection toiletry case. He never left anything here. Never took a shower, unless it was with me, for sex. He came on Friday, stayed Saturday, left Sunday evening.

I wasn't home. She was home.

My head was spinning, breaking. My heart was... numb. I wasn't sure how my heart would react, how my soul would react, when reality caught up to me. I didn't care. I finished my tea, sipping calmly, and then poured another cup. While that one was cooling off, I put *Billy's* phone back under the pillow. But not until after I'd changed two tiny little things. "Sweetheart" was now "COCKSUCKER" and "Ever" was now "GONE."

It was 4:30 a.m., and I finished my tea, dressed in comfy clothes, tied my hair in a bun, and left. I drove to Cranbrook, went straight for the private studio. Locked the door and pulled the blinds and turned on the ventilation fan and changed into my paint shirt, just the shirt. No bra, no underwear, no pants, just the button-down shirt, bare feet. Sleeves rolled to my elbow.

And I painted. Caden's face appeared, sad for me. Angry for me. Needing me.

And I painted Will as a twisted demon, all black shadows and flames. And Will's blue eyes. No. Not Will. Not anymore. Billy. Billy fucking Harper.

I painted without seeing what I was doing. Shapes and colors, back to abstractions, back to what excised the demons from my soul. Hard reds and angry yellows and burning oranges, swathed across the most massive canvas I could find, a ten-by-ten I'd stretched, intended for a self-portrait project. Raw anger on canvas, confusion and rage and some strange sense of…freedom.

A key scratched in the lock. I didn't turn around; only Eden had a key.

"Felt you needing me," she said, wrapping her arms around me from behind. "Is it Will?"

I slapped a vivid path of blue so hard it spattered on my shirt and cheek. "*Billy*. It's Billy."

"What'd he do?" Eden didn't sound surprised. She'd met him a few times and didn't like him. She'd said he reminded her of Adam Levine: a quintessential hot douche.

"I've known he was lying to me about something for a long time. All the signs, you know?"

"Jealous? Possessive? Hides his phone?" Eden had dated a guy her senior year, the first-chair violinist. Rob. She'd found out after a year and a half of dating that he'd cheated on her with the second-chair violinist, a bitchy, acne-scarred, insanely eccentric girl named Nina.

"Yeah. So I'm not surprised, really. Just…pissed off."

"Who is it?" Eden did her usual thing, strolling around the room flipping through my various drying canvases.

"Some girl named Kelly. That's all I know. And I think he lives with her."

Eden stared at me in shock. "He *what?*"

"I went through his phone. Found a text message conversation with '*sweetheart*,'" I emphasized the word with as much sarcasm as I possessed, "and she said if he, quote, 'comes home now,' she'd blow him until he can't see straight. 'Comes home' being the operative phrase here."

"Shit. What a douche-nozzle."

I snorted. "Douche-nozzle isn't strong enough."

"Douche commander?" Eden suggested.

"That might work. Commander of all the douches." I tossed the paintbrush into a sink and rinsed it, scrubbed the paint off my hand and face.

"What are you gonna do?"

I shrugged. "I don't know. Shove his trumpet up his ass?" I rested my forehead against the wall, suddenly exhausted. "What should I do?"

Eden turned me around and pulled me into a hug. "Come stay with me for a while. We'll watch *Notting Hill* and eat a gallon of pistachio ice cream."

"Hugh Grant usually cheers me up." I pulled away and gathered my clothes. "Love you, Edie."

"Love you too, Ev." She watched me dress. "I honestly expected you to be crying when this happened."

"You knew it would?"

"Not knew. Just suspected. Like you would have listened if I'd told you?"

I huffed a laugh. "True. I'm not going to cry. I'm not sad. I don't know what I am. Angry, more than anything. Confused as to why."

"'Cause guys are all assholes."

"True."

I told Eden I'd meet her at her place. I had to get a few things. Namely, my dignity back. And some clean panties.

Billy was still sleeping when I returned. It was seven in the morning, Sunday. He normally slept until eight on Sundays. I wasn't quiet as I packed clothes into a bag, my phone charger, some toiletries—but no makeup—and then, finally, he woke up. Rubbed his eyes with a fist. Naked, sexy as hell with his hair mussed and falling in his bright blue eyes, morning erection bulging against the sheet. And a douche commander.

"Whassup, babe? Going somewhere?" He stretched, letting the sheet fall away, pushed at his erection, stretching it, too. I couldn't look away, because hot was hot.

In an effort to exert control over the conversation, I tossed his jeans at him, covering him. "Over to Eden's."

"Why?" He went still, hearing the ice in my voice.

"How long have we been together?"

He didn't even have to think. "Two years in July."

"And how long have you been fucking Kelly behind my back?"

He hung his head, pinching the bridge of his nose. "Shit."

"I read the texts between you and your *sweetheart.*" I put so much vitriol into the term that it dripped poison. "I hope you have fun in Arlington."

"Ever, listen—" He stood up and shoved his legs into the jeans. He winced as he did so; he hated going commando. He found his shirt on the floor and put it on, too.

"Don't. Just tell me why." I set my bag on the floor in the doorway, and went back to my closet, unearthing the paintings of Cade, one by one, ranging them around the room.

"What is that? What are those? Is that—? That's him, isn't it? That asshole you write those fucking letters to."

"You don't get to talk to me about Cade. Just tell me why. I would have understood if you'd said you'd met someone else. I would have made it easy."

"It's hard to explain, Ev."

"Try."

"Honestly? I don't really know. I like you. You're funny. Weird. Hot. Amazing in bed. But...you're—you're cold. Closed off. Like there's this barrier just beneath your skin that I can't get past. You don't let me in. You don't tell me anything about yourself. You just hang out with me, fuck me, and that's it. There's no emotion to you. You're just...ice."

I couldn't breathe, couldn't speak. Couldn't form words. I tried anyway. "You—in the text. You told her I was delicate."

"You are. Ice cracks easily. Even the thickest ice will crack under enough pressure. If I dumped you, I thought you'd—"

"Crack?"

He shrugged. "Yeah."

"So instead you shack up with some *whore*, and don't bother to break up with me? Spend the weekends with me, the week with her. Twice the pussy for the price of one." I clenched my fists at my side, refusing to crack. I was close. He knew me all too well. This was too much pressure. If he'd just dumped me, it wouldn't have cracked me. I would have refrozen and been fine. This...this was too much.

"It's not like that—"

"Then what's it like? You just stayed with me for the sex? Why else? If I'm so cold, so closed off, that's the only reason, right?"

He ran his hand through his hair. "No, Ev. Like I said, it's hard to explain. I didn't want to hurt you." He was staring at the floor. Lying.

"God, you're such an asshole. Just get out. Don't come back." I grabbed my bag and whirled around.

He followed me, yelling. "Quit acting so innocent. You and that Caden guy. The letters. And you were painting his face? Like, seriously?"

"Oh, like it's even close to the same thing?" I shoved him, hard, slamming my palms against his chest and shoving him backward so he tumbled over the back of the couch. "I met him *one time,* almost *five* years ago. We write fucking letters. And barely that anymore. So don't even try to make out like I was cheating on you with a piece of fucking paper."

Billy righted himself, scrambled around the couch, and rushed me, rage on his face. I felt panic race through me as he raised his fist, closing in like a freight train. I cringed, shrinking back against the wall. He stopped at the last second, his fist still raised, face a rictus of rage, blood trickling down his face where his cheekbone had been cut open by the corner of the coffee table.

He sagged, backing away, turning in place with a shocked and horrified expression on his face. He leaned against the window, fists on the sill, forehead against the glass. "You know what, Ever? The truth is, I stayed at first because I hoped you'd open up. I thought maybe you and I could really be something. Like we could fall in love, if you'd just open up a bit. And then I met Kelly, and she was…everything you're not. She had these…emotions that you just won't show. I'm a guy, I know I'm not supposed to care about emotions, but there it is. She was open. She talked to me. She has friends, Ever. A life. She doesn't have secret pen pals, secret paintings." He shot a glance at me, turning slightly to look at me. "You want truth? Yeah, by now it was…habit. I was afraid of breaking up with you. You only had your sister, and I was…worried. And plus, yeah, it was also the sex."

"But mostly, it was the sex."

"Does it matter?" he demanded, yelling. "Does it really matter?"

I stood up, collected my bag, and stuffed my feet into my UGGs. "No. I guess it doesn't. I'm leaving. Just get out. Get out of my apartment, out of my life."

He grabbed his bag and his shoes. "That'll be easy. I was never really *in* your life to begin with." He sat down, put on his socks and shoes, spoke as he tied the laces of his Nikes. "You wanna know something?

You act like I'm so evil for cheating and lying. And maybe I deserve that. Sure, I'll take that blame. But ask yourself why *you* stayed with *me* all this time. If you were never going to really let me in, never really give me any of yourself, your heart, then why were you with me? Why did you keep me around? You could have ended it anytime. You never did. Ask yourself why, and if it was really so different from what I did. You may not have spent time with this guy in the letters and the paintings, but it was still a part of yourself you were hiding from me and giving to someone else. And *that*, if you ask me, is the real down-deep definition of cheating."

And then he was gone, and I was alone, and his final words were clanging in my head.

The knowledge of his cheating and lying couldn't make me cry. But those words, the truth in them… *that* made me cry.

When I got into my car, I connected my iPhone via USB cord and turned on Pandora. The first song to play? "Delicate" by Damien Rice. Wonderful.

once more unto the breach, dear friends

Caden

Alex passed me the joint, and I held it low as he made the turn onto Beaubien. Took a hit as we cruised past empty buildings and burned-out warehouses and graffiti-tagged storefronts, clusters of people on street corners. I was waiting for Alex to start talking. He'd been moody lately, going from manic to mopey, frantic and frenetic to dark and depressed.

Throughout my first year at CCS, Alex had remained my only friend. I had classmates and teachers. Lab partners and assignment groups and critique partners. But no friends except Alex. He didn't ask questions, just accepted me. Showed me his favorite diners and restaurants. Bought me beer since he was twenty-two, let me smoke his pot and didn't question when I didn't want to. I smoked because he did. I did like the high, but only when the loneliness got too much. Alex could only take so much of a place in my life. He was a buddy, someone to hang with. We'd sketch in silence, me at the kitchen counter, him on the couch, classic punk music playing from his iPod dock. I didn't really love punk, but it was Alex's thing, and it grew on me. Sort of.

So now, with Alex in a depressed phase that was lasting for more than a week, I was worried. And I didn't know how to handle it except to let him talk when he was ready.

He had to pull into an alley to roll another joint before he was ready to talk. I didn't smoke that one. It was all his, clamped in his lips as he circled through Detroit, cruising the midnight streets, going places we had no business going. And then he found a particularly dark street, most of the houses boarded up, drove down it at barely fifteen miles per hour, his headlights off, head craned out the window, counting houses. He found the one he was looking for, I assumed, when he pulled to a stop in front of it.

"Wait here." He got out of the car and closed the door behind him.

I felt anxiety rise in my gut. This was not the place for a white kid from Wyoming. "No, Alex, I'm not—I'm not staying here. It's not—it's not safe."

"Don't be a pussy. If anyone bugs you, tell 'em you're waiting for me. They know me here. Don't get out, just hang. I'll be right back."

"What are you going to do?"

He shot me a disgusted look through the open window. "What the fuck you think I'm doing? Having tea with the queen? Buying drugs, you hick." He smacked the door with his palm. "Just chill, bro. You'll be fine."

And so I sat, in a beat-up old Monte Carlo, pot smoke curling up around me from the smoldering roach in the ashtray, on a side street in Detroit at one-thirty in the morning. The streetlights either didn't work or flickered, lending an eerie stop-motion effect to the night. A red two-door classic Buick, long as a battleship and throbbing with bass, rolled past me. The windows were down, two shadowed faces peering at me with curious eyes. They slowed as they passed me, not even two feet away. My heart thudded in my chest, my pulse pounding and my stomach flopping. My eyes met those of the driver, and I held his gaze steadily. I didn't nod and I didn't look away. After an eternity, he lifted his chin at me and gunned the engine, vanishing around the corner.

I heard a gunshot somewhere in the distance. Sirens. Laughter from the house where Alex was buying drugs. Hard drugs, I realized. This was not the kind of house one went to with the intent of buying a bag of weed.

Another car passed, and this one didn't stop or slow down, and they didn't look at me. Fifteen minutes passed, and they felt like an hour. Eventually Alex came out, sidling slowly, a lazy grin on his face. He slid into the driver's seat, fumbling at the keys, and then leaned his head back.

"You drive," he said. "I'm blazed."

"All right. Not sure where I'm going, though." I got out and circled around while Alex slid over.

"No problem. I know where we are. I'm just too strung out to drive."

"What kind of drugs?" The question slipped out. I couldn't help it, and I was glad it had emerged.

"Does it matter? I ain't offerin' you any, that's for fucking sure. You're too nice for this shit."

"It matters. What are you on?"

He snorted. "Dude, what planet you live on? What kind of drugs do you think I would buy from a house like that, in that neighborhood? Don't you ever watch *Cops*?"

"Crack?"

"Yes…sir." He blew out a long breath. "You mad, bro?" He flopped his head to one side, grinning at me.

"Not mad. Worried, though."

"Don't be. It's just a little, to take off the edge."

"Edge of what?" I knew very little about Alex. Just that he had deep, dark waters inside him, and he did drugs to ease some pain I would never know, quiet voices I would never hear. For all that he was given to rambling and sharing awkward personal details, usually of his exploits with Amy, there were certain things he never discussed.

"Life, man. Just life." He stared out of his window, watching the dark, dilapidated houses pass. Every once in a while he'd direct me to turn one way or another. "I grew up in this city, man. Never left, never will. Mom was born here, Dad was born here."

"Yeah?" I sensed a confession coming.

"Yeah, man. I know her. Detroit, I mean. Her dark secrets. Things you can't imagine. You don't belong here. I do." He peered sideways at me. "Just finish your schooling, man, and get out. Don't get sucked into my world. Don't smoke my pot. Don't drink my beer. Don't listen to my secrets. They'll eat you up, man. They'll pull you in."

"Give me more credit than that, bro." I recognized a street and turned onto it, cruising slowly. "What's bugging you, man?"

Alex didn't answer for almost half a mile. "I'm falling for Amy, dude. Remember the agreement I made with her? I can't tell her. I don't know how. I thought it was just fuckin', but it's more. I can't tell her, because she don't want that. She's so goddamn cute, Cade. For real. You ain't met her, but she is. The thing about writing a book? That shit drives me crazy, but I love it. I love teasing her about it. I want her to write it. I want her to be this amazing writer. And she will be. But if I tell her I accidentally fuckin' fell in love with her, she'll call it all off, and I'll lose her. She don't wanna be with no crackhead." His words were slurred, sounding unlike himself, thick with the urban Detroit accent. "She knows exactly what I am, and she won't want no part of it."

"How do you know?"

"'Cause I asked her. If she ever thought there was more for her, for me. She laughed and said no. I was good in bed and fun to smoke down with, but she couldn't be with me for real. It wouldn't work, she said. She just smokes for fun. When she graduates, she'll give it up and get a real job, a real life. It's just a college phase for her, she said. It ain't that for me, and she knows it. It's life for me. This is all I'll ever be."

"It doesn't have to be, Alex." I turned again, bringing us around toward our apartment. "You're a talented artist and damn good bass player. You could get bigger gigs if you tried. Find a better band."

He flopped his head in a sloppy negative. "Nah. I'd lose my shit on the road. I'd be dead of an OD in a fuckin' week. The groupies would be nice, though. I've always wanted to bang two chicks at once. Amy ain't into that, though. I asked."

"Dude, don't scare me." My heart was falling away, out of the bottom of my chest.

"I'm in deep, dude. I want her bad. I'd go clean for her, if I thought that would make a difference. I'd try, at least. But she has ambitions. Teach, write. She wants to be a professor of literature. Write for fun. Ambitions like that don't include a crackhead bass player."

"You're not really a crackhead, right? It's just a little, you said."

Alex laughed, leaning his head out the open window. "Dude. Get a clue. All addicts say shit like that. It's how you know an addict."

"Then why are you at CCS?"

"A desperate attempt to legitimize myself, I guess. Got a scholarship. Loans for being dirt-ass poor." He leaned forward, peering at the ashtray. "Where's that roach? I know I had a roach."

"Haven't you gotten high enough for now?" I couldn't help asking.

He shot me a look, one that spoke of depths of desperation I'd never realized existed within him. "Don't. Do *not* get in between me and my buzz, bro. You're my roommate. Not my friend. You don't know jack shit about me."

That hurt. I drove in silence. "So tell me," I said finally.

Alex found the roach, shut his window, cupped the butt-end of the joint between his lips, tilted his head to the side, and lit it, inhaling deeply. "Sorry, Cade. That was shitty. You know you're my bro." He blew out, opened the window again. "Not much to tell. Mom was an addict. Raised me and my little sister alone. Teen mom, no education. Same old story you hear all the time. Never knew my dad, had a parade of Mom's boyfriends in and out of my house. Some nice, some…not. A few hit her, one hospitalized her. One raped my sister. That was during my gangbanger years, and he…well, let's just say he regretted it not too long afterward. Pot, booze, crack, it was just life. The streets, gangs. Whatever. I graduated high school, barely, because Mom was unfortunate in her life and her choices, but she wasn't stupid. Neither am I. Just…dumb. 'S a difference, I think. Mom raised us best she could with what she had. But…she was trapped, you know? 'Cause of me and Annie. So I learned to use art to deal. I think you know about that. I got out of gangs when I was sixteen. Turned to art, graduated. Eventually got a scholarship to CCS. Found music, and that helps. But there's a part of me that's just…dug down deep into the roots of what this city means to people like me. It's a prison world, sometimes. Like in fuckin', what was that movie? The Riddick movie. Shit, that's what it was called. *Riddick*.

A prison world. There's beauty here. Life. Love. But for some of us, it's all we'll ever know."

He took a long drag, held it until I thought he would pass out, and then let it trickle from his nose. "You're here, and you don't belong."

I had no response for any of that. I parked in the lot outside our apartment, and Alex lurched out of the car, inside, into his room, closed the door.

I thought about writing Ever, but I didn't. I hadn't gotten a letter from her in weeks. Maybe that was done.

And then, the next morning, there was a letter from her in the mail. Addressed from Cranbrook Academy of Art.

Caden,

It's been a really long time. On both sides. Why? Are we not doing this anymore? Did I say something to upset you? Are you okay?

I broke up with Will. He was cheating on me. Living with someone else and fucking me on the side. Which is weird, because I thought it was the other way around, you know? That if he was getting some on the side, I was the main girl in his life, and the other girl was the one on the side. But...no. It didn't work that way.

I miss your letters.

I miss you.

Draw me something? Please?

Yours, (am I, though? Am I anyone's?)

Ever

I sat at the kitchen counter, staring at the letter, at the address. At the deep-seated pain between the lines of her letter, of her words, haunted sadness in the spaces of her words.

Yours, (Am I, though? Am I anyone's?)

What a sad interjection. Tragic. And I understood it completely. The cry, the petition hidden in the soul, unscreamed, unuttered. The cold within and the numbness, going through the motions and using art to feel anything. I knew all this was true for her, even though she'd said none of it.

I drew. It was her style, abstract. Lines on paper, arcs and whorls and slicing and cutting and no design. Until…until the end, when I set the pencil down, the abstract lines on paper formed two words, buried within tangled barbed wires and thorny vines: NOT ALONE.

I sprayed it to set it, put it in my room, and went to class, thought about her through art history and theory and calculus. I went home—still no Alex, no smoke, no music—and sat down to write.

Ever,

You are someone's: Your own. Don't belong to anyone but yourself. It's the only way. Those are wise words from a fool who can't use his own advice. I'm sorry about Will. I'm sorry he hurt you. He didn't deserve you.

I'm trying to write, but my words have dried up. Sorry. Just...sorry. Paint. Paint me something.

Always yours,

Cade

And I sent it. Despite the contradiction. With the drawing, I sent it, and I went back to evening class and spent hours in the studio, trying my hand at acrylics, letting my head and my heart empty onto white space, knowing it would never fill the space in my soul where my mother and my father belonged, knowing somehow, along the way, I'd been broken so I could never find peace or true friendship or love.

A week later, I found him.

Ever

I was more fucked up about Billy than I'd thought I'd be. Days at Eden's turned into a month, and then I jerked myself out of it and had Dad sell my apartment. I moved out and got myself assigned to a double dorm room on campus. My roommate was as erratic in her hours as I was, so I never saw her.

I painted, and I refused to cry, refused to believe I was that hurt, that lonely. I threw myself into painting. Hours with the brush and canvas, until instructors and janitors had to kick me out. Until Eden had to remind me to eat. To sleep.

When I got Cade's letter, I nearly did cry. When I saw his drawing, the rose thorns speaking to my loneliness, I did cry. Just a little. Two or three tears, sniffed away.

And then I painted. Something daring. Baring.

I painted myself. A self-portrait, in my studio. In my painting shirt, the top four buttons undone. Baring skin, baring cleavage. The shirt draped mid-thigh. A brush reaching for the viewer, the other hand freeing a button. Unclothing myself, one button at a time, while I painted myself for him. I let it dry, packaged it in a wooden brace and wrapped it in thick plastic wrap, and sent it to him still damp, unwilling to wait, to chicken out.

The title of the painting, written in black sharpie along the bottom of the frame: *BEAUTIFUL?*

A plea.

Three days later, he sent me an acrylic piece, and it took my breath away. It was part abstraction, part portrait. The edges were blurred colors, black near the top and along the left side, fading into a yellow-orange glow on the right side and near the bottom edge. At the center was a pair of eyes, my eyes. Vivid, stunning, arresting. My cheekbones, lit by the yellowish glow from the right side of the piece. Candlelight, I realized. And the blackness? Parts of it were matte black, parts were textured with strands of lighter shades. Hair? Yes, it was my hair, lost in the darkness.

The title: *BEAUTIFUL.*

Two days later, I got an overnight UPS package, thin, wide, and heavy. I brought it into my room, cut open the box with a steak knife, and pulled out a thick wooden frame, similar to that which I'd packaged Cade's painting in, stuffed with packaging air bubbles. It was a mirror.

It was old, probably an antique, spotted and pitted. As I pulled it out, the reflection of the ceiling wavered and wiggled, and then I righted it so I could see my own reflection. And there, surrounding my face, was a web woven of Sharpie-inked words: *lovely, talented, beautiful, needed, loved, smart, funny, kind, thoughtful, fascinating, dedicated, wondrous, wonderful*…the list went on. The words were tangled, letters overlapping, the "N"s in "funny" used to create "needed" and the "D" in "needed" used in "dedicated" and so on, all the words intertwined like a briar or a spiderweb, all inscribed on the mirror to surround my features.

I held it together long enough to hang it in my room over my bureau. And then I sobbed. Just… bawled.

I was doubting everything about myself. My talent, my looks, my appeal to men. It seemed like everything about my life was a lie. If Billy could lie to me for so long, in such a huge capacity, and I was so gullible and stupid as to not even realize it, what did that say about me? If I wasn't enough for him, who could I be enough for? What did this Kelly have that I didn't? Was I really a cold, closed-off bitch? Good only for sex on the weekends?

Did he close his eyes when we were together and picture Kelly, because he wished I was her but was too afraid of my delicacy to break up with me?

Was I delicate?

I didn't know anything anymore.

And this mirror…it didn't magically restore my self-esteem, but it sure did help. Mainly because it proved, if nothing else, that Caden thought I was all of those things.

Why his thinking that about me, feeling that way about me, made me feel so much better, I didn't dare examine too closely.

I stared at myself in the mirror, examined the pattern of his handwriting, wondering about Caden. About his feelings. About what would happen if I suddenly showed up at his door. Wondering if he still had feelings for me, like I did him, on some deeply buried level.

I was afraid. That was the raw reality.

Until this moment, I'd had other things to distract me. School, Eden's drama, Billy. Now Eden was living her own life, contained, seeming fairly happy as a single college girl. School wasn't the same kind of distraction, not anymore. I painted, I studied art, some other necessary classes, but it wasn't enough to distract me. And Billy was gone. Gone. And I was alone, and all I had were Caden's letters, his words and the emotions written between the lines. He was all I really had, in some strange way. He was all that comforted me.

That wasn't true. Eden was a constant comfort. She'd taken me in and let me wallow in my anger and self-pity, and then she'd gently encouraged me to get out there and get over it. By gently encouraged, I mean she shoved me out of bed one morning and told me to quit docking around and feeling sorry for myself, that the Lord Captain Douche Commander Harper wasn't worth my time or energy and I had to get over his sorry ass.

Which worked, to a degree. It got me off my ass and out into the world, got me painting and going to the gym to work off the gallons of ice cream I'd eaten while watching sappy romantic comedies and anything featuring Channing Tatum.

But Eden's advice and tough love didn't address the inner psychological damage Billy had done to me, which went deeper than I'd ever imagined. I'd never been truly in love with him, so how could his lie so badly shake the entire foundation of my life and my emotional sanity?

And why did Caden's letters and his art and the precious gift of the mirror do so much to heal me?

And why was I so afraid of pursuing more with Caden? Why did I keep shying away from an IRL relationship with him?

The last two questions I had answers to, at least: because if I tried for something with Cade and it didn't work, or he lied to me, or he let me down, if he failed to measure up, failed to be the magnificent specimen of manhood I'd built him up to be in my mind, I'd be devastated. Wrecked. And then I wouldn't even have him to get me through my heartbreak.

And so I painted. All the hurt and the confusion and the darkness went onto canvas.

the scent of death

Caden

Dread. Fear. The scent of death. I knew these things. I knew them all too well. I stood outside Alex's bedroom door, feeling them all rage through me. My knees shook, trembled like leaves in the wind. My fist was curled around the tarnished brass knob, paralyzed there, refusing to twist and push.

The wood of the door was splintered and rough against my forehead. My breath was a ragged influx of panic, a terrified soughing exhalation. I knew what I would find on the other side.

He'd come home two days before, eyes glassy and heavy-lidded, flesh greasy and sallow, unwashed, stringy hair lank around his face. He'd slammed his

bedroom door behind himself, and I'd heard the
plastic-cracking sound of a bottle of whiskey being
opened. The rasping hack of a three-pull swig straight
from the bottle. Heard a lighter scrape and flick and
whuff into life, inhaling. Coughing exhalation. The
scent that wafted to me then was not the familiar
pungent, innocent smell of pot. No, it had been thick
and dark and poisonous.

I'd pounded on the door with my fist. "Alex! Let
me in, man."

"Fuck off, Cade. Leave me alone." His voice had
been thin and wavery and fragile.

"Talk to me, Alex."

"I told her, man. Amy. I told her. I told her I was
in love with her." He'd coughed, took a hit. To cover
the sob, I think. "She said exactly what I thought she
would. 'Sorry, but you're just not my type for something serious.'"

"Shit, man. That sucks."

He laughed, a mirthless, aching sound. "Yeah. It
sucks."

He hadn't responded after that. I'd heard him
in there, listened at the door every once in a while.
He'd been silent for hours now, and I was worried. I
knocked on the door, hesitant at first, and then with
increasing urgency. I finally got the courage to twist
the knob. Locked. I found a paperclip at the bottom

of my backpack, unfolded it, fed it into the tiny hole at the center of the knob, popped the lock out.

I didn't believe in God or anything, but in that moment, I prayed. "God, please. Don't let me find him dead."

I opened the door, knowing, despite my prayer, exactly what I would find. And I did.

He was on the bed, on his back. A fifth of Jim Beam lay empty on the floor to the right of the bed. His right hand lay stretched out down his thigh, curled slightly open. His pipe sat on his palm, along with his transparent yellow lighter. He was shirtless, and mucus-yellow vomit spilled down his mouth and over his throat, onto his pillow. His eyes were open, staring at the ceiling. Lifeless.

I sank to my knees, unable to breathe or to cry or to do anything.

Eventually, I dug my phone from my pocket, dialed 911.

"Nine-one-one what is your emergency?" The operator's voice was flat, female, brusque.

"It's Alex. My roommate. It's not an emergency, though. He's already dead."

"Can you tell my why you think he's dead, sir?"

"He OD'd. On crack. He's dead. I know he's dead. I can see it. Smell it. I didn't know who to tell. He's dead. Someone needs to come get him." I heard myself speaking, but that part of me was disconnected from the part of me that was on the floor, on my knees, staring at dead Alex, another death.

I'd known he was on drugs. Why hadn't I gotten him help? Why hadn't I made him go to a clinic? See a doctor? I should have—I should have done something. I wasn't sure what, but something. He wouldn't have liked it, he would have hated it, hated my interference. We weren't friends. He said so himself. Just roommates. He'd apologized after saying that, sure, but I think it was true. He was my friend, but was I his? Could I have saved him?

The operator was speaking, and I couldn't hear her, understand her. I rattled off the address and let the phone fall to the floor. After a span of time I couldn't have measured, didn't care to measure, I heard feet, voices, felt someone push past me, pull me to my feet and out of the way to the couch. They spoke to me, whoever it was. A guy. Young, black hair. Not young, though, now that I looked at him. Maybe thirty? Brown eyes that spoke of having seen things like this all too often.

"Hey. My name is Kevin. Can you come outside with me?"

I followed him outside, answered his questions. Cops, their questions. Yes, I'd known he was using drugs. No, I didn't use drugs. I didn't mention having smoked pot with him once in a while, because that didn't seem to matter. I told them they could look through my room. Why did they need to do that? Because of the drugs? I wondered idly if they would arrest me for having not helped Alex quit smoking crack. I knew he was depressed, upset about Amy. But...

Was it my fault? I didn't know. I thought no, and then I thought yes.

I saw disapproval in the eyes of the paramedics and the cops. Had they ever had friends they couldn't help? He was my roommate. That's all. I realized I knew nothing about him. I didn't know if his mom was still alive. If his sister was alive. If he had anyone at all. Other than me, and I'd sat in my room writing an art history paper and worrying while he overdosed on crack and drowned himself in whiskey.

Eventually everyone left, and I was alone. I threw the vomit-stained sheets and pillow away, and then left Alex's room, closed the door. Was I supposed to try to find his mom and sister? Would the cops do that? I didn't know. I sat in the living room, on the threadbare couch, listless. I wondered if they'd taken the bag of pot and metal pipe Alex kept stashed in the old cigar box on the coffee table.

I checked; yes, it was gone. That was probably good. For the best. That wasn't me anyway. But it would have been nice to float away from the world for a few minutes.

What did I do now? This was Alex's apartment. Would they kick me out? I had nowhere to go. Of course, I had money enough to get my own place, but that wasn't the point. I had no one. Nowhere to go.

I went down to the mailbox, grabbed the latest letter from Ever, and trudged back up to the apartment, sat on the couch with Ever's letter in my hand. Stared at the address until the letters blurred and wavered and shook. Ever. Ever. I couldn't write to her. Not about this. Not another death. Another dead body haunting my memories. It was all too much, and I'd written her about it all.

Her name kept ringing in my mind, like a bell.

Ever. *Ever*. **EVER**.

I found myself in my Jeep, Mom's Jeep Commander. I found myself on I-75 heading north. Past Holbrook, Caniff, then the Davison, 8 mile. Yeah, I knew where my car was taking me. 14 mile, Rochester Road. Square Lake Road; exit, make a left on Michigan, south on Woodward Avenue. Silence in the car, silence except for my breathing, which sounded slightly panicked and erratic.

What the hell was I doing?

I blinked, and then I was turning right into Cranbrook Academy of Art. I meandered, wandered, got lost, and eventually found the studios and the adjacent dorms.

What the *hell* was I doing?

I couldn't make myself stop, though. I found her door. Knocked. No answer. Knocked again. Shit. What if she wasn't here? And then the knob turned and the door swung inward, and my heart lurched in my chest, skipped a beat or four, and my stomach dropped away.

a kiss upon your flesh

"Hello? Can I help you?" It wasn't Ever. It was a pretty, heavyset girl with blue-streaked hair and horn-rimmed glasses, a charcoal pencil behind each of her ears and one in her hand, charcoal on her hands and streaked on her forehead, smudged on her fingers.

"I'm—" My voice cracked, and I tried again. "I'm looking for Ever?"

"Studio seven." She peered at me, a curious expression crossing her face. "You're the guy from her paintings."

"Paintings?"

She tilted her head. "God, you're even hotter in person." She pointed across the street. "Studio seven. That's where she always is." And then she closed the door in my face, not rudely, but with finality and the absence of mind of a distracted artist.

I couldn't quite figure out that interaction, but my feet were carrying me across the road. I found studio seven. The door was locked, but I heard music from inside. I knocked. Everything stopped, my heart, my thoughts, my pulse, everything halted. The music continued, the lock scraped and the handle twisted, the door swung inward.

I was left breathless. "Just a Kiss" by Lady Antebellum played.

She was wearing nothing but a white button-down shirt, paint-spattered and smeared, the top three buttons undone, showing her porcelain white skin and a generous hint of cleavage and her long, thick thighs beneath the hem and her hair like ink hanging loose around her face and on her shoulders and her eyes green as sunlit grass and luminous jade.

A paintbrush in her hand, tipped with bright red. Crimson dots on her cheek, emerald smeared on her chin, cyan on her cheek.

I don't wanna mess this thing up…

The song was speaking to me, so perfect, exactly what my mind was shouting, pleading.

She stood frozen in the doorway, eyes searching me, unbelieving. "Cade?" The paintbrush clattered to the floor.

"Ever." It was a whisper in the afternoon sunlight.

Everything inside me, every molecule of my body was on fire as I closed the space between us, instinct and need taking me over and operating me, moving my legs and causing my arms to lift, my hands to close around her cheeks, gently, so tenderly, electric fire blazing from the touch of fingertip to her flesh, and now her eyes were close and so bright and caught up with wonder and her hands were on me, on my back and the nape of my neck and I was kissing her, kissing her, god, I was kissing her.

Something in my soul splintered open. Her lips were heat and moisture and tasted of cranberry. She kissed me back, no hesitation, no doubt, nothing but pure response and awestruck passion.

Nothing had ever felt so cataclysmic, so fraught with atomic power. I couldn't breathe for the kiss, hadn't taken a breath in an eternity, and it didn't matter because now, suddenly, she *was* my breath. I'd never kissed anyone before this. Her fingers tangled in my hair, pulled me closer, deeper. She rose up on her toes and wrapped one arm around my shoulders, and I couldn't do anything except lift her up, catch her with my arm beneath her thighs and under her ass, and I kissed her, felt dizzy from the way she devoured my breath and my kiss and my need and returned it and hadn't questioned my presence or this sudden kiss, had only responded in the way I needed so badly.

Somehow we were moving, and I heard the door slam closed and felt her hand return to tangling in my hair and there was a couch beneath my legs and I was tumbling backward, sitting down and sliding to my back, holding on to her, refusing to relinquish a single point of contact, and she was on top of me, above me, all around me, her hair a night-black curtain around our faces; her lips were desperate against mine and her tongue was frantic inside my mouth and she was making these tiny little sighing sounds that made me mad and wild and primal with need.

"Awake My Soul" by Mumford & Sons played, and yes, I was waking up for the first time, my soul expanding and learning to breathe.

She pulled back, just enough to speak, her lips moving against mine, her eyes wet and so close to mine. "Is this real?"

"Yes."

"Are you really here?"

"Yes."

She whimpered and buried her face against my throat. "Don't—don't lie to me. Don't let it be a dream."

My hands were on the backs of her thighs, her flesh hot as coals and softer than silk. "Ever…" I didn't know what to say. I was praying it wasn't a dream just as fervently as was she. "It's real. Say my name so I know it's real."

"Caden." She lifted her face to look at me. "Cade."

Then, "Why are you here?" She threaded her hands in my hair, her thumbs on my temples, her lips, between words, touching featherlight kisses to my lips and the corners of my mouth.

"I couldn't...I don't know—I couldn't take it anymore."

"Take what?"

I brushed her hair from her eyes and tucked it behind her ears. I'd known the feel of her body for all of my life, it seemed, known the possession of her flesh for as long as I'd drawn breath. "The loneliness. The memories. The need for...for something I'd never had. The need for something to fill the hole inside me." All of that was the raw, unvarnished truth, but it wasn't all of the truth. "I've always told you everything. Mom died, and I wrote you. Dad died, and I wrote you. And now...and now my only friend died, and I couldn't take any more of it, couldn't take it all alone."

"Who died? How?" She brushed her thumb over my cheekbone, and I shivered from the touch.

"Alex. My roommate. I've never had friends. Never made friends. Except you. And he...he OD'd. I found him dead in his room. And I can't take it anymore, can't stand to bury him, too. Fuck. I'm... I'm alone. Always alone. And I can't—I can't take it anymore."

"You're not alone. You've always had me. And how did you know I needed you?" She said this in a whisper aching with vulnerable fragility. "I was losing my mind. Doubting everything. Doubting myself. Doubting…life. And then you show up and…and I was too afraid to go to you, afraid you'd—you wouldn't want me, you didn't feel—"

"Ssshhh." I stopped her. "I do. I always have."

"Then why…why are we just now meeting? Just now doing this?" She shook, her shoulders betraying the tears she hid against my shirt.

"I don't know. God, Ever. I don't know. Why?" I held her and felt my own eyes sting with tears. "So close, for so long. Why did we never—"

She heard the break in my voice, heard the tears. Lifted her face and let me see hers and pressed her lips to mine and we kissed, our tears mingling. "I don't know. It doesn't matter now. It doesn't matter, not anymore. You're here. I'm here. We're…we're here." She breathed a shuddering sob/sigh and clutched my neck. "Don't go. Please. *Please.* Don't ever leave me."

This was an outpouring between us, an unleashing. It was as if a lifetime of pent-up need and imprisoned love was finally unfurling once-pinioned wings and taking flight, finding freedom in the far blue forever of the sky.

"I won't."

She pinned my eyes with hers. I saw need in her jade gaze. "What is this, with us?"

"I don't know." What words could I use? I'd just met her after five years of letters. But I knew her, and I needed her. "It's…everything. It's—"

"That's what I need. I need everything, Cade. I need you…your everything. Your always." She sounded as if the words were being tugged from her, drawn involuntarily from the depths of her soul. Like she didn't want to say them, to admit such need, but couldn't help it.

I knew exactly how she felt.

"Is this crazy?" I asked.

"Yes. It is." Her forehead touched mine. Both of us had our eyes shut tight. "But it's not. We've divulged to each other our deepest secrets, the most vulnerable truths. We journaled to each other for five years, holding nothing back. At least, I never held anything back from you, and I don't think you did, either—"

"Neither did I. We haven't been writing as much lately, I guess, and when I found Alex, I just couldn't—"

"I needed more than letters. I didn't know what to write. Billy…he cheated on me, lied to me, and it fucked me up in my head so bad, I don't even know how to deal with it. And I dreamed of you, and I can't get you out of my head. I paint you all the time. Even when I was with Billy, I would paint you when nothing else made any sense, when I couldn't get another piece to work right, I would paint your face. Again and again, and it always helped, and then I found out about Billy lying to me and cheating on me and I just—I just—I thought about you, about what if there was more, what if I showed up at your house—"

"Why didn't you?"

Ever rested her head against my shoulder, pillowing her face between my bicep and my pectoral muscle, and my hands were on her waist, one near her hip and the other on the small of her back. So familiar. Like holding her was my whole eternity, like we'd always held each other this way. But we hadn't, and it was exhilarating. It was *Ever*, actually Ever, and her body was so soft against mine, warm, her weight a perfect pressure, her breasts crushed against me, and I wanted so much, but there was more to say.

"I was afraid."

"Of what?"

"That you'd...stopped caring about me. That way, I mean. This way. You said you'd had a crush on me, and that it was a literary love, but did that mean more? I didn't dare ask, because I was with Billy at that point and I—I don't even know why I didn't ask, why I didn't—" She stopped abruptly, curled her fingers into fists in my shirt, raw emotion consuming her. "Why did we waste so much time, Cade? *Why?*"

"I don't know, Ever." I ran my hands up her spine and back down, stopping at her waist. "I wish I knew. I wish I'd been with you all this time. I've—I've never stopped feeling this way about you."

She lifted up and our eyes met. We were still lying on the couch, her on top of me. Her partially unbuttoned shirt hung free, and I could see she wasn't wearing a bra, wasn't wearing anything, was bare beneath the thin scrap of cotton. My body was on fire. "What way? Tell me, Cade. Tell me how you feel. We've never shied away from the truth with each other. Let's not start now."

"But...we haven't—we haven't seen each other since we were fourteen. Fifteen? We're basically meeting each other for the first time. How can I... put all that out there so soon? How can I even be feeling all this so soon? It's crazy. It's...so much. My head is spinning. My heart, all of me is spinning."

"Me too." She was completely on top of me, her arms beneath her, propping her upper torso on my chest. Her arms were barred on either side of her breasts, which bulged out of the shirt. I was mesmerized, torn between her hypnotic eyes and her tantalizing breasts. "But...all that time, all those years we've known each other. I know you, Caden Monroe. I know who you are. This is right, and I'm not afraid of it. I'm afraid of losing it. That's all I'm afraid of now. Losing you. So what is this, for you? What am I to you?"

I opened my mouth to speak, but no words came out. I hadn't said those words in so long. Never to anyone but Mom and Dad.

Ever's eyes speared into me, drilled, dug, devoured. Denied me the ability to lie, to hesitate, to withdraw or to shy away or to do anything but admit it all, bare it all, risk it all.

"This is love, Ever." The words tumbled out, and I was rocked to my core by the admission. "I love you. Since I met you at Interlochen, I've loved you."

Ever

The smell of oil paint hung thick in the air. Cade was a muscled hulk of man beneath me, hard, huge, and rugged. My insides were coiled tight, had been since I opened the door to see him standing there, backlit by the late afternoon sun. He was wearing a faded pair of Levis, the kind of worn, faded look that only comes from actually being worn hard, not the expensive, pre-faded look of Billy's $150 jeans. A tight black T-shirt hugged Cade's torso, which was thick with cords of muscle. He was work-hardened, life-toughened. His hands on my cheeks were rough and callused, just like in my dream, but so gentle.

His eyes, pure amber, were liquid heat, searing me, demanding all I had, all I was, and giving the same back to me.

He wanted me.

He loved me.

He loved me? How? How could he? How could he know that? I'd demanded he tell me how he felt. And how did I feel?

"I love you, Cade." I didn't tack on the "too." It wasn't that I loved him as well; I loved him. I'd always loved him, but for some reason I couldn't understand I'd ignored that fact for five years.

He seemed to shudder as he absorbed what I'd said. "For real?"

I couldn't help but laugh at the raw wonder in his voice, the sheer shock. "Yes. I do."

"Why?"

"Because our souls belong together. Because... because after everything you've been through, everything you've endured in your life, you're still here. You're strong. You're...you're all man. You're talented, but humble. You know me. You know my secrets. Things I could never tell anyone else. You've been there since I was a kid, a girl figuring out who she was, and now I know who I am, and you are part of that. Our letters have been a part of me, a part of my maturing, part of who I am as I've grown up. Which means *you're* a part of all that, part of me. That's why

I love you." It was so easy to say that phrase somehow. I'd thought it would be hard.

A dusting of black stubble coated his cheeks, off-setting his amber eyes. His skin was tanned from endless hours in the sun, and his gaze on me was unwavering. I could dive into his eyes and stay submerged there, drown in his expression.

His mouth worked, as if he was trying to speak but simply couldn't find the words. All I could see, though, was the way his mouth moved, the way his lips were slightly chapped and swollen from kissing me, the way his five o'clock shadow shifted with the movement of his facial muscles. He had high cheekbones and thick, full eyelashes, fluttering dark against his skin. I wanted to kiss him there, kiss the tender place just beneath his eyes.

I could, couldn't I? I didn't have to wonder, to dream, to imagine. I let my face descend and my lips touch his eyebrows, the ridge at the corner of his eyes, delighting in the sharp intake of breath he made as my mouth caressed his skin, the way his hands tightened on my waist.

He'd been so careful to keep his hands on my back, on my waist, and his eyes on mine, constantly tearing his gaze away from my tits and my flesh. I wanted more. I wanted it all. I *needed* it all. All of him. I needed to unwrap myself and let him delve into me, I needed to fly free into the high heaven of his body, his touch, his caress and his love.

I'd never felt that, the true caress of love. I'd felt the grip of lust, of lascivious ardor.

He tilted his face and caught my lips, and his kiss was a tide, a rolling wave overwhelming my breath and my thoughts in crashing fervor. I arched my spine and pressed my breasts against his hard chest, lifting my ass, seeking his touch there. I opened my eyes and pulled away from his lips, seeing need in his eyes to mirror my own, and I wished I knew how to get him to unleash himself, to quit holding back.

"Ever…" His voice was so deep, smooth and dark and rich. "God, you're so…much. So beautiful. I feel drunk from kissing you. Like touching you makes me high. I'm dizzy from your skin."

The poetry of his words made me quiver and shudder and made me clutch him and kiss him compulsively. I nuzzled his throat, felt his Adam's apple bob as he swallowed, kissed the hollow of his throat and the side of his neck and up to the crevice behind his ear and then the hard ridge of his jaw. "You're all there is, all I know. All I need." I whispered the words with my lips brushing the shell of his ear. "And I need more of you. All of you. Now. I need it…all, now. Please, Cade. I've needed you for so long. Don't make me wait anymore."

"I'm...I'm broken, Ever." His words cracked as he spoke them. It was admission torn from the bottom of his soul.

"Me, too. Let's heal each other. Put each other back together again."

"Here?"

I moaned in frustration. I didn't want to be reminded of reality. Of the fact that my private studio space was unlocked and that there were windows cracked open so sound could escape, even if the blinds were drawn closed. "No. God. Goddamn it." I slid off him, and as I stood up, I relished the way his eyes raked down my body and back up, and then his gaze locked on mine, as if embarrassed to be caught looking at me.

I held out my hand to him, and he took it in his, his palm engulfing my fingers. I drew him to me, pressed my boobs against his chest. "You can look, Cade," I told him. "Look at me." I freed a button, and felt myself spill out, the edges of the shirt just barely covering my nipples.

He let his eyes leave mine, slide down, and his breath halted as he saw my nearly bared breasts.

"Touch me," I whispered. My heart hammered, my pulse sent haywire by my daring, my need for him.

He touched the pad of his index finger to my collarbone, dragged it across the bone, sliding the edge of my shirt aside. Down, then, his finger moved, and his eyes were on mine as he moved the shirt away, and then my left breast was bare to the air and to his gaze and to his touch, and I was breathless. His hand cupped underneath my boob, and then he lifted its weight and the heel of his palm brushed my erect nipple, sending sparks through me. He flattened his hand over my breastbone, and then slid the other side of my shirt away and caressed my right breast, and then he was on his knees in front of me, kneeling before me, and his fingers were freeing the last few buttons and his lips were on my skin, his mouth grazing my navel.

I threaded my fingers through his hair and tried to remember to keep breathing. He kissed upward, dragging his lips across my flesh, which pebbled with goosebumps. His hands curled around my waist and slid up the bare skin of my spine, pulled me closer and then his mouth was touching too-gentle kisses to the round underside of my breast, and now my lungs filled with an abrupt *whoosh*, which turned into an eager moan as his lips closed on my nipple. He sucked it into his mouth and I was gone, gone, aching all throughout my body, fire blazing a trail from my tits down to my core, and as he tugged on my nipple with his nimble lips the line of heat grew hotter and the pulling within my core loosed a torrent of damp, slick need between my thighs.

"Cade, Jesus, Cade...." I breathed, "don't stop, please, don't ever stop..."

He moved his mouth to the other breast and I was dizzy, my knees weak, and his palms were skating up and down my back, holding my shoulder blades and curling under the shirt fabric over my shoulders and down again, to the upper swell of my ass.

"Hot," he murmured when he realized I wasn't wearing panties. His mouth touched an electric kiss between my breasts and then moved down, and my entire body was...what was beyond fire? What was hotter than flame?

He pulled his gaze away and his mouth away, and I whimpered at the loss of the hot wet slide of his lips against my skin, but I was rewarded by the raw heat in his gaze as he stared at my privates. He licked his lips, and his hands on my hips tightened their grip, dimpling the flesh with some sort of control he was trying to exercise over himself..

"Talk to me, Cade." I needed affirmation from him. I needed to know his thoughts, to know how he felt. I needed, simply, to hear his voice.

"I want you, Ever." His voice shook. "So bad. You were beautiful when you were fifteen. You're...Jesus fuck, Ever, you're a goddess now. Let me worship you."

"Please?" I could barely speak.

My button-down painting shirt was hanging from the crooks of my elbows. His mouth devoured my navel, the inward curve where my hip and my thigh met. I shivered and shook, curled my fingers in his hair and panted, heard tiny mewling moans emit from my throat as his kisses slid down my thigh and back up, across my belly, low. I trembled in his grip. His hands rested on my hips, held me still. I needed his touch; I placed my hand on his, moved his palm with my finger twined in his to cup my ass, my head tilted back, my eyes closed, my breath coming in shallow gasps of ragged passion.

He took the hint and took the taut round weight of my ass in both his hands, caressed the flesh, cupped, tested the firmness with his fingers, ran his palms underneath and lifted each cheek, traced the crease with sliding fingers, dipped in through the keyhole gap and ignited trembling need into an inferno.

I let my feet slide apart, opening for him. "Cade? More. Touch me. Please."

I had no problem begging him. I'd beg him until he sated the ravenous hunger within me for his touch, for his kisses, for his caresses and his love. I needed this, more than I'd ever needed anything, and he was being so slow, so careful, exploring me with thoroughness that left me shivering with impatience.

He held onto my ass and kissed my pubis, down over the close-cropped hair, and I was limp in his touch, quivering all over, barely able to stand, yet I found the strength to grasp his shoulders and widen my stance. "Yes…" I whispered, "please. Kiss me. Right there, please, Cade." I loved saying his name, loved whispering his name with such sexual heat.

And then he pulled his mouth away. "I thought we were moving somewhere more private?"

I could have screamed. "I don't care…not now. I just need you."

He let his forehead rest against my belly. "I don't want to share the sounds you're making for me with anyone else. I don't…I don't want to be interrupted. I don't want you to be embarrassed later."

He was thinking of me, protecting me from my own impatience. I did indeed feel a rush of embarrassment as I realized anyone could walk in. I'd unlocked the door to let him and hadn't relocked it. Eden had a tendency to visit me without warning, and so did Ms. Meier, my mentor.

I pulled him to his feet. "Come on. My room."

"But your roommate…" He buttoned my shirt from the bottom up, missing a button, so it was crooked.

"She'll leave. Or we'll have to close my door and be quiet." I tugged my yoga pants on, grabbed my shirt, bra, and shoes off the floor, and led Cade by the hand across the road to my dorm room.

Steph was on the couch, a thick textbook on her knees, glasses on top of her head, a *Doctor Who* episode playing on TV. She glanced up as we entered, took one look at Cade's mussed hair, my misbuttoned shirt and clothes tucked under my arm and the fevered expression on my face, and shot to her feet. "I'll just...go to Mark's," she stammered, ducking her head as she vanished into her room, packed a bag in record time, and stuffed her feet into a pair of clogs. "Text me when it's...safe." And with that, she was gone.

I locked the door behind her, flattened my palms against the door, and leaned back against it. "Now we're alone." I'd been in such a hurry, but now I wanted to delay the moment, revel in the heat in his eyes, the obvious bulge at his zipper, the pounding excitement racing in my veins.

"Very much alone," Cade said, taking a step closer to me.

I reached for him, but instead of pulling him against me and kissing him, I grasped the hem of his T-shirt and lifted it up, over his head and off, memorizing his unique scent as I tossed it aside. My eyes devoured him. I'd seen the evidence of his build through the shirt, but nothing could prepare me for the dizzying splendor of his bare torso. I let my head thunk against the door, my gaze raking over him. Broad shoulders, thick, heavy arms and bulging pectoral muscles, rippling abs, a hint of a wicked V-cut peeking above the waistband of his boxers. Every muscle was hard and huge and defined, but not from hours in the gym, rather from hard work, the natural muscle of a strong man who knew how to use his body, and did. He looked like he could wrestle a bull to the ground, carry a foal on his shoulders, lift a bale of hay with ease.

After his shirt was gone, he unbuttoned three buttons on mine, then stopped. "I buttoned it crooked," he said with a laugh.

"I know," I said. "You were kind of distracted."

I ran my hands over his shoulders, down his biceps and back up, over his pecs, down his abs, splaying my fingers and tracing the lines of his abs. His gaze was locked on me, his hands resting on my hips, waiting to see what I would do. I looked up to meet his eyes. His mouth fell open and his chest expanded with a huge inbreath as I crooked an index finger inside the elastic of his underwear, following the curve of his waistline from hip to hip, and then back to center. I undid the button of his jeans, drew the zipper down. He wasn't breathing now, holding the breath he'd taken, his hands bunching the cotton of my shirt in tight fists. I ran my hands between his jeans and boxers, caressing his tight ass and pushing the denim down in the same motion. He was wearing skin-hugging gray boxer-briefs; he was hard for

me, and he was *huge*. A dot of moisture darkened
the stretchy fabric where the tip of him touched it,
leaking.

I swallowed hard, able to see every glorious inch
of him outlined by the gray material, and I wanted it
all. I reached for the elastic band, but he pinioned my
wrist in his massive hand. With the other hand, he
deftly unbuttoned the last three buttons of my shirt.
He let go of my wrist, brought both of his palms
to my face and slowly closed the distance between
us, pressed his hungry lips to mine, kissed me till I
swooned. His palms slid down the arch of my neck,
over my shoulders, brushing the shirt away. I straightened my arms and let it fall free.

I was naked before him.

He continued to kiss me while his hands explored
me, searching my curves in earnest. Sliding down my
arms, around my neck and down my spine, following the curve of my ass, the backs of my thighs and
around to my quads, squeezing gently the generous
flesh and muscle there, and up, tracing in a teasing,
tantalizing slide the crease of my pussy, making my
knees quake.

My own hands were not idle; I dragged my finger down his straining length, over the stretched cotton, and then was unable to pretend any longer and
impatiently drew his underwear down, down, and he
stepped out of them, and we were both bare for each

other. I took his lower lip in my teeth and grasped his thick cock in my fist, eating his groan with my kiss and sliding my palm down his length.

"I wasn't thinking about...this...when I knocked on your door," Cade murmured, "so I'm not...I don't have anything. Protection, I mean."

I squeezed gently, caressed his hardness, learning the length of him, the girth of him, the way he lay straight up against his belly and the bulbous mushroom head, springy under my touch. "It's fine," I said, "I've got an IUD."

"Thank god," he said.

He bent and kissed the side of my neck, and I leaned back against the door, displayed my throat for him. His mouth descended, and I held onto the base of him, just holding him, waiting and desperate to see how he'd touch me, what pleasure he would give me, what bliss he would infuse into my eager body. His mouth followed my flesh to my nipple, brought it to diamond hardness with a single kiss, tongued it, nibbled it, and I moaned at each wet touch of his mouth. One hand on his cock, I wrapped the other around his neck and held him against me, arched my back to get more of his mouth on the flesh of my breasts.

"Your tits taste so good," Cade mumbled. "So good. They're perfect tits, Ever. Just perfect."

"I love your cock," I said, breathless. "It's so big, so hard."

"I want to hear you come." He slid a hand between my thighs, and I spread my legs to allow him room. "Can you moan for me? Say my name when you come, Ever."

"I love the way you say my name." I slid my fist up and down his length as slowly as I could, savoring the size and silky perfection of him in my hands. This was Caden, my Caden, real, here, in my house, his cock in my hand and his fingers delving into my folds. "Yes, Caden. Yes. Touch me there. I'll come for you."

I'd never spoken this way before. Not ever. No matter how good it was, I never spoke this way, and it had never, *ever* been this good. This wasn't even sex yet, this was foreplay, and my life was changed, my notion of pleasure altered, my idea of passion shattered and remade.

I moaned loud when his finger slid into the tight wet space of my pussy, and louder yet when he curled his finger and found the perfect spot and caressed me there, so gently, so slowly, as if he knew exactly how to touch me, how to make me come. He knew my body, knew it as if he'd always made love to me.

My fist was pumping his cock steadily now; I cupped his tip with my palm, rolled the leaking pre-come around and spread it, caressed his length, my fingers loose around him, just barely touching, and my other hand was in the hair at his nape, holding his head against my chest, his lips kissing my boobs all over, licking my nipples, paying homage to my tits.

He grabbed my hand and brought it away from him, pinned it against the wall, his muscles tensed and straining, his breath coming in short panting gasps. "I...I almost lost it," he muttered through gritted teeth. "It's been a long time, and I want you so bad. You're so fucking gorgeous, and you touching me that way, I almost came all over your hand."

I heard the embarrassment in his voice. "I want you to come," I said. "I want to feel that. On my hands, on me, in me, anywhere. I don't care. We have all the time in the world."

I worked my hand loose from his grip and grasped his erection in my fist once more, brought him to the weak-kneed, gasping, trembling cusp of coming within a few slow strokes of my fist. I brought my other hand down from his neck and cupped his balls in my hand, whimpering as his fingers inside me brought me to the edge, like he was, together at the edge of orgasm but holding back, not ready to fall over yet.

Suddenly I was in the air and my legs were wrapping around his waist and my arms around his neck and he was at my entrance, his mouth on my tits and his breath hot and his hands hard and strong holding me by the ass, my back against the door, growling with the effort to hold back. He lifted his gaze to my eyes, saw the tears I hadn't known were there until just that moment.

He froze. "Ever? What's wrong? What did I do?"

I shook my head, buried my face against his neck. "No, nothing. I'm…so ready. I'm sorry I'm crying, I don't know why I am, but it's from all this being so much, so intense, so infinitely more incredible than I even hoped or dreamed or fantasized it could be." He was poised at my entrance, and I was gushing emotional vulnerability to him. "I'm sorry, I'm sorry, I just—god, don't stop. I want you inside me. Make love to me, Caden."

He swiveled, holding me, strode easily across the living room, around the couch and the TV still flickering, forgotten, and stopped at the junction of the bathroom and the two bedroom doors. I gestured at my door and he pushed through it, kicked it closed, set me with utter gentility on the bed. I scooted back, knocking the throw pillows aside and kicking the blankets down, reaching for him, begging him to join me.

He stayed where he was, though, one knee on the edge of the bed, staring at me. "I want to remember this moment," he said. "You, there on the bed, reaching for me, naked, so perfect. No one has ever looked at me the way you're looking at me."

"Like I love you so completely it almost hurts?" I asked. "Like you're the center of my universe?"

It baffled me how my feelings for him could expand with such dizzying hyper-speed. It wasn't so sudden, though, I realized, watching him climb onto the bed and crawl to me like a powerful, primal animal, lean and agile. It had been there all the time, I just hadn't seen it, refused to acknowledge it, and all the while it had been building and growing silent and unseen inside me, a well of potential bubbling and simmering, ready to boil over, and now he was here with me, and he wanted me, loved me. And god, Jesus, he was so much *more* than I could fathom. His size and power and looks and the intensity in his gaze and the tenderness of his touch and the hunger in his kiss…it was all so much, too much. He overwhelmed me, and I nearly wanted to retreat away into my head, into my art, simply because I was in some way afraid, like he'd admitted, terrified of giving in to him and letting him take over my life and my soul and my body and having it taken away from me somehow.

He approached me like a hurricane, with inevitable might. His shoulders rolled as he crawled toward me, his hair hung over his eyes and his biceps rippled and his deltoids shifted like a prowling tiger's, and his immense manhood jutted straight forward, bobbing with his motion, wagging side to side, hard and long and thick and straight and heavy. Watching him move was sheer eroticism, sexuality in motion, and my body responded. My nipples turned so hard they

ached, and my loins clenched, my cleft went damp
with desire, hot with anticipation.

My mouth fell open as his hands planted on
either side of my hips, and my eyes went half-closed
and I couldn't look away from him. He licked his lips,
and then his hands circled over my thighs and parted
them, spreading me wide. I blushed, shifted, wanted
to close my legs, embarrassed. I was on full display
for him, and his eyes were roving over me, examining me, seeing every fold and crevice and drop of
wetness and curl of pubic hair, and I couldn't bear
the scrutiny.

"You're beautiful, Ever," he whispered. "All over.
I want to taste you."

"Taste—taste me?" I squeaked the question, a
panicked whisper gone wrong.

Oh, I knew what he was suggesting. Obviously,
I did. But Billy and I had always been too impatient
for oral sex. Or he had been, at least. He'd kiss me
and touch me down there, and I'd touch him, and
then we'd fumble out of our clothes and then he'd
be there, inside me, and then it would be over. We'd
found variations over time, of course, but other than
the one time Billy had asked me to go down on him,
oral sex had never come up. Now I wondered if it
had something to do with Billy's girlfriend. His *real*
girlfriend, since I was just his piece of ass on the side.
If he went down on her, but not me, because that

would violate some odd sense of not-cheating ideas he might have.

I pushed those thoughts away, the errant thoughts of my brain gone off the rails, distracting itself to get away from the fear. Why was I afraid? This was Cade. My Cade. The boy I'd drawn with at Interlochen. The man I'd dreamed about, painted, shared everything with via handwritten letter.

My Cade.

And he wanted to go down on me. I met his eyes, and he was waiting, palms on my quads, fingers gently digging into the insides of my thighs, his thumbs brushing slowly up and down the outside of my core, gently stroking millimeters away from my labia.

"Ever? Are you okay? If you don't want me to, I won't."

"I'm just…nervous."

He laughed, a confused, amused huff. "Nervous? Why are you nervous about this? I want to. I don't expect you to ever go down on me if you don't want to. I *want* to do this to you. I want to make you come like this. I want to feel you squirm and hear you moan." Realization dawned on him. "Wait. Have you never…have you never had anyone do this to you before?"

I could only shake my head, for some reason embarrassed to admit it. I didn't want to discuss what I had done and what he had done with anyone else.

Not now. Not in so intimate a setting, so intense a moment.

Cade must have realized I wasn't going to say anything, that I couldn't, didn't know what to say, so he lowered his mouth to just above my knee. "Stop me if you don't like what I'm doing."

His thumbs continued their gentle stroking, and his lips touched the inside of my knee, kissed upward an inch, and then the other leg in the same spot, and his mouth was hot and almost ticklishly tender on my flesh, but I liked it, felt a subtle response in my core. He kissed up my thighs, one side and then the other, and as his mouth neared my privates, his tongue began to flick out and touch my skin with each kiss, and then he paused and mouthed my inner thigh near the crease of my leg, pushed slightly so I stretched my leg higher, open wider, and he kissed there again, tongue laving me, and my insides began to heat up, uncoil, and then his mouth touched my pubis, and I heard a sigh release from me. Across, down the other crease of my thigh, down my thigh, back up, and then he hovered over my slit and breathed on it, his hot, damp breath making me shiver. And then he kissed my lips, my lower lips, and I moaned. Yes, I moaned very gently, almost inaudibly, and I knew that this would wreck me, undo me. My inner muscles were twitching and the wetness of need was pulsing through my privates, and he was only kissing, actually kissing, lips touching lips, no tongue yet.

Tongue, oh, shit, oh, god, his tongue speared into my pussy, and I gasped, a sharp surprised intake of breath, and my fingers instinctively tangled in his hair, and my hips lifted of their own accord. He pulled his mouth away and then brought it close, licked up my opening with his tongue flat and strong and pushing through, in, and another slow swipe of his tongue, farther in, and I was panting. Again, and again, he merely licked me, and I was coming undone already, and then he brought his thumbs to my labia and pulled them apart and his tongue flicked my clit, and I could only writhe helplessly and listen to myself moan, loud, wanton sounds of pleasure that I had no control over. His tongue hit my clit, flicked it, flicked it, then ran in quick circles around it and I felt my hips begin to move in time with his tongue. My moans were nonstop, gasping noises and increasingly desperate groans.

He slid a finger into me, one finger slicking deep into my channel and curling up, and now I didn't merely moan or groan or even shriek, I outright screamed, head arcing back and my spine leaving the bed and my hips pushing up, shoving my quaking pussy into his mouth. I was holding his head against me, I knew it and couldn't make myself loosen my hold, couldn't exert any control over myself. I was lost, completely helpless. I couldn't stop shrieking as his finger stroked that magical spot, finding it unerringly, and his tongue worked in increasingly rapid circles around my clit.

It began low in my belly, a knot of something hot and tight unfurling, billowing outward and downward. It was an orgasm. I knew that. I'd had countless orgasms before. Self-induced, and otherwise. I knew an orgasm when I felt it. But this…this was something else. My previous orgasms had been summer rain, brief and gentle. This…this was a thunderstorm, raw power raging through me.

Cade slowed the stroke of his fingers and the circling of his tongue, and I whimpered, thrust my core against him. "Cade…oh, fuck, Cade. Please. More. I need…I need…"

"Come for me, Ever." His voice was a husky whisper, his breath hot on me.

"Please, Cade. Make me come. I'm so close."

He curled his finger against my wall, sought and found that perfect spot and his tongue did something I couldn't fathom to my clit, and I felt the edge approaching, a balloon expanding inside me, a volcano nearing eruption. And then he sucked my clit into his mouth and tugged, suckled, and his fingertip massaged inside me, and I didn't even try to hold back.

I came with a deafening shriek, a scream that embarrassed me with its erotic, breathy desperation. It wasn't an explosion—it was all of me coming apart, shattering. I couldn't breathe to scream suddenly, and I was dizzy, spinning, my insides clenching, and he didn't relent, didn't stop or slow, kept sucking and flicking with his tongue and massaging with his finger, and I was arching off the bed and my hips were driving up and down.

I had to stop him, had to, I simply couldn't take it anymore. It was too much, too intense, and I would die if he didn't let me catch my breath. I fumbled at him, tugged him up to me.

But he didn't relent even then. He poised above me, and I saw through dizzy eyes his hot gaze and his chest heaving and something wet slicking his mouth and cheeks. My essence, on his face. It was hot, for some reason. I wondered what I tasted like to him, smelled like. I lifted up and kissed him, tasted myself, musky and pungent.

And then he was there, at my entrance, and his hands were on either side of my face and he was waiting, and I couldn't speak, was still too flustered and breathless from my explosive orgasm to form words, so I shifted my hips and pushed against his thick tip, gasped for air as he slid inside me.

I was spread open by him. He entered me slowly, filling me carefully. I felt myself stretching, almost painfully, as he pushed in to me. I watched his face, watched his expression turn to pure wonder, and I knew my own face mirrored the emotions on his.

"Oh…Ever…" he rested his forehead against mine, breath coming in slow deep gasps. "You're… you're so tight, so hot and wet and tight. You're heaven, Ever. This is…being inside you is—it's heaven."

I could only pant as his cock stretched me and filled me past bursting. I couldn't understand how I'd thought I knew what pleasure was until this. What ecstasy was until now, until I'd felt the perfection of Caden's cock inside me.

I had to try to communicate this to him. He needed to know how this felt for me. "Cade, Caden. You…this is…everything." Wow, that was eloquent. I tried again. "Your cock, I've never—never felt anything like your cock inside me. I could come again just from feeling you slide into me. Feeling you inside me like this is…it's home. It's where I belong, where you belong."

I felt a tear prick, and he kissed it away, didn't question it this time, and I knew he could see the wonder and the ecstasy and the love on my face. He was buried to the hilt inside me, our hips flush. He didn't move, though, just held there, deep inside me, and lowered his mouth to mine and kissed me. It felt like my very first kiss, in a way, that kiss with his cock inside my pussy and his tongue inside my mouth and his palm skating over my cheek and down my chest and covering my breast. His fingers caught my nipple and twisted it gently, and I moaned, and he finally slid out partway, hesitated, and then thrust in.

"Yes!" The word shot out from my mouth, unbidden. "Oh, god yes, Cade. Again. More. God, please, more."

He moaned then, and the sound of his moan made my pussy clench around him, the pleasure I heard in his voice as he drew back and pushed in. I couldn't stop the whimpering moan, didn't try to. I was going to be loud, I knew I was. So loud. I didn't care. The whole world could hear me, and I wouldn't care. He was all that mattered, his huge erection inside me, moving, filling me and completing me and driving me wild was all I cared about.

"Talk to me, Cade," I whispered. "I need to hear your voice. I love the sound of your voice."

"What do you want me to say?" He punctuated his question with a slow thrust, all the way out, only the tip remaining inside me, and then all the way in, a slow sliding thrust that made me gasp.

"Anything. Whatever you're thinking. Whatever you're feeling." I clutched his shoulders and wrapped one heel around the back of his knee. "Talk dirty to me. I like it when you say nasty things to me."

"You're so tight, Ever. Every time I slide into you, I can't believe how tight you are, how perfectly I fit inside you." He was finding a rhythm now, thrust, pause, thrust, pause. "Do you know how good your pussy tasted? Do you? Like sugar. So good. I love the sounds you make. I love hearing you moan. I *really* love hearing you scream."

"I've never been so loud before. I didn't know I *could* scream like that." Both heels around his knees, now, and my hands clawed into his shoulders as he started to drive into me in a steady rhythm. "Oh, yeah, like this. I like this. Don't stop, Cade. Fuck me like this forever."

"It's not fucking, Ever. It's love. Never just fucking."

"I know. I know. God, do I know. Love me like this forever, then." I kissed his shoulder, and then his neck, and let my fingernails scratch down his back. "But…I like talking like that with you. I don't know why. I've never talked, during. And I like it."

I knew I shouldn't keep talking about what I'd never done before, but I had no filter, no control over my words.

Caden shifted so his weight was on one forearm and his hand traced across my chest and palmed one of my tits, and began toying with my nipple.

"Yes, Cade. I love it when you play with my tits. Put your mouth on them. Your tongue."

"I never knew skin could taste so sweet," he said, lowering his mouth to my left boob, taking my nipple between his lips and worrying it. Then he seized the erect, hypersensitive nub in his teeth and bit gently, and I shrieked, arched my back, and bucked my hips against his. "Your tits are so amazing. So fucking amazing. Just the right size, big and round and heavy, and your nipples, fuck, I love the taste of your nipples. They're so sensitive—you go crazy when I do this." He demonstrated by sucking my nipple into his mouth and tugging it, stretching it, and I moaned, crashed my hips against his, driving my pussy up against him, around his cock.

"You know me…it's like you were made to fuck me."

"I was," he breathed. "I was made to fuck you. I was made to love you, to hold you, to kiss you, to fuck you, to make you come and watch you sleep and keep you safe. And I will always, *always* do all of that."

His rhythm was faltering, stuttering, and his voice was going husky, his eyes closing. I tilted my hips and wrapped my legs around his hips and set the rhythm for him, my head tipped back and my pussy sliding wet and slick around his thickness, and I was moaning and he was groaning and our bodies synched in rhythm, met in furious passion, and I moved us faster, rocking my body against him. I'd come for him, and now I wanted—needed—to feel him come. I needed to know what he looked like when he lost control, what it felt like when his cock unleashed and his body shuddered against mine.

So I drew it from him, refused to let him slow down, refused to let him hold back. I bucked against him, encouraging him with my body to move faster, to give me more.

"Fuck me, Cade. Fuck me harder. Come for me. Right now." I whispered it in his ear, and he obeyed me, fucked me harder, fucked me like I'd never felt before, and it was still not enough. "Yes, like this… oh, god, baby, oh, god, Cade, you're gonna make me come again."

"Do it," he rasped, "do it for me. Come for me again."

"No, *no*." I moved faster, set a frantic, pounding rhythm, whispering in his ear all the while. "Not until you. I can't, not until I feel your come inside me. I won't come until you do."

"I'm close, Ever."

He planted his fists beside my ear, and I kissed one of his wrists, threaded my fingers in his hair and clawed at his tight, iron-hard, pulsing ass and pulled him to me, jerked with my legs against his madly thrusting hips and let my voice whisper in his ear, saying whatever came out.

"God, I feel you. You're so close, baby. Don't hold back. Don't stop. Never stop. Fuck me, Cade. I love it. I love this so much. Keep fucking me."

I'd never talked like this before, never even thought this way before. It belonged to Cade. Something about Cade unleashed a beast within me, a frantic sex-demon that took control of me. I didn't even say the F-word, almost ever, and now it was coming out of my mouth nonstop. But Cade responded to it—it made him crazy, made him grunt and groan and gasp and made his body rock against me, and I was so close to coming, but I couldn't, like I'd said to him, I couldn't come again until I felt him explode inside me.

And then…he detonated. His rhythm faltered and his hips jerked, crashed into me. He groaned in my ear and his cock pounded into me, and his mouth pressed helplessly against my breastbone.

I held his head, clutched his face to my flesh and rocked with him, feeling something in my very soul open up and envelop him, tangle and twine with him, felt something inside him unfurl and reach out and enter me, some invisible but tangible and real essence clasping and braiding around my soul.

"Oh, god, Ever…I love you…" he gasped, coming and coming and coming.

I felt the flood hit my inner walls and still he came, tensing and jerking and panting, but still moving, quick desperate thrusts, and I came, too. It was as if the tidal wave of his come reacted with my essence and exploded, a violent reaction that completely subsumed me.

I screamed, screamed, came and came and whimpered and felt him still thrusting inside me, post-orgasmic quakes, tiny thrusts. I met them with my own strokes, milking the hardness of his cock and coming so hard I was blinded and breathless, unable to even continue screaming as wave after wave of raw energy twisted through me.

"I love you…I love you…I love you." I chanted it as we moved together, ecstasy fading into kiln-hot bliss. "I love you so much, Cade. How can I love you this much, so suddenly? It's like I just met you, but I love you. How is it possible?"

"I don't…I don't know." He was slowing, slowing, went still, rolled with me so I was pillowed against him, his cock slipping out of me, a loss I felt intensely. "But I feel it, too. Exactly that. I don't know how it's possible, how I could love anyone so much. I feel like…maybe this is stupid, but I felt like when we came together just now that our souls… met. Connected, somehow."

I put my palm to his cheek and turned his face to mine, locked eyes with him. "I felt it, too. It happened. We fused. Our souls fused."

"That was…it was like nothing I've ever felt before." Cade's hand smoothed down my side, rested on my hip. "From the very first moment I opened the door and saw you, I had to kiss you. I had to touch you. I didn't know how you'd feel, and I was terrified, so scared. I don't even mind admitting it. But I couldn't *not* kiss you. And from that moment, when our lips touched, everything has been just so *much*. So fucking intense. And that…making love…it was…I don't even know how to put it."

"Earth-shattering?" I suggested.

"Yeah. Exactly. Earth-shattering. Whatever I've felt before just…doesn't even exist, doesn't even register." His hand went into motion again, sliding up my side and down, resting on my hip, then daring over the side to cup my hipbone and slide in farther, his fingertips brushing the trimmed fuzz of my pubic hair.

I wondered idly if he'd want me to shave it. I'd thought about shaving myself before, but never had had the courage to go that far. I touched his chest, let my palm wander down his stomach, felt his tight hard abs and then the similar scratchy stubble of his closely trimmed groin. I toyed with the stubble, running my fingertips over it, my fingernails, down around his flaccid cock and beneath. I wanted to know what every inch of him felt like. I cupped his sac in my palm, ran my thumbs over his balls and then cradled the limp but still-impressive member in my hand.

"God, I love the way you touch me," he mumbled, post-orgasmic drowsiness in his voice.

"That works out, since I love touching you. You have a beautiful cock."

"It's not very impressive right now."

I giggled. "Yes, it is. It's beautiful like this. And it's just glorious when it's hard." I rested my cheek against his chest, stared down at him, at the lovely sight of his cock in my pale white hand.

"Keep doing that, and it'll be glorious all over again."

"That's what I'm hoping." I continued to toy with him, fondle him.

His hand stroked my flesh, as far up as he could reach, as far down. He traced the line of my pussy, and I shivered. He ran his hand up my belly and cupped one of my boobs, and then the other, twiddled my nipple and then the other.

We both fell asleep like that, touching each other.

no need to breathe

Caden

I woke up slowly. I felt a weight against my chest, on my side and on my thigh. Warmth, softness, something tickling my nose. What was it? It was unfamiliar. I slept alone, always slept alone. But this felt so good. So good. I didn't want the comforting weight and intoxicating softness to go away.

Ever. It was Ever. I was in bed with Ever. Relief and amazement and joy rushed through me. And then I felt a surge of panic as I worried that everything had been a dream, had been a fantasy. But then I remembered that it was real, and it had been real. Real, and perfect. Beyond perfect, something I didn't have a word for.

Love. She loved me, and I loved her. We'd made love, and she'd begged me to never stop fucking her. It hadn't sounded wrong or dirty when she said it, only erotic and incredible.

I opened one eye to see Ever draped on top of me, her head on my chest, her arm across my stomach, her leg thrown over my thigh. Her hair was splayed across my neck and tickling my nose, and her breath was warm on my skin. I didn't dare move, didn't want to disturb her. But I couldn't help touching her. Her skin was like silk, like sun-warmed satin. Pale and fair and smooth. I touched her shoulder, and she murmured in her sleep, shifted, and her hand slid down my stomach to rest a hair's breadth from my cock. Oh, holy hell, how I remembered the way she'd fondled me as we'd fallen asleep, the way she'd cradled me in her hand and stroked me so lovingly, not to arouse but to caress.

And now, with the memory, my cock was thickening, going hard and aching with turgid heat as I slid my palm down her arm, down her side to her hip. Her beautiful hip, bell-curved, and her ass, just begging to be touched. I cupped her ass cheek, closed my eyes in bliss, inhaling hard as I palmed the fullness of it and down to the other cheek, back up, to her hip, down her thigh.

She shifted again, and I froze with her hipbone in my hand, on the way to relearning the sumptuous glory of her pussy. She mumbled in her sleep, and I felt a moment of panic as I worried that she'd think she was with *him* and say his name. But she didn't. She slid her knee up, her palm down, sliding her hand between my now-hard cock and stomach. She murmured again, and this time I made out her words: "Cade. Caden. Don't go, please…don't go…"

"I'm here," I whispered in her ear. "I'm not going anywhere. Not ever."

"Need you," she responded.

"I need you, too."

"Touch me." I wasn't sure if she was awake or asleep or in between. "Touch me, just once, before you go."

"I'm not going anywhere." I let my hand slide down low over her belly, down to her pudendum. "I'm here forever now."

She moaned sleepily, a sound of pleasure. I slid my hand up her stomach and between her breasts, cupped her tits in turn, feeling my cock twitch as I palmed the heavenly softness of her boobs. Her nipples were soft and flat now, but as I ever-so-gently slid my fingertip across one, I felt it lift and thicken. Ever moaned again, and I involuntarily lifted my hips, wanting her to touch me, to grasp me. Her hand was *so* close, right there beneath it, touching it, but not giving me the kind of pressure I needed.

I played with her tits, cupping and squeezing them, twiddling her nipples, trying to make them hard. She moaned again, and again, and then rocked her hips against my leg, grinding on my thigh.

"Cade…god, Cade." She was sounding more lucid now. "I don't want to wake up. I don't…don't want it to be a dream."

I put my lips to her ear. "It's not." I traced a line down her body to her core, dipped two fingers between her thighs and slid them up her pussy. "It's real. I'm here…we're in bed together. Wake up and touch me." It was a selfish thing to say, but it was also an attempt to alleviate the pain I heard in her voice as she begged for her dream to be real, thinking I'd go away when she woke up.

She stirred, grinding her hips against my thigh again, and then her head moved, slid off my chest and onto the pillow. I paused with my palm cupping her breast. Her eyes fluttered, opened, slid closed, and then jerked open again.

"You're real." She sounded amazed. "I thought…I was so afraid it was a dream, that it had all been a dream."

"I know," I said. "I felt the same way. I had to touch you to make sure you were really real. And then once I started touching you, I couldn't stop. Your skin is addictive."

Her stunning green eyes, still sleepy, searched my face. A tinge of fear touched them suddenly. "You won't—you won't ever lie to me, will you, Caden?"

"*Never*," I said, vehement, "not ever."

"Not about anything? Swear to me you won't ever lie to me. I couldn't handle it."

"I promise you, Ever. I will not ever lie to you. No matter what, not about anything."

"Good." She rubbed my chest, caressing my pectoral muscles and the ridges of my abs, moving her hand in a circle, each circuit bringing her hand closer to my cock. "Tell me something true."

"Like what? What do you want to know?"

"Do you have any fantasies? Things you want to do that you haven't?"

I furrowed my brow in thought. "Yeah, I guess I do."

"Like what?"

"You want me to tell you my sexual fantasies?"

Her lips curved in a seductive smile. "Yeah. I'll trade you, though. I have some, too. You tell me yours, and I'll tell you mine."

It was hard to isolate my fantasies and put them into words. I opened and closed my mouth, but nothing came out. I took a deep breath and reminded myself that this was Ever, who knew just about everything about me. The only things she didn't know were to do with Luisa, and I knew as uncomfortable as it might be, we'd eventually share those things too. I tried to think of something I'd always wanted but never gotten, never had the courage to ask Luisa for.

"I guess one thing would be…just—different… positions." My heart was thudding in my chest. Ever just watched me, clearly expecting more detail than that. "I'd like to be with you in different positions, other than me on top."

Ever's hand continued its teasing path around my torso, brushing the tip of my cock with the edge of her hand now. "Yeah? What positions?"

"You on top. Or…from—from behind."

Her eyes widened. "From behind? Like…" Her breath hitched. "You mean…anal?"

"No! I just meant normal, but from behind."

"You wouldn't want the other way, though?"

"Maybe someday. But that wasn't what I meant."

She bit her lip. "So you want me on my hands and knees?" Her voice was teasing, her eyes laughing, but I could tell she was serious as well.

"In more ways than one," I answered, in the same teasing tone of voice. Her expression shifted, turned serious and almost hurt. "What is it? What's wrong?"

She licked her lips nervously. "This is one of those truth things. I've never…I've never gone down before." She shrugged, trying for nonchalance and failing. "It came up once, but I wasn't ready. Or just afraid. And…that was it."

"That was it?" I sensed more to the story.

"Yeah."

I touched her cheek. "Hey. It's me. Tell me. No holding back."

"He got mad when I said no. Not like, *angry* angry, just irritated. Like he couldn't believe I'd be so selfish, that was kind of the undertone he had. And it never came up again."

I felt anger rush through me. "Ever, listen. That's *your* choice. Always, *always* your choice. I just want to be with you. If there's something you don't like or don't want, tell me. Please." I made sure her eyes met mine, that she saw my sincerity. "Don't ever be afraid to tell me anything."

She turned into me, buried her face against my chest. "I'm sorry. That ruined the mood."

"Ever, baby. No. Don't be sorry. I want the truth. I want us to always be honest." I wrapped my arm around her shoulders and held her tight. "Besides, we can get the mood back. It's fine, okay? We have all the time in the world. Nothing matters, just us."

She nodded. "Hey, would you mind if I took a shower?"

I shrugged. "Go ahead, please. Take your time."

She lifted up to kiss me, but she kept it brief, and then left the bed. I felt a stir in my cock as she walked away, her wide hips swaying and her hair loose. So sexy, so beautiful. I couldn't believe I'd been so lucky as to be with her, to get her body all for me. I lay in bed and drowsed, listening to the sounds of the water, imagining her skin all wet, black hair in slick strands against her fair skin. Some day we'd take a shower together, but I sensed she needed some time alone to push those thoughts of Billy away.

I'd nearly fallen back asleep when I felt the bed dip under her weight at my feet.

"You want to take one?" Ever asked.

I opened my eyes and sat up. She was wrapped in a red towel, with her hair in a turban in another towel. She was wiping at her face with a small round piece of cotton.

"Sure. That sounds great, actually." I couldn't take my eyes off her, though, as she stood up and unwound the turbaned towel from her hair, bent over, and rubbed her hair with the towel.

I got out of the bed and moved to the doorway, but stopped to watch her. I'd never had this before, this kind of intimacy of day-to-day things shared. Ever sensed something and looked up at me, running her fingers through her hair.

"What?" She smiled at me, her eyes loving but quizzical. "You're watching me very intently. I'm not going anywhere, I promise."

"It's not that," I said. "It's just…I've never done this before." I leaned against the doorway, trying to seem casual in my nudity when I was anything but. In the heat of the moment, when passions were raging, it was easy to be naked. Here, now, with conversation ranging to personal subjects, it was much harder to be so bare and vulnerable with her.

"Done what?" Her eyes roved over me, as if she couldn't stop looking at me, even while we were talking. I knew how she felt.

"Stayed the night. The whole…sharing a space thing."

She tilted her head to one side, confused. "I'm not sure what you mean."

I sighed. "Well, with Luisa, we never had our own place, you know? I stayed with Grams and Gramps, and she lived with her uncle. Most of the time, we hung out either in the spare room over the stables—which wasn't really a bedroom, just a loft with a cot—or it was outside, on a blanket."

"Really? Outside?"

I nodded. "It was…the best place for us to go to get privacy. Ride out a mile or two, out to the middle of nowhere where there was nothing but cows and horses and birds."

"So you've never slept the whole night through with someone before?"

I shook my head. "Nope."

"Well, I've never done it outside. So maybe together we can...fix those things for both of us."

I smiled. "I'd like that. I just love watching you. Seeing you dry your hair, everything."

She licked her lips, a motion I was learning to correlate with nerves, a sign she was about to do something she was afraid to do. Her hair was hanging in damp black strings around her shoulders, the red towel wrapped tight around her chest and hanging to mid-thigh. Her eyes met mine, and she didn't look away as she moved to stand a couple feet away from me, hooked her fingers into the knot of her towel. My mouth went dry, and it was suddenly hard to swallow as she tugged the end of the towel free, slowly unwound it from around her torso, grasping the other edge and holding both now, keeping them closed. And then, with a twitch of her wrists, she dropped the towel, and she was naked. My cock immediately responded, hardening and lengthening at the sight of her lush curves and the dark circles of her areolae and the heavy weight of her breasts and the solid muscle of her thighs, her eyes like jade pools, hot on me.

"Jesus, Ever." I could barely whisper. I simply couldn't believe she was meant for me, that she was giving me this incredible gift of her body, her passion, her love. "You are...just the most gorgeous and the sexiest woman I've ever seen in my life."

"That was absolutely the right response." She sashayed toward me, her tits swaying with the accentuated sway of her steps.

My cock was rigid now, achingly hard. She kept her eyes on mine for a brief moment, and I saw resolve in them, and hunger. She licked her lips once more, and then she was sinking to her knees in front of me. For a moment I couldn't react, could only stand stunned as she wrapped both her fists around my erection.

"Wait, Ever. No. You don't—you shouldn't—"

She slid her fists down my length, then stroked me hand-over-hand. "I want to. I want to try this." She looked up at me. "Have you ever had this done to you?"

"Yeah. A couple times, not a lot." She moved her eyes away from mine, down to my cock, watching her own hands as they moved on me. My throat was dry, compulsively swallowing as she caressed my cock with her hands. I found my voice again. "Ever, seriously. I just want you. Us, together—"

"Unless you *don't* want this, shut up and let me do it before I lose my nerve." She moved her face closer, and my heart rate ratcheted up to a thunderous hammering. "I'm scared. I'm scared of doing it wrong. That you won't like it. That it won't be as good as when—"

"Baby. There's no right or wrong. Not with us. And there's no comparing, either. Anything and everything you do, *we* do, is better than anything I've ever known. So if you want to try it, then god, I'm not gonna say no. Just…don't—don't bite me."

She laughed. "I think I can manage that much."

Another nervous flick of her tongue over her lips, and then she was shifting forward, her fists around my cock, and she was lowering her mouth to me, wrapping her lips gingerly around the tip. I swallowed hard and held completely still, my fists clenching at my sides. Her mouth was…shit, god…so hot and wet. She made an "mmmmm" sound, and moved her mouth away.

"That's…not so bad. You actually kind of taste… good. A little like me. Like…like when I kissed you after you went down on me."

"You taste so good. I can't wait to do that again." I closed my eyes as she put her lips around me again, taking me in to just past the groove around the head. "I can't wait to lick your sweet pussy again." Talking dirty was foreign to me. Talking during sex at all was strange. It had always been silent and quiet before.

She moaned, and the sound and the vibration sent a shock of pleasure through me. "I really, *really* liked that. You are welcome to do that as much as you want." She stroked my cock with one hand, from the base up to her lips, and back down, and a groan left me. "You like that? Am I doing this okay?"

"Fuck, Ever. *Fuck…*" I could barely form words. "So good. So—oh, Jesus—*so* good."

She was moving her mouth on me now, her lips tight around the head of my cock, down to the groove and back up, sliding her fist slowly, so slowly up and down my length. I couldn't believe she was doing this. This was Ever, my Ever. My beautiful, perfect Ever. I glanced down, watched her hair around her shoulders and tangling against her cheeks. As I watched, she paused to pull an errant strand of hair from her mouth. I pushed my fingers into her damp, thick hair and pulled it away from her face, held it gently, gingerly, at the back of her head. She flicked her eyes up to mine, spat me out of her mouth.

"Guide me. Show me how you like it. Just… be gentle." She took me in her mouth, took me in deeper than she had yet, nearly half of my length in her mouth, her fingers around me and moving up and down my length.

I held her hair out of the way, not applying any pressure, just holding her hair. "You could…you suck, a little, if you wanted. Like it's a sucker."

She sucked then, gently at first, and then harder, and then she moved her mouth up and bobbed back down, sucking all the while. I groaned, moaned, gasped as she did this faster, taking me deeper, until I knew I had to be near the back of her throat.

"Don't—oh, shit—don't gag yourself. God, that feels so good."

She took me from her mouth and gazed up at me. "Good. I want you to like it. I want you to love it. I want—I want to make you lose control, like you did me." She took me in both hands again and stroked me, using her leftover saliva to slide her fists around me. "What else would make you feel good?"

I didn't say it, but I was thinking that with Luisa, when she'd done this, she'd made it quick, fisting me into bucking, sucking me until I came. Ever was… she was going slowly, and we were in unfamiliar territory. Everything about Ever, about being with her, making love to her, touching her, was new for me. For her, too, I was pretty sure.

"I don't know. It's never…never felt this good before. Not sure how it could better." She stared at my cock and watched as she did the hand-over-hand motion again, which made my knees buckle. "That—I *really* like it when you do that."

She did it again, kept doing it, squeezing me in one fist and sliding that hand down, and then replacing it with the other as soon as there was room at the tip of my cock. She put her mouth to me, worked her tongue and lips around me, leaving saliva wet and slick around me, and then did the motion again, and now I couldn't stand it, couldn't keep my knees locked. Each erotic slide of her fists around me left me breathless, brought me closer to the edge, and with her head out of the way I could see her hands on me, and for some reason seeing her small white hands on my cock was so hot, so insanely hot that it made me even crazier.

"What if...what if I did this?" she said, and then cupped my balls in one hand and pumped my cock at the base with the other, and then licked me with her tongue, a long, fat swipe of her tongue up my length, and again, and then the tip, and I knew she had to be tasting the pre-come I felt leaking from me. She continued the pumping motion, squeezing my balls gently, massaging them. Her tongue moved up my length, licking me like it was ice cream, and then she said, "You do taste good. I kind of like this, actually. I like the way you react to everything I do."

I couldn't respond, couldn't speak. She'd taken me in her mouth again and was matching the rhythm of her fist around me with a bobbing of her head, sucking and moving and sliding her fist around me, and I felt the rising desperation inside me, the coiled tension building.

"I'm—I'm close," I said. "I'm gonna come soon."

"Good," she murmured, "come hard. I want to feel that. I want to taste you."

She didn't relent, and my knees were weak. I had to brace myself on the doorposts to stay upright as she began to stroke my cock with both hands, sucking on the tip.

"That…just like that. I'm—so close now. Fuck… god, yes, Ever. God…oh, god, oh, shit—"

She kept the pace, sucking on the head of my cock and moving both hands on the length, and I was on the verge, right there, and I opened my eyes to watch.

"I'm coming, oh, fuck, Ever, I'm coming…so hard, right now!"

I exploded in her mouth, and she plunged her mouth around me, took me deep as I released inside her, keeping one fist around my base and working me hard, swallowing, pumping, sucking, moving, and I could only groan and curse as she drew ecstasy from me in dizzying waves.

She finally let my cock leave her mouth with a soft *pop*, and looked up at me. "You came…a *lot*." She said it with a smile.

I was embarrassed by that, feeling almost ashamed that she'd swallowed all of that. "Sorry—" I started to say.

She interrupted me. "No, I liked feeling you lose control like that. I didn't mind the taste, either. Mostly, I loved feeling you enjoy it so much."

I pulled her to her feet and tugged her into an embrace. "It was so amazing. Thank you, so much."

"I'm glad I did it." She tilted her head to meet my eyes. "You can ask me anything, you know. If you want anything with me, just ask."

"You, too."

I kissed her then. Kissed her deeply, and tasted myself on her breath. I kissed her to prove something, but I wasn't sure what. Her hands curled around my shoulders, and she kissed me back as if she'd been drowning and my kiss was the air she needed to live. I moved her toward the bed, intending to give her what she'd given me.

She stopped me, though. "Take a shower." She put her palms on my chest and pushed me away, as if tearing herself away from me. "I know how much better it made me feel."

"Are you saying I stink?" I teased.

She leaned toward me and sniffed. "A little?" She grinned and pushed me toward the bathroom. "Go. There are towels in there. My shampoo isn't girly-smelling, and there's normal bar soap, too. So you won't come out smelling like a girl."

I closed the bathroom door, but didn't latch it or lock it. It was definitely a girl's bathroom, full of curling irons and hair dryers and little paintings on the wall, cases of makeup and bottles of eyeliner or some other goop. The mats on the floor were lavender in

color, and the hand towels matched, but the folded
shower towels stacked in the cabinet under the sink
were varying in colors. I set a black towel on the
toilet seat and adjusted the water to just cooler than
scalding. I stepped in and soaked for a moment, then
looked for the shampoo. There were no less than
eight different bottles of different kinds of shampoo, conditioner, shower gel, exfoliating something
or another, all kinds of other things. The one that
seemed the least girly was vanilla-scented, so I used
that.

It was as I was rinsing away the shampoo and
letting my mind wander that it hit me.

Alex was dead.

I'd let myself forget. Pushed it away. A flash of
memory hit me like tidal wave. Alex, on his back,
eyes glazed open, the room smelling of death and
vomit.

I tried to rein in the memory, the panic attack.
I couldn't, though. Image after image hit me: Alex,
alive, smoking a bowl, laughing as he exhaled a cloud
of smoke; Dad, driving his truck, me in the passenger, seat, letting out a rare laugh at something I said;
Mom, at the stove, cooking pasta; Alex, dead; Dad,
dead; Mom, dead. I saw their last moments, their last
breaths. It became a rolling montage, a series of lightning strikes hitting me one after another.

The water went lukewarm, and I felt my knees give out. I hit the bottom of the tub in a heap, trying to breathe, trying to stop shaking.

I'd kept it together for so long, kept it all pushed away, put away. Locked deep down. Numb. And now Ever was there, threading her beautiful smile and stunning eyes and tender love throughout me, her passionate hunger for me, and it was unlocking all the secret rooms where I'd hidden those memories, and it was all coming out at once, and it was too much.

I felt the water turn off. I was sweating, but I was cold. Shivering, aching, gasping.

"Cade? What's wrong?" Ever, on her knees outside the tub. Her hand on my wet shoulder, brushing the hair from my eyes.

"They're all…they all died. Mom died. Dad died. Alex died. They all left me. Mom left me. Dad left me. Alex left me." I heard the words but couldn't stop them or control them. "I watched them all die. I found Alex. Hours before I came to you. I found him. I knew he was in bad shape, but I didn't think he'd—I didn't know. I didn't know. And Dad just gave up. At least Mom fought. She tried to stay but couldn't, at the end. It took her. The cancer took her. Dad…he just couldn't take it without her. Couldn't live without her, and so he just gave up, just fucking stopped living."

"Cade, honey. I'm so sorry."

"Everyone left me."

"I'm here." She pressed a kiss to my cheekbone. "I'm here. I'm with you, Caden. I'm here with you."

I gasped for breath, fought to get air into my lungs, fought to slow my heart. "Ever?" I knew it was her, but it came out as a question. "You can't die. You can't give up. I think I get now why Dad gave up."

She put a hand underneath my shoulder and pulled at me. I sat up, worked to get out of the tub. As the panic attack left me, I felt wetness on my eyes, tears. Shame hit me. After what Ever had just done for me, I went and had a panic attack, and I was crying now. I tried to hide, but there was nowhere to go. I was naked still, wet. She unfolded the towel and rubbed my chest with it, my stomach, my shoulders, my back.

I tried to take it from her, but she wouldn't let me. "Ever. I'm—I'm okay."

She gave me the most tender, most gentle, most loving smile I'd ever seen, glowing bright on her lovely face. "Let me."

I dropped my hand and kept my eyes on her, feeling the shame at her seeing me cry twist into something else. "I'm sorry," I said. "I'm—I'm more of a mess than I'd thought, I guess. It just, it hit me. Alex, then Mom and Dad, and it all just—I don't normally cry—"

She brushed the towel over my face, dabbing at my forehead, my cheeks, then over my head, going up on her tiptoes to reach my hair. "Don't apologize, and don't be ashamed. Please?"

It felt so, so strange to have her there in the tiny bathroom with me, dressed in nothing but a tiny, slinky red thong, so gently drying me with a towel, her eyes gazing at me in a way that seemed as much a tender caress as the touch of her hands upon my skin.

"It's just…you're seeing me at my worst, and we just…had such an amazing experience together, and I feel like I'm ruining it with that stupid—stupid panic attack. I've never had that happen before, and I couldn't stop it, it just hit me. And I don't want you to think—"

She wrapped the towel around my waist, and I tucked it in place. Her palms rested on my chest and she pressed her body up against mine. "Cade, you're allowed to be upset about things. You didn't ruin anything. And what kind of love would this be between us if I couldn't see you at your worst and comfort you?"

I touched my forehead to hers. "Thanks."

She lifted up, kissed me. "Thank you for…not pushing me away, I guess. I think a lot of guys would have freaked out. You let me in, told me what you're feeling. That's how it should be."

I vowed that's how it always would be.

Ever

Two weeks later, Cade and I were sitting in the same side of a booth at National Coney Island, sharing disgustingly good cheese fries. It was 2 a.m., and we'd just spent the last two hours exhausting each other in the best possible way. I was sated, pleasantly sore, and ready to jump him again as soon as we went back to my dorm. Which could be tricky, since Steph had broken up with her boyfriend and was home more, which meant we had to stay in my room afterward or put on clothes, as well as having to be quiet when Steph was around. I especially wasn't very good at being quiet. I'd never had that problem before, but Cade seemed to have a talent for making me scream.

He'd continued to flat-out refuse to let me come to his apartment, which wasn't really his. He was staying month-to-month at the apartment he'd shared with Alex, but he'd expressed several times how much he hated it. It reminded him of Alex, of finding him. He was spending as much time at my dorm as he could, but with his own classes and Steph's presence, it wasn't as much as either of us wanted, and it was rarely as uninhibited as we would have liked.

"Maybe this is crazy," Cade said, dipping a liquid-cheese-product-coated fry in ranch, "but...what if we got our own place?"

I tried not to choke on my Coke. "Um…what?" I turned to look at him. "You mean move in together?"

He shrugged, and I could tell he was trying to sound casual when he felt anything but. "Yeah. I mean, I know it's only been two weeks, but…is it really that big of a stretch?"

I didn't answer right away. I'd had the same thought, but hadn't voiced it. It seemed a little crazy to be considering moving in with the boy I'd been dating for barely two weeks. "Our relationship isn't exactly normal, though. It's not like we met two weeks ago. Not really."

"Is it crazy to you?" he asked.

I mimicked his attempt at nonchalance, succeeding about as well. Meaning, my heart was hammering. "Yeah. But everything about us is crazy. Right? I mean, is it normal for two people to fall in love as quickly and intensely as you and I have?"

"No, I'm not sure it is exactly normal." He glanced at me. "Does it seem like it would be rushing things?"

"That's my worry. What if this is…I don't know, a honeymoon period or something?" I rushed the next words out. "I'm not saying I don't want to. I do. I really do. I'm just…this whole thing between us scares me sometimes."

Cade threaded his fingers through mine. "Me, too."

"You really want to live with me?" I asked.

"Yeah. Absolutely." His amber gaze was serious and intense. "I want everything with you. I want you all to myself. I want to have our place and be able to lock the door and keep you in bed with me until we can't move anymore. I want to be able to watch you walk around naked all day. I don't want to have to leave you to get more clean clothes. I want to spend every moment of my life with you."

I melted, sank against him. "Don't you ever get tired of me? Don't you ever want your own space?"

He shook his head. "No. I miss you every single second I'm away. I have trouble focusing in class because I want to be home with you. I want to do homework together. I want to cook dinner together. I don't want space. I've been alone for so long, essentially on my own, even if there were people in my life who did care." He eyed me with curiosity. "Do you need space?"

I squeezed his arm. "No! That's not my point. I just...I feel the same way. I just didn't want to seem clingy, or too...too needy, I guess. Like I can't be away from you for an hour without getting all mushy. But I can't. I am clingy. I am needy. I was just...I wanted you to know that you can have your space, if you need room to breathe."

He leaned his head against mine. "I don't have any need to breathe. You are my breath."

I heard a coughed laugh of disbelief from behind us. I turned in place to see a middle-aged man sitting alone, wearing a faded Van Halen T-shirt and a tattered trucker's hat. "Sorry, I'm not trying to eavesdrop. You two are just so fucking sweet it's making my teeth hurt. You should just get married and get it over with. Seriously." He shook his head, jamming a huge bite of gyro in his mouth and continuing to talk around it. "I can honestly say I've never felt that way about anyone. I didn't think it was real. You two are like...fucking Hollywood romance characters or some shit."

Cade and I laughed as we slid out of the booth and paid our bill, but I saw a thoughtful look on Cade's face as we drove back to my dorm. We let ourselves in, only to stop in awkward shock. Steph was on the couch, on top of a guy I'd never met before, riding him. They were both completely naked, his hairy legs bent, feet braced against the arm of the couch, Steph leaning back, face tipped up to the ceiling, hands in her now-burnt orange hair, massive tits bouncing as she rocked on her new boyfriend/latest fling, moaning loudly.

She heard us come in, gasped in shock, leaned down over the guy, with her hands covering her boobs. "Oh, my god!" she shrieked. "I'm so sorry! I thought you'd be gone longer."

I had no idea what to say, what to do. Cade pulled me into a stumbling walk, into my room, and closed the door behind me. As soon as the door latched, I heard Steph moan, heard the slap of flesh and the grunts of her guy. I hurried to plug my phone into my dock, cranking up the volume until I couldn't hear my roommate's sex noises. "Bulletproof Weeks" by Matt Nathanson isn't really blast-it-until-you're-deaf music, but it served the purpose.

I collapsed onto my bed, laughing. "Oh…my… god. I could've gone the rest of my life without seeing that."

"Yeah, it was kind of a shock."

I grabbed his arm, shaking him. "I knew Steph was pretty stacked, but…Jesus, did you see the size of her boobs? They were *huge!*"

Cade colored. "Couldn't help but notice them," he mumbled, then grinned. "I prefer yours."

I slapped his arm. "You'd better!"

"You're the one who asked me if I'd seen them," he pointed out. "I couldn't *not* see them. They were… rather prominent."

"Why do you like mine better? Hers are bigger."

He frowned. "Well, they're attached to you, for starters. And it's not just about size. You ever see pictures of those ladies who get, like, triple-F implants? There's nothing sexy to me about tits the size of basketballs. They're just these big, fake, plastic…things.

Yours are the perfect size. Big, round, soft. They bounce and jiggle. Fake tits don't. And yours…god, I don't even know if I can put it into words. Like I said, they're *you*. Part of you."

I leaned into him. "Good answer, babe."

He laughed. "Not hard to get that one right. I love you, and I want *you*." He made a face. "I think you should help me erase the mental image I've got going on, though."

"Yeah?" I pulled down on my V-neck, exposing more of my cleavage. "Like this?"

He bobbled his head from side to side. "It's a start. Maybe a little more."

I lifted the hem of my shirt up so the bottom of my bra and a little skin showed. "How about now?"

"I think maybe if you got rid of the shirt entirely, it'd be better." He scooted back on the bed, put his spine against the wall, crossing his arms over his chest, eyes on me.

"If I take off my shirt, you have to take off yours," I said, grasping the hem of my shirt in preparation to strip it off.

"Fair enough." Cade had his off in a blink, chest muscles rippling as he tossed the shirt aside. "Your turn."

I peeled mine off more slowly, wadded it into a ball, and threw it at his face. He put it to his nose and sniffed, then set it aside. "Is the mental image gone yet?"

"Nope. I think I still need to see more of you."

I grinned at him. "Well, then, maybe you should take off more of your clothes. I have my own mental images going on, you know." I faked a shudder. "Those skinny, hairy legs…" He laughed, slid off the bed, and stood directly behind me. I swiveled on the bed to face him. He unbuttoned his jeans in a flash, but I stopped him. "Slowly. I like to watch you undress, too, you know."

He frowned, as if this hadn't occurred to him before. Then he shrugged and unzipped his jeans, more slowly this time, teasingly. When the zipper was down, he glanced at me, then rezipped and drew it back down again before tugging the denim down around his hips. I couldn't help biting my lip as the bulge in his boxers was revealed, and I lifted an eyebrow at him, expectantly. He tugged the jeans back up, then grabbed the waist of the jeans and the boxers together, shoved them down together, baring his semi-rigid cock for me. Then back up, just as I was beginning to contemplate using my mouth to make him all the way hard. I'd used my mouth on him a few times since that first time, but never to orgasm. He'd always stopped me so he could get inside me, so he could come inside me. I loved the way he'd pull me away desperately, muscles tensed, eyes hot, the way he'd plunge into me and move slowly, deliberately teasing us both.

He pushed his jeans off, just the jeans this time, and stepped out of them, then crossed his arms and waited. I stood up, my boobs touching his chest. I couldn't resist kissing his skin, his chest just above his nipple, just once, and then I unbuttoned my own jeans, unzipped them, stepped out, kicked them aside. He reached for his boxers, but I stopped him.

"Let me." I pulled the elastic waistband down around his hips, to his thighs, to his knees, sinking downward with them so I knelt in front of him, glancing up with a sultry smile. Before he could move, I had him in my mouth, sucking hard and taking him deep, just to the point of gagging. He dipped at the knees, and then I stood up, satisfied with my handiwork. He was hard as rock now, standing upright against his belly.

He mimicked my maneuver, pulling my panties down and going to his knees as he lowered them, putting his mouth to my core and flicking his tongue through my entrance, once, twice, three times, just enough that I shuddered and felt myself go wet with anticipation.

I still had my bra on, and Cade was watching me expectantly as he stood up. I reached behind myself, freed the clasps, and shrugged my arms out of the straps, and then it was gone, at my feet, and Cade's hands were on me, caressing my skin, thumbs brushing my nipples, bringing them erect.

Cade pulled me against him, crushed his mouth to mine and kissed me as though starved, despite having made love to me less than two hours before. No matter how many times we had sex, he always made love to me as if for the first time, as if he couldn't ever get enough. He kept kissing me, and every time I thought he'd break away and push me to the bed, he would renew the kiss, his hands chaste on my back, my waist, holding me against him.

Finally, my own desperation had me breaking the kiss first, pushing at him, shoving him to the bed, to his back, crawling over him and straddling him. He shifted beneath me, and then I felt the broad head of his cock against my folds, and I breathed a sigh as he lifted his hips, pressing the tip inside me. I moved away from him, though, making him wait the way he'd made me wait. I smiled down at him, my hands on his chest, my hair hanging in loose black waves around his face. His palms skated over my skin, up my spine and down, over my hips and thighs and up to my tits, cupping them and squeezing them and lifting, pinching my nipples and moving downward. I kept my weight forward, letting the tip of his erection stay inside but not letting him in any further.

I was only teasing myself, though. I wanted him deep; I needed his fullness within me.

"God, Ever. I need it. I need to be inside you."
He lifted his hips, but I moved with him, away from
his questing thrust.

"Hold still," I murmured. "Just wait." He froze,
and I pressed a kiss to his mouth. "In fact, don't move
at all. Let me do everything."

He slid his hands to my hips, gripped me in the
bent crease where thigh met hip. "I'm not sure I
can…"

I fluttered my hips, slight, small movements, not
enough to let him in, but enough to tease him. "Try,
my love."

I waited until he was still beneath me, and then,
in a single swift motion, impaled him deep. He filled
me, stretched me, and I had to let myself adjust to his
size. I couldn't breathe, my mouth wide and brow
furrowed as I felt his huge, thick cock buried inside
my pussy. I shifted my weight forward, palms flat on
his stomach, and he slid out of me, inch after inch
of silky hardness carving against my sensitive folds.
I paused with him nearly slipping out, and then
crashed my hips against his, and he groaned with me.
The next thrust was slower, and when I had him
poised at my entrance a third time, I buried my
face against his neck and adjusted myself so he was
stretched away from his torso. This time, when I slid
down his length, his thick shaft dragged against my

clit, and I couldn't help the gasping whimpers that escaped me.

I did it again and again, slowly, so slowly, my clit stuttering against his sliding erection. I clawed my fingers into his muscles as I felt a climax rising inside me, but I refused to hurry, refused to relax the stretching of his cock. He was groaning, trembling. He wanted to thrust, wanted to take control, but he was obeying me, letting me do what I wanted.

"Are you close?" I asked. "I'm almost there."

"Yeah," he grunted, "I'm so close."

"Come for me, Cade," I said, sliding down his length.

I felt him strain, shift slightly, saw the desperation in his eyes. "I can't," he groaned. "Not like this, not stretched like this."

"Does it hurt?"

"Not really. It just...I'm there, but I can't—can't—"

I interrupted him with a gasp, pressing my lips to his and stealing his words, his breath, feeling the climax approaching like the edge of a storm. I moved slowly still, pressing my clit against his length, greedy to feel the way his hardness felt inside me, the way it made me shiver and twitch with each inch of him sliding inside me.

Between one breath and another, orgasm washed through me, exploding inside me, taking control. I sank down on him, burying him deep. I was so wet, so slick, and he shuddered inside me, deep, so deep. I clamped my teeth together and fought the scream that was bubbling in my throat. Everything inside me shook and twisted, heat billowing through me. I leaned back to sit on my shins, lifted up and sank down, again, and again, rocking my climax harder and harder, and then I felt him explode, felt his cock throb and thicken and unleash, felt the hot flood of his come, and I lifted and sank, screaming through my teeth. Cade was moaning with me, hands on my hips, helping me lift up and jerking me back down, crushing our hips together, slamming his cock into me.

I couldn't hold myself upright any longer and fell forward against Cade's chest, my body trembling, pussy quaking, muscles like jelly, and still Cade was thrusting, coming, groaning, and then he, too, was still and gasping.

After several silent, breathless moments, I shifted so he slipped out of me and I rolled into his embrace. "So, does this mean we're moving in together?" I asked.

He didn't answer immediately. "I have an ever better, crazier idea."

I knew what he was about to say, and my heart stopped, because I knew I'd say yes. "Okay?"

"Marry me?" I opened my mouth to speak, but he kept going. "Before you say yes, I'm not saying let's get engaged. I'm saying…let's elope. Get

married, like, tomorrow. Buy a condo in Royal Oak
or something. Just…fuck it, start our lives together.
I'll never want anyone but you, never love anyone
but you. I want our lives, our every single day to be
spent together, as one."

I felt tears prick my eyes. "Don't fuck with me,
Cade." I heard the anger in my own voice, the fear
and the doubt. "Are you serious?"

He rolled on top of me, pinning me to the bed,
his flame-hot amber eyes blazing. "I've never meant
anything more in my life. I've never—never wanted
anything so much. I know it's completely batshit
insane. I knocked on your door two weeks ago, and
now I'm saying we should fucking elope. I knocked
on your door and saw you for the first time in four
years and knew I'd never love anyone else. Two weeks,
yeah, but it might as well be a lifetime."

I wrapped my arms around his neck, my legs
around his. "Yes, Caden. Yes. Yes." I breathed in his ear.
"Yesyesyesyes. A thousand yeses. A million. Forever
yes."

"I don't have a ring. I don't even really know
where you go to get married when you elope except
Vegas, and we both have midterms coming up.
But—"

"I don't care. I don't need a ring. I just need to be
your wife." It felt so crazy to say that, it just toppled

out of my mouth unbidden, and it made me giddy and terrified.

Cade buried his face against my throat and laughed. "Shit, that sounds…insane and amazing. My wife. Husband and wife. Ever Monroe."

"Ever Monroe." It sounded…perfect. "God, I like that."

"Me, too." He kissed me then, and I kissed him back until neither of us could breathe, but there was no need to breathe, for we had each other, sharing breath, sharing minds and hearts and bodies and eternities.

forever and always

"You're insane," Eden whispered to me. "Are you sure you want to do this?"

It was four days after Caden's impulsive afterglow proposal, and we had a signed marriage certificate, my twin as a witness, and we were standing in a tiny chapel connected to a quaint bed and breakfast Caden had found online that had "elopement specials" and a last-minute opening. He'd thrown this whole thing together in a matter of forty-eight hours. I'd expected a county courthouse justice-of-the-peace wedding, but of course, Caden had surprised me.

"It might be a crazy last-minute elopement," he'd told me, "but you still deserve at least a little romance."

He'd told me to go a salon and get "done up," as he'd put it, and let him worry about everything. So I had, and I'd found myself begging Eden to come with me, to get our hair and nails done. She'd agreed to the manicure, since I was paying, and had listened skeptically as I tried to explain. She hadn't quite understood, but she was my twin and she'd come with us to the B&B as our only guest and witness.

I stood on the far side of the doors of the chapel, dressed in a simple sleeveless, off-the-rack wedding dress with a plunging neckline, clutching a bouquet of roses, trembling.

"Ever?" Eden shook my arm. "Are you okay? You don't have to do this. He'll understand."

I couldn't breathe. I was about to get married. To *Caden*. I was still trying to figure out how this had happened, how I'd gone from weekends with Will and hidden paintings of Cade and sporadic letters to insane, earth-shaking, life-changing sex with Cade, to getting married, all in less than a month.

Was I completely crazy? Was I going to wake up and regret this? Should I tell Cade we should wait?

I pictured myself telling him I wasn't ready, and knew he'd love me, understand, and not even blink. But...

I *was* ready. I was terrified, nervous, jittery, but I was also excited, giddy, and eager. I wanted to see his face as I walked the short aisle toward him, in a dress he hadn't seen yet.

I gripped Eden's hand and squeezed, meeting her concerned eyes. "I want to," I told her. "I'm ready. I'm just…nervous."

"Nervous? Shit, I'd hope you'd be nervous," she said. "You're about to get married. You're not even twenty! You haven't even told Daddy."

I didn't want to think about my dad. I hadn't spoken to him in over six months, not because I was mad, but because we simply didn't talk. He still worked insane hours, I was at school, and we just… we didn't have anything in common. "And I'm not going to."

"Don't you think—"

I whirled on her. "*Ed*en. Shut up about Dad. I'm getting married to the man I love, and that's all that matters."

She raised her hands. "Okay, okay. Not like *I* want him here, either. Shit. It's not like he's been exactly present—"

"I don't want to talk about him. I want to talk about Caden. I want to go out there and say 'I do.'"

Eden pulled me into a hug, her dyed blonde hair tickling my nose. "As long as this is what you want. Be happy, that's all I care about. You love him? He loves you? Good enough for me. It's fucking crazy, but if it's what you want, then I'll support you. I might even be a little jealous. He *is* pretty hot."

I mock growled at her. "Back off, bitch, he's mine."

Eden laughed. "I thought we were supposed to share everything! Can't I just....borrow him for a few minutes?"

I glared at her. "Eden...seriously. Not funny. We haven't even shared *clothes* since we were twelve."

She snorted. "I was *kidding*, Ev. Jeez." She pushed me toward the door. "Go on, then, you damn lunatic. Go marry your man." She moved behind me, adjusted the hem of my dress, and then opened the door for me.

I took a deep breath and fixed my eyes forward, locking on the tall, broad, ruggedly gorgeous man waiting for me. Less than twenty steps later, I was facing Cade, holding his hands, staring into his amber eyes, barely hearing the words of the officiant. I heard the prompt to repeat the vows, though, and managed to get all the words right without crying. What did me in was hearing Cade say the vows, seeing the sincerity in his eyes and hearing it in his voice. He promised to love me till death do us part, and I knew he meant it. I couldn't help crying then, just a little. A few quiet sobs, my finger brushing the tear away before it smudged the makeup Eden had so carefully applied.

I slipped the ring on his finger, and he did the same to me. Our wedding rings were simple white gold bands, picked out together. I didn't have a diamond, and I didn't care. I only needed Cade. He'd promised he'd get me one at some point.

We kissed, and both the officiant and Eden looked away when the kiss went on far too long.

When we finally broke apart, breathless, Cade brushed a thumb across my cheekbone. And then he took my left hand in his left hand, reached into the pocket of his tuxedo coat, and held out a ring. A thin white gold band, a tiny diamond sparkling in the sunlight. I stared at him in shock, but couldn't speak, couldn't breathe, could only watch as he slid the ring onto my finger, nestled it against the wedding band.

"It's not much, but you deserve a diamond, even if it is the smallest one Zales had."

I threw my arms around his neck and held on, whispered against his throat. "It's perfect, Cade. So perfect. Thank you. God, you're amazing."

"You may have said you didn't need a diamond ring, but that doesn't mean you didn't want one, right?"

I shrugged. "Yeah, I guess I did, a little. I mean, yeah, of course I wanted a diamond ring. Every girl wants a diamond ring on her wedding day."

"I just want you to be happy." His eyes sparkled, and he lifted me up, spun me around. "You're officially, permanently mine, Mrs. Monroe."

"Forever and always," I murmured, brushing his lips with mine.

Caden

We'd stayed in the B&B the night before our wedding, and we had it for one night more, but I had other plans. It just depended on Ever. I didn't tell her where we were going, and when I told her it was one last surprise, she just smiled at me and squeezed my hands, turned up the radio, and let the wind from the open window of my Jeep buffet at her hair.

I pulled into the parking lot of a condo building in downtown Royal Oak, led her into the foyer and up the elevator, to the sixth floor. Ever was quiet, her fingers tight in mine, eyes scanning the walls of the corridor as we walked together. I knocked on 619, and a slim, older woman with sharp gray eyes and red hair in a tight bun answered the door.

"Caden, Ever, please come in." She shook my hand, and then Ever's. "Congratulations, you two. Young love is a beautiful thing."

Ever glanced up at me. "Caden? What's going on? Where are we? Who is this?"

"I'm Lisa Scott. I'm Caden's real estate agent."

Lisa had been the one hired by my parents' estate lawyer to sell their house, and she'd been the first one I called when I'd come up with my idea. She'd been working nonstop for three days, but she had everything ready.

"Real estate agent? Did I know you had a real estate agent?" Ever asked. She was confused, and I understood the trepidation I heard in her voice.

"Lisa sold Mom and Dad's house after Dad died. I was in Wyoming, so she did everything for me." I turned to face Ever, took her hands in mine. "Trust me?"

She nodded, taking a deep breath and letting it out. "Of course I trust you. I'm just…confused as to what's going on."

Lisa took over. "Well, why don't we start by looking around?" She ushered us into the living room, pointing out the open-plan kitchen, stainless steel appliances and dark granite countertops, sleek cabinets, the floor-to-ceiling windows along one wall of the living room.

There were two bedrooms, a master and a smaller one, and I kept silent as Ever looked around, poked into closets and the en suite bathroom with the dual sinks, the second bathroom off the other bedroom.

"What is this, Cade? Why are we here?" She waved at the condo. "This place is incredible, but… there's no way we can afford this. My dad gave me some money to live on when I got accepted to Cranbrook, but it's not enough to even put a down payment on a place like this."

I ducked my head, not wanting to explain. Lisa left us alone in the master bedroom, and I took a deep breath. "When Dad died, there was…life insurance. I was living with Gramps, working for him, and he was paying me ranch hand wages. Between that and the life insurance payout, I've been able to pay off school. I've got enough to get us this place, but I wanted to make sure you liked it first."

I saw the shock, then watched her work through it. "This place is expensive, Cade. I love it, but…is it a bit much?"

I shrugged. "Mom and Dad's policy was…well, not so much that I'm, like, idle rich for the rest of my life. Not even close. But it's enough. I can buy this place and still finish school. If we both work and go to school, we'll be fine. Especially since I'm buying it outright."

Ever turned away from me and stared out the window at the traffic on Main Street. "Are you sure? I mean, isn't that…all you have? Of them?"

I stood behind her, wrapped one arm around her shoulders, buried my face in her hair. "It's just money, Ev. It's not…it's not *them*. It's not their memories. Do you want to live here with me?" I whispered in her ear, and she turned her head to the side, nuzzling

against me. "The second bedroom can be your studio. You can paint there in that sexy shirt of yours all
you want. And then I can come in here and take it off
you and make love to you on the floor."

She giggled. "We could get a couch in there, and
then you can fuck me on the couch, and then I can
keep painting, naked, and you can watch."

"I like that plan." I burrowed through her black
locks and nibbled her ear. "So is it a yes?"

She nodded. "Yes, baby. Yes."

Lisa had the paperwork ready, and the keys. After
everything was formalized and finished, she left, con-
gratulating us again.

We spent the next several days picking out furni-
ture and filling our new home with our things, hers
and mine, and now…ours. Through it all, I found
myself marveling at the fact that this beautiful, sen-
sual, talented, incredible woman was my wife, mine
forever. Day by day, we found a pattern. We'd get up
early, eat breakfast together, go to our separate classes,
come home and make dinner together and study
together, and draw and paint and watch TV together.

Then, about a month after we moved in, on a
Saturday, I was out looking for work, something
close to home that I could use to supplement the
insurance money with, which I knew wouldn't last
forever. I'd been gone all day, filling out applications
and dropping off my resumé. By four o'clock, I was

exhausted, stressed out, and sick of smiling for strang-
ers. I drove home, let myself in, and kicked off my
shoes, calling for Ever. She didn't answer, but I heard
music blaring from her studio.

I slipped in, closed the door behind me, and
watched her paint. She had on the shirt, nothing
but the white button-down, her fine ass swaying to
the beat as she painted, the hem brushing the backs
of her thighs. She paused in her dancing to examine her work, then dabbed her brush into a splotch
of pink and dragged it across the canvas, nodding.
"Flapper Girl" by The Lumineers came on, and she
moved with the song, her brushstrokes mimicking
the rhythm of the song.

I wasn't sure how long I leaned against the door
and watched her paint, and I didn't care. Time was
irrelevant. Only Ever mattered.

In the silence between songs, Ever heard my foot
scuff the carpet, and she whirled around, smiling at
me, waving with her brush, inadvertently smearing
paint on her forehead. I laughed, closed the space
between us, my feet crinkling the tarp she'd put
down.

Ever watched me approach, her eyes widening,
her breathing going shallow. I took the brush from
her and the palette, set them down on the tarp. She
reached for me, noticed paint on her fingers, and
withdrew her hand. I grinned at her, took her hand,

and wiped the paint on my cheek. She laughed, and took her fingers from me, brushed at her shirtfront to clean them. I stilled her hands in mine, and then pressed a kiss to her neck, to her throat, above the hollow of her clavicle. She inhaled, pressed her palm to the back of my head.

I freed the top button of her shirt, then the next, pausing to kiss each patch of flesh. Another button, and now her breasts were bare, her nipples hard buttons in my mouth. Another button, and two more, and then there was nothing between us, the shirt hanging open, loose on her shoulders. I glanced over, made sure the blinds were closed; she was mine, and I wouldn't share the sight of her naked body with anyone. Especially not with what I planned to do with her.

I stepped forward, into her, and she backed up. I took another step, and she matched it. Finally, her back was to the mirror she'd had me hang on the wall behind her easel for her recent project, a series of self-portraits.

"Turn around," I told her.

Ever obeyed, and I watched her eyes widen as she saw us, her torso bare between the edges of her shirt, her tits heavy and pale, the dark pink circles of her areolae with the erect nipples, her flat stomach and wide hips. She sucked in a breath as I ran my hands down her body, over her boobs and down her belly, over the tight mound of her pussy. She'd shaved it recently, and I loved the feel of it freshly shaven, smooth and soft, the labia just begging me to open them and kiss them and slip between them.

"You see us?" I asked her. "You see how gorgeous you are? How perfectly you fit in my hands?"

She nodded, her nostrils flaring, her green eyes darkening with heat. "I need you. Get naked for me, Cade. Touch me. Put your cock in me."

I stripped quickly, and she turned in place, wrapped her hands around my cock, stroked me, fondled me. I stopped her when she moved to take me in her mouth. "Unh-uh, baby. Not this time." I pivoted her to face the mirror. "Like this. Watch us."

I slid my hands on her body, palming her breasts, then down to slip a finger into the folds of her pussy. She moaned, arched her neck and back, writhing into my touch. Her eyes closed.

"No, Ever. Open your eyes. *Watch* us."

Her eyes snapped open, and she watched my fingers move inside her, stroking her clit, digging deep to find her perfect spot and bring her to the cusp of orgasm. I gripped her hips and pulled her ass toward me. She widened her stance, shifted forward, keeping her eyes on me, on us, and I watched us in the mirror, too, as I slid my cock against the soft silk of her pussy. Her mouth dropped open in a silent scream as I plunged deep into her, fucked deep in a slow slide.

"God...Cade. *Cade*. Yes—fuck, fuck, yes," she groaned and growled, her palms flat on the wall beside the mirror.

I had to work hard to hold back, to go slow. The sight of her bent over in front of me, her ass spread wide and crushed against me, it made me wild. Then my gaze went to the mirror, and I could see her tits swaying and bouncing and jiggling as I thrust into her, a glimpse of my legs between hers, her face, her eyes wide and her mouth open and her expression primal and hot and desperate, and I had to fuck her harder, and she took it and begged for more, for me, pleaded my name.

I slid out of her tight wet pussy, watching the slick movement of my cock going in and out, and I nearly lost it.

"Cade...god, I love this. I want more. Dirtier. Do something crazy. Something dirty. Fuck me, Cade. I like it dirty. Fuck me dirty..."

I gasped and groaned, hard-pressed to stop from coming when she talked to me like that. "What—what do you want, baby? What do you want me to do to you?"

She started pressing back into my thrusts, her eyes locked on mine in the mirror. "I don't—oh... *god*...spank me? Touch my ass?" I caressed her ass as I slid into her pussy, and then smacked her left cheek, not hard, but enough to make a resounding *crack*.

Ever shrieked, but it wasn't a pained sound. "God, *yes!* Do that again!" she gasped. I spanked her again, and again. "Touch me, Cade. You know what I want." I did. I knew. I slowed my thrusts, focused my muscles on holding back, and then slid my middle finger down the crease of her ass. "Yes. Like that. Touch me. I know I'll come *so* hard."

I found the tight, hot knot of muscle, pressed my finger against it. Ever shuddered, her counter-thrust strokes stuttering, faltering. She gasped, moaned, and then lifted up on her toes, moving her ass against my finger.

"You like that?" I asked. "Does that feel good?" I pressed harder, wiggled my finger, and felt the knot loosen, and my fingertip slid into her asshole.

Ever groaned long and hard, pressed her head against the mirror, trembling all over. "Yes, Cade…it feels so good. You don't even know. You're inside me, filling me all over. Everywhere. I'm gonna come so hard. You fit inside me so perfectly, so right, and your finger, fucking my asshole, it's *so* good."

I had to slow, tense, hold back, on the verge of exploding inside her. I wanted to feel her come first. I wanted us to come together. She was close, and I wanted her there with me.

She pushed away from the mirror, opened her eyes, and met my gaze in the mirror. I worked my finger deeper inside her, and listened to her moans go louder and longer as I thrust my cock inside her.

"Talk to me, Cade. I need to hear your voice when I come."

I reached with my free hand, cupped one of her big, swaying tits. "You feel so good, Ever. So good." I wasn't as good at talking dirty as she was. It took me some time to work my way into it. "I love watching your tits bounce when I fuck you like this."

Ever shifted her rhythm, going from smooth and slow to hard and fast, accentuating the motion of her boobs. She did it for me, and I responded by trying an in-and-out wiggle of my middle finger, mimicking the way my cock moved inside her.

"Yes, baby, like that. I love that." I let go of her breast and watched them both move, jiggle, and sway. "I'm so close, Ev. I'm gonna come soon. I can't hold it back much longer."

She was breathless, and both of us were sweating, our skin sliding and our sweat mingling. "Don't hold back, Cade. Come for me right now. Fuck me so hard that you can't stop."

My finger was inside her to the first knuckle, and I slid it incrementally deeper, and she groaned with every motion of my hand. "I love your ass, Ev. Your asshole is so tight, I almost can't move my finger any more." I felt the impending explosion rise within me, and felt my words loosen, tumble out without direction, felt my hips start to piston harder, felt her ass bounce with every thrust, watched in the mirror as her tits bounced so beautifully with the rhythm of our love. "I'm right there, baby. I'm so hard, so deep inside you. Jesus, fuck, I'm coming, baby. I'm coming, Ever, right now. Come with me, love…"

"If You Want Me" by Glen Hansard and Marketa Irglova played in the background, my brain tuning in to the music abruptly.

"Caden…Caden…" Ever rocked back into me, matching my thrusts with her own, matching my need and my passion and my hunger, satisfying me perfectly even as she made me want her even more. I felt her quake, felt her pussy tighten around my cock, felt her body shake and shudder, felt her asshole clamp down around my finger. "I'm coming, my love…I can feel your cock exploding inside me, Caden. Fuck me harder, don't stop, please don't stop…"

Her words made me wild, primal and unstoppable, and I came in that moment, exploding with the rhythm of her words. She was chanting my name, pushing back into me, thrusting against my gliding cock, panting, screaming. I couldn't take my eyes off us, off my reflection above her and behind her, her face straining and her breasts moving and her soft pale skin, and nothing, nothing had ever been this good, not ever.

Our eyes locked as our mutual orgasms collided and our souls merged, coalescing through our gazes.

Time slowed and stopped, and the love I saw shining in Ever's luminous jade gaze was indescribable, overflowing and overwhelming and at once potent and so tender. I tried to let my own expression flow with how I felt, the upwelling surge of passion for this woman, this amazing person who had given herself to me so completely, so trustingly. Our movement slowed, and I slipped out of her folds, gathered her against me. My knees shook, sweat beaded on my skin, my breath came in gasps, but I lifted her in my arms and carried her into our bedroom, settled her gently on our bed. She burrowed into me, let her hand skate over my skin.

"I love you, Ever. I wish those words were stronger, I wish I had some way of expressing it better."

She tilted her face to look up at me. "You just did, baby."

I grinned. "That *was* pretty fucking intense."

"You mean it was pretty intense fucking?"

"That, too." I kissed her temple, her forehead, her cheekbone. "But it was more than fucking, Ever. So much more."

She shrugged. "It's just a word, Cade. For us, everything we do is…*more*. We have sex, and it's making love, because that's what it's expressing, every single time, whatever kind of sex it is. Whether it's hot and hard and dirty, or soft and slow, it's making love. It's fucking. It's boning. It's shagging. It's…all the slang words, I guess. It's pure and it's perfect and I love it, whatever you call it. I just like the word 'fucking' because it…I don't know, it turns me on for some reason. I don't know if I can explain it any better than that. I love fucking you. I love being fucked by you. Because it's you and me, it's not…it's not less, or less important, or anything because of what word we use."

She kissed my breastbone, and her hand smoothed over my stomach, found my cock, and fondled it. Her mouth was hot and moist on my skin, her hand soft, her fingers caressing and manipulating me into arousal. I wondered, as she kissed my torso and fondled my growing erection, if I would ever get used to this with her, if I would ever take it for granted, if I would ever get tired of it. I couldn't see how that would be possible. Every time we made love, every time I kissed her, it felt better than the last time. Every time we came together, I felt closer to her than ever, more intertwined with her, more tangled up in her.

"Don't—don't ever leave me, Ever," I whispered, fiercely, desperately, needily.

She paused, glanced at me. Her eyes blazed. "*Never*, Caden. Never. I promise you. I'll never leave you."

Ever

"Little House" by Amanda Seyfried played in the studio, the soft strains floating to us. Cade's eyes were closed, but I knew he wasn't asleep. I couldn't close my eyes, couldn't take my gaze from his body. I couldn't stop touching him. He was growing hard in my hand, slowly responding to my touch. I wanted this to last forever, this feeling of anticipation, completely sated, flush with his love, yet still ravenous for him, ready to feel him inside me again, fill me again, sate me all over again.

The only thing in the way was having to pee. I whispered, "Be right back," to him, heard him murmur an acknowledgment, and went into the bathroom to pee and clean up a bit. When I came back, he'd rolled to his side, facing me, watching me approach through slitted eyes. I added a sashay to my hips for him, and melted at the smile he gave me.

It was intoxicating, the way he wanted me, the way he needed me, responded to me. The slightest touch, a kiss, a simple caress, and he would moan, growl, go hard. I could bring him to the edge of coming within seconds of touching him.

It was just as dizzying a high belonging to him. I was his, completely. He knew me, owned and controlled my body, my pleasure. I gave him everything I had, and he did the same for me, and together, we knew total ecstasy in every touch, every kiss, every moment spent naked and writhing together.

All this passed through my mind as I climbed into our bed, twisted to lie on my side, slid my back against his front. He kissed the round of my shoulder, pulled my hair away and kissed my ear, my neck. His hand cradled my breast, and I felt my nipple aching for his touch. I shimmied my hips against his groin, and felt the rewarding prod of his hard cock thick against my ass.

I wondered, briefly, about that, having him in me there, but then his fingers danced over my belly, distracting me, and I moaned as his touch tripped down over the shaved mound of my pussy and between the tender, sensitive lips, and his touch brought heat billowing through my core, the slick, wet heat of desire.

"Oh, god, Cade…" I moaned, "I need you."

"I'm so hard it hurts," he whispered in my ear. "Already. What do you do to me?"

"Same thing you did to me."

I was rocking into his hand by that point, writhing on his two middle fingers, panting and riding the verge of orgasm. I reached behind me and grasped his hot, silky hard erection, shifted my hips and draped my leg over his thigh. He bit my earlobe and breathed my name, "*Ever…*" and then I felt his huge cock glide into me, and I was complete again, filled by him.

With no words spoken, only mutual understanding, we rolled together so I was lying on him, my spine against his chest, my knees bent and my head arched back over his shoulder, my ass against his groin and his cock deeper inside me than it had ever been. His fingers were still circling my turgid, throbbing clit, pressing lightning into me, drawing heat from me, making me so wet his thrusting cock slicked and slipped and squished.

"God…damn, Ever, you're so…juicy." He laughed at his own words. "So wet for me. God, do you feel the way I slide inside you?"

"I feel it…I feel it. You're so deep, Cade," I gasped, "almost too much, but so perfectly too much. Go slow, baby. So slow. Slow as you can. Love me slowly."

He moved sinuously, slow as the coursing of the stars in the sky, loving me with every inch of his body, fingers in me, cock in me, hands on my belly and my breasts, tweaking my nipples into diamonds, kissing my neck and my ear. I twisted my head and his lips met mine and he was all around me, beneath me, kissing my breath away, stealing my soul with his mouth on mine, except my soul was his already.

I came, a first slow pulsing glow, and he kept gliding glacially slowly into me, kissing me, making out as we made love, tongues dancing, his palm cupping my breasts, caressing them and kneading them and his fingers circling my clit, dousing me in wet desire.

Another pulsing orgasm, stronger now, followed by a third like a crashing ocean wave. I didn't understand what was happening, those small cresting climaxes, one after another, each building upon the next.

They were waves, I realized, not orgasms, but the buildup to one so massive it would shred me.

I slid my body against him, pressing my heels into the bed to move away, crushing my hips down against his up-thrust, clutching at him with my hands over my head, holding his face to mine, imprisoning his lips to my kiss. Wave after wave struck me, broke through me, and I couldn't breathe for the potency of each new climaxing swell, and still he loved me without speeding his pace, a tireless rhythm, a slow sine wave of bliss.

I began to grow frantic as the waves of ecstasy neared their apogee. I moved against him, sought speed and friction and pressure, but he never relinquished the slow pace I'd begged for. I panted into his mouth, not kissing him now but merely gasping, biting his lower lip, writhing helplessly on top of him.

There was no way to measure how long we moved together that way, in silence except for our breathing and our bodies' slide and the faint music playing in the background. We were silent, uncharacteristically silent, feeling something being created in this timeless moment together, this desperate, catalytic fraction of eternity.

I felt his body tense and his muscles go iron hard beneath me, felt his cock swell inside me and his motion go staccato as he neared his release.

My hands were around the back of his head, pulling myself up on the column of his neck, lowering myself with ever more forceful movements, and I felt him cruising into me, crushing into me, delving deeper and harder, not faster, only with more power and more force.

Our mouths were touching and open, sharing gasped breaths, eyes meeting and sparking, and I couldn't fathom what was happening, what this was, how I could feel his very essence within my mind, expanding in my heart, how our souls could meld with the heat of our bodies' union.

Cade, in orgasms past, came with a soft grunt, a low groan or growl, a curse or a breathed whispering of my name. I was the loud one, the screamer.

Now I felt a growl begin in his chest as his cock drove into me, and I heard my own voice begin to groan wordlessly. We moved in perfect sync, ultimate unison, matching stroke for stroke, our voices raising louder and louder until Cade was growling like a lion and I was shrieking breathlessly, abandoned to him, to us, to this.

Louder still, Cade bellowing and roaring, me screaming.

The waves were one now, a blasting, fiery inferno torching every synapse, every molecule, my belly clenching and my pussy clamping down around his cock, and I felt him lose all control with a shout, fucking into me with such power that my body shook and spasmed and yet I met his urgency with my own, rolling my hips, all my weight on his chest and my frantically digging heels, grinding into his thrusts with all the strength I had, feeding the frenzy in us both, the nuclear reaction detonating within us, a wild mad frisson, becoming something unknown heretofore, something like the moment that had begun the whirling of the universe, an instant of creation that cannot be caught by mere words, something true and pure and past the scope of human comprehension, a tearing of the veil between heaven and earth so that as we moved in erupting love we saw into eternity together, we saw the face of God, the fabric of infinity.

I wept, and felt his tears on my cheek.

His eyes blazed amber, wet with tears I knew matched my own, love made liquid and escaping through our pores as sweat, our eyes as tears, our most intimate places as the juices squeezed from passion.

"Ever…" he breathed, and I heard the susurrus of words unspoken thick in those two syllables.

"Caden," I whispered, and let my eyes refract the love I felt bursting from my being.

Silence.

Breath, sweat, tears, love.

Purity of connection.

Eternity.

We slept, dreamed, twined together in body and in spirit.

an arpeggio, descending

Caden

'Twas the night before Christmas…and the roads were complete shit. Actually, it was the night before Christmas Eve, but close enough. I've always hated that stupid poem, except for the way Clark Griswold recites it in *National Lampoon's Christmas Vacation*. Ever and I were on our way home from shopping and a late dinner, driving through a blizzard. The snow was so thick I couldn't see the lines on the road ten feet in front of me. I was going barely thirty on I-75, wishing I didn't have to pee and cursing the snow. Ever, in the seat beside me, had her feet up on the dashboard, her phone casting a white glow on her face. She was texting someone,

Eden most likely. My wife and her twin had been fighting for the last week, arguing via text message about whether Ever and I were going to go to Mr. Eliot's house for Christmas tomorrow morning, and whether we were going to tell him we'd gotten married. Ever didn't want to go, and *really* didn't want to tell him. She didn't see the point, she claimed. She hadn't seen her father in months; he hadn't made any attempt to contact her, hadn't come to see her. I'd never met Mr. Eliot, except that one time in the parking lot of Interlochen, nearly six years ago.

I understood her anger, her frustration. She and her father had essentially parted ways many years ago, and hadn't mended the distance. She claimed she wasn't angry at him, not for anything in particular, she just didn't care to see him. I didn't quite believe that. He was her father. She was hurt that he'd checked out of life, that he'd rather work a hundred hours a week than see his daughters, his only family. Not having any parents of my own anymore, I wanted her to try to fix things with him before it was too late, before she lost him and realized what she was missing only after it was gone.

I'd told her this, of course, and it had become our first real fight. I'd held my ground, become impassioned, upset at her stubbornness, her refusal to even admit that she was pissed off at him, and she in turn had been mad at me for trying to force her into something she didn't want to do. It had been a fight that lasted three days. Three days of tense silences and cold shoulders.

We'd gone shopping today and to dinner. It had been…awkward, since she still wasn't talking to me, really.

I leaned forward against the steering wheel, peering through the snow, preparing myself to say whatever it took to end the standoff.

"Look, babe," I began, glancing at her, "first off, I'm sorry for upsetting you."

"It's fine," she said, not looking up from her phone.

"Clearly it's not." I sneaked another glance at her. "I just…I don't want you to have any regrets. You'll regret it if you don't fix things with him."

"If this is your attempt at an apology of some sort, it's not going so hot for you. Just sayin'."

"Can you please put down the phone and talk to me?"

She sighed, and finally looked up at me. "I *am* talking to you. I don't have to turn off my phone to talk to you."

"You're not listening to me."

"You're not saying anything worth listening *to*." Ever slid her feet off the dash and stretched. "God, this weather. It's gonna take us another hour to get home at this rate." It was normally not even thirty minutes from our condo in downtown Royal Oak to Somerset Mall, but it had already taken us that long, and we weren't even halfway home yet.

"It's insane, that's for sure." I rubbed my face. "Ever, listen. I'm sorry. It's your decision, your life, your business. I won't say anything else about it. If you don't want to go to your dad's place tomorrow, that's fine with me. I love you, and I just…I wish you'd make an attempt with him before it's too late." Her gaze hardened, and she opened her mouth to speak, but I lifted my hand in a gesture of surrender. "You know how I feel, and that's all I'll say. I don't want to fight anymore."

She leaned her head back against the headrest and closed her eyes, swallowing hard and blinking. "I don't, either. It's been killing me, fighting with you." She leaned across the console between us and wrapped her arm around mine, rested her head against my bicep. "I was so mad, because I don't want to *be* mad, but I can't help it. *He* walked away from *me*, Cade. From us, Eden and me. He's worked seven days a week, from five in the morning to ten or eleven at night, every day since Mom died. Sometimes he sleeps at work. He doesn't talk to us. Doesn't call us or text us or send emails, sure as hell doesn't come see us. He stopped caring, Cade, and I don't know *how* to fix that. He's my dad, and I love him. Or…I want to. But I don't know how you're supposed to love someone who isn't there and doesn't want you, doesn't love you back."

I hated the tears I heard in her voice. "I'm sorry, honey. I'm so sorry. It's bullshit. I know it is. And I don't know how you're supposed to fix it, either. Maybe…I don't know. Just go over there with me tomorrow, and try to hash it out. Tell him how you feel and that you want your dad back. I don't know. I'm not trying to tell you what to do, babe. I'm just—I hate seeing you upset, and I know this thing with your dad is harder on you than you're letting on, even if it is way deep inside."

"You're right. I know you're right." She took several deep breaths, sat up, and wiped her eyes. "Fine. Okay. We'll go. But I'm not even going to try and approach the fact that we got married. Not that I'm ashamed, I just—"

"One step at a time," I cut in, "I get it. For real."

She twined her fingers in mine. "Thanks, babe. I love you."

I glanced at her, smiled. "Love you, too. Together, one day at a time, okay?"

She nodded, and we drove home in silence, more companionable now.

Ever

Cade was nervous, tense, picking at his food and bouncing his foot under the table. Dad was… the same. Not looking at anyone, not talking, just shoveling food into his mouth. Eden was gamely try-ing to make small talk, but it kept falling flat.

"I saw this movie the other day," she said, taking too big a swig of wine. "I don't even know what it was called, but it had Ryan Philippe and that red-head from *X-Files*, what's her name, Gillian...Gillian Anderson? Yeah. And it had all these other famous people in it. I don't remember the whole cast. It was made a long time ago. Late nineties, maybe? And it was just about all these different people going through different things. And Ryan Philippe's char-acter, I think it was him, he said something really cool. He said, 'Talking about love is like dancing about architecture.' It just struck me as such an inter-esting thing. Because you can't really talk about love, can you? Not really. I don't think so, at any rate."

I rolled my eyes and glared at her, mentally will-ing her to shut up. She caught the hint, of course she did, but she ignored me, chattering on.

"I don't even remember the name of the movie. It was on some obscure cable channel, late at night." She paused to drink more wine. "It wasn't Ryan Philippe's character, now that I think about it. It was...Angelina Jolie. That's who said it. I wish I could remember the name of that *fucking* movie."

"*Playing by Heart*," Caden put in, not looking up. "I watched it, too. It played on, like, one of the sixteen random Starz channels in the middle of the night. That movie had fucking everyone in it. Sean Connery was in it. So was…what's his name, a character actor kind of guy. Jay Moritz? And Ellen Burstyn, too."

I glanced at him, trying to hide my irritation. "When did you watch that?"

He shrugged. "Thursday? You were asleep. I couldn't sleep, so I flipped channels, landed on that movie. It was good, in a disjointed kind of way."

Dad let his fork drop to his plate with a clatter. "Are we still talking about this movie?" He pushed his plate away. "What does that movie have to do with anything?" He addressed the last part to Eden.

She frowned back at him. "I was just…making conversation. All of you are being so awkward. Someone's got to say *some*thing."

Dad rubbed his hand through his thinning hair. "No one's being awkward, Eden. It's fine. We're all just eating."

"Dad. Not being awkward? The tension in here is so thick you could cut it with a knife."

And so it would begin. I glanced at Caden, who was still picking at his food, not eating but pretending to.

"There's no tension." Dad swirled the red wine in his glass, staring at the sloshing liquid.

Eden sighed and tilted her head down, placing her palms flat on the table. "Seriously? No tension? How could there *not* be tension? We haven't seen you since our birthday over the summer."

Dad grimaced. "I've been—"

"Busy," Eden finished for him. "I know. The problem, *Dad*, is that you've been busy for our whole lives."

"Eden, now is not the right time for this conversation. We have a guest." Dad gestured at Caden with his glass.

"Yeah, but he's basically family now, too, so…" Eden slammed the last of her wine in a long gulp.

I cringed, wishing she hadn't brought that up.

Dad frowned in confusion. "He's Ever's boyfriend. I hardly think that qualifies him as family just yet." He shot an apologetic glance at Caden. "No offense, son. You seem like a good kid."

Caden hated being referred to as "son," I'd come to learn. He kept his voice even, however. "None taken, sir." He didn't correct Dad, and I was glad he didn't. Now was *so* not the time to have that particular conversation.

Eden glanced at me, and then Caden, her expression baffled. "Ev?"

I had to distract her. "Dad's right, Eden. Now is maybe not the best time for this. Caden doesn't need to hear it."

"But—" Eden began.

"*Eden.* Drop it. Please." Dad stood up. "How about pie?"

"No!" She stood up, knocking her chair to the floor. "I don't care if he hears. He knows about all this, I know he does. Things are *not* fine. They haven't been fine since Mom died."

Suddenly, you could hear a pin drop. The grandfather clock in the formal living room across the foyer from the dining room tolled seven times.

"Eden…" Dad began.

"*No.* I'm not gonna drop it. You walked away after we buried Mom. You know you did, I know you did, and Ever knows you did. You checked out."

Caden stood up, grabbed his plate and mine. "I'll just…I'll clean up."

"Sit down, son," Dad said, not taking his eyes from Eden.

"I'm not your son." Caden set the plates back down and resumed his seat. "All due respect, sir, but don't call me that, please."

Dad slumped into his seat. "I didn't walk away, Eden—"

"The fuck you didn't!" Eden yelled. "You checked out! You all but abandoned us!"

"I kept a roof over your head, didn't I? I paid for your cars and your apartments and your college educations." He pinched the bridge of his nose. "So don't tell me I abandoned you—"

I couldn't keep quiet anymore. "That's all well and good, but it doesn't replace *you*." I tried to keep my voice reasonable, calm. "I'd rather have been poor and had you."

"You *had* me," he said.

"No, we didn't!" I couldn't keep the shout from escaping. "You were gone! Always gone! And you never came back. Not really. You work, and that's it. You don't—don't call us. Don't come over. Don't act like we're even—even—even your daughters."

"And how much effort have you made, either of you, to reach out to me? This can't all be on me."

"You're our father!" Eden cried. "You were… you were supposed to be, at least. Now? Now you're more of a memory than anything else. Just as much of a distant memory as Mom is."

Dad buried his face in his hands. He took a deep, shuddering breath, and then another, and then his shoulders began to tremble. Eden and I exchanged glances. What were we supposed to do now? Tell him it was okay? That we understood and forgave him? We didn't. I didn't, couldn't.

He stood up, head bent down still. "Just a memory, huh? Well. I—I'm sorry I let you down." He moved away from the table, shambling and shuffling as if he'd aged a hundred years in the last five minutes. "I'm—sorry. That's all I can say, right? Sorry." And then he was gone.

Silence reigned, a thick, impenetrable presence at the table.

"Great job, Edie. Way to ease into it." The sarcasm dripped from my voice, and I didn't try to stop it.

My twin glared at me. "How would you have done it? Oh wait, you *wouldn't* have, would you? You would've just sat there with your *husband*, which Dad doesn't even know about, mind you—and said nothing. Done…nothing."

"I was going to…I was waiting for the right time, Eden! I was going to…make it a conversation, not a fight!" I was yelling now.

"Because that would have worked *so* well!" she yelled back at me, eyes full of unshed tears. "Sometimes there just is no easy way, Ever. Maybe you wouldn't know that, though, since everything's always come so easily to you."

My jaw dropped open. "Easy? *Easy?* What the fuck are you talking about? What's come easily to me? Losing Mom? Getting my heart ripped open by Will—Billy—whatever the fuck his stupid name is? You think that was easy? You think basically losing Mom *and* Dad at the same time came easily to me?"

"You were never anything but an easy *fuck* for Billy Harper," Eden shot at me, "and everyone knew it but you. You brought that on yourself. And you know what? You wanna know what's even more fucked up? Even though I *knew* that Billy never gave a shit about you, I was *still* jealous of you, because you got him when no one else could, and it just *happened!*

He just—just wanted you. No effort on your part. He *wanted* you. Not me, *you*. We're supposed to be *twins*, but you get *every*thing. All the friends, the guys chasing after you, the looks. You've had *him*"—she jabbed her finger at Caden—"almost your whole life, and you even took that for granted until it was almost too late. So yeah, I think everything comes easy for you."

"I don't think that's quite fair, Eden," Caden said, standing up now.

"I wasn't talking to you!" Eden shouted. "This is none of your business, so shut the fuck up!"

"Hey!" I pushed Caden back and stood between him and my sister. "Don't talk to him that way! This is his business. My business *is* his business. What the hell is wrong with you?"

She seemed to go weak, suddenly, leaning on the table with her head hanging between her arms. "I don't—I don't know. I just—I wanted this to be a…a nice Christmas. For once. Not just you and me, but…a family. Some kind of a family again. It's been just you and me the last few years, you know? We'd come over here, but Dad would…he would be spaced out, and he'd go to bed early, or he'd have a phone call to make or emails, or something. Anything to avoid being with us. And I thought—I thought now that you have Cade, you'd…we could…" She trailed off, picking up her empty wine glass and tipping more from the bottle into it. "I guess I just thought we could be a family again. I guess I was wrong." She turned away from the table, taking her wine glass with her, and left the dining room.

I stood in silence, tears threatening, heart breaking, confused, hurt, lost. Only, I had Caden's arm around me, so I wasn't completely lost. "Let's go home," I said.

Cade just nodded and went to gather our things and start the car while I cleaned up a little. I cleared the table and wrapped the leftovers, leaving the dishes for Eden. It was our way, the way we'd split the duties since we were little girls. I hated doing dishes, and she hated clearing the table, so it worked out, and now we didn't even have to discuss it. I found Caden waiting in the car for me, "Pitter Pat" by Erin McCarley playing on the radio via his iPhone plugged into the auxiliary USB port.

We'd put our money together and bought a car as our Christmas present to each other. It was a two-year-old Ford F-150 with low miles. It had been time to get a different car; the Jeep simply had…too many memories attached to it. We wanted something that was only ours, his and mine.

I sat beside him, listening to the music, watching the thick flakes of snow fall slowly in an impenetrable white blanket.

"You didn't need to yell at her for my sake," he said finally, as the song ended. "She was just upset. She didn't mean anything by it." He put the truck in reverse and backed out of Dad's driveway.

I frowned at him. "You're my husband, Cade. Of course I'd defend you. No matter who it's against. No one gets to yell at you."

"Except you?" he asked, giving me a small, teasing smile.

"Except me."

We folded our fingers together and drove through the snow, listening to music together. I felt myself dozing, felt my eyes getting heavier and heavier, closing.

"We'll be home soon," Cade said. "Just rest, love."

I let myself drift, eyes flicking open every once in a while to glance at Caden, focusing on the road, peering through the snow.

Then I heard him curse suddenly, felt the truck shift sideway, turning, sliding. Tipping.

It was strange how the snow muffled the sound of screeching brakes. I opened my eyes to see the white air through the window, and then the blacktop of the road, somehow beneath me, and my hair was hanging down around my face. Cade's arm was on my chest, pressing me into the seat. There was silence, strange and distorted and twisting.

I didn't feel the impact. There was a crash, and then silence again, thicker, deeper silence. I tried to open my eyes, but all I could see was darkness. I felt the blackness of night somehow within me, somehow all around me, becoming me.

I wasn't cold, or hot, or in pain. I was only me, darkness.

Silence.

Caden

A car, a little gray Hyundai, half in the thick snow on the shoulder, half in the road. Stuck, tires spinning vainly. It came out of nowhere, suddenly there in the snow-haze, just there, too late. I hit the brakes and spun the wheel, panicking, feeling the ice beneath my tires, the same ice that had probably put the Hyundai in the ditch.

Ever was asleep beside me, so beautiful, at peace as she slept. Holding my hand, her fingernails painted deep crimson. Her fingernails, painted deep red. Dark red.

Blood red.

Blacktop hit my tires, replacing ice, and then it was too late, the truck was sideways and moving forward, spinning, tail dragging out around and forward, traction control fighting to catch the tires on the ice, but four-wheel drive didn't help you stop, didn't stop you from spinning.

My stomach dropped, and we were airborne. I slammed my arm across Ever's chest, an automatic reaction in an attempt to keep her from leaving the car through the windshield, even though she was wearing her seatbelt. Sky and ground traded places, once, twice, and then we hit. The passenger side crashed into the ground, the window shattering. Something wet splattered against my face.

Snow?

No. It wasn't white. It was hot and sticky.

The airbags deployed, sudden explosions of white.

The truck rolled again, across the ground, ice and snow sluicing over me through the broken window, through the smashed windshield, and now my window was shattering and I felt a million razorblades slice my skin, my arms, my face, my chest, felt the weightlessness of going airborne, and I had a sudden flash of memory, seeing the drop on the left hand side of the road, a stand of trees, a fence line and the industrial buildings farther beyond.

The next impact hit my side, slamming me into the ground and into the car. The shattering window had ripped open the airbags, and glass shredded me once more. Heat, pain, not just pain but agony. Rolling, rolling. Tumbling, twisting.

Another slam, this one stopping us abruptly. The passenger side was facing the ground, leaving me in the air, hanging by my seatbelt.

The passenger side.

Ever.

Silence. No screams. Why wasn't she crying? Moaning? Something.

"Ever!" I writhed, wriggled, felt something spiked through my left forearm, digging into my side and my thigh. Piercing me, pinning me in place.

"EVER!" I thrashed, felt myself tear open. Inside, outside; shredded.

Pit. Pit. Pitpit. Red droplets falling.

I twisted in place, trying to see her. I managed a glimpse. Wished I hadn't. Couldn't help looking again. An ocean of red beneath me, Ever's black hair. White skin. Porcelain stained crimson.

"NO! NO!" I flailed my body, felt whatever was through my forearm rip free, raw torment pulsing through me.

I grabbed whatever it was, felt slick metal, pushed at it, straining every muscle I had to bend it away from me, feeling faintness steal over me, through me, agony blinding me. I saw bone through the gash in my arm. I managed to reach for Ever, nearly able to touch her.

She was limp, so still, so silent. I heard screaming, wordless and hoarse, coming from me.

"EVER!…EVER!" I fumbled for the seatbelt latch. "Please, baby, wake up! Wake up!"

There was so much blood around her. Mine? Hers? So much blood. Her face was painted crimson, her hand, flung out through the shattered window, was sliced into meat, dripping red. Her jeans, torn and ripped and red.

Oh, god…oh, god, her head. So much red, and white flecks, bits.

My throat went raw, but still I screamed, screamed, flailed and thrashed, trying to reach her, but still pinned and unable to free myself, each motion costing me blood and agony and consciousness.

I heard sirens. Voices.

Somehow, impossibly, the radio was still playing. "Cosmic Love," Florence + The Machines: *"No dawn, no day, I'm…twilight…shadow of your heart…"*

"Ever! Get Ever!" My voice felt faint, sounded distant. "Get her…save—save her…"

"We'll get you both out, son, I promise. Just try to stay still, okay?" His voice was calm and steady, but I heard the tension underneath.

Son. I hated that. *Don't call me "son."* Couldn't get the words out.

"Save…save her. Please…Save her."

Something moved, shifted, and pain lanced through me, pulling another hoarse scream from me. The torture was too much. Agony overwhelmed me, darkness sucking me under, flesh ripping and bones grinding, metal screeching, a saw screaming and whining, metal on metal.

So dark, so cold.

Everything hurt, everything hurt.

Ever. Ever. Ever.

Ever.

fiat concordia discordiam

White. Silence fading into ambient noise.

"He's awake, Dr. Miller."

How did they know I was awake? I wasn't sure I was. But yes, the whiteness was a ceiling. The whiteness was also snow falling through the window to my left.

Pain, dizziness.

I coughed, glanced around the room. A short woman with a blonde bob and blue scrubs came in, a stethoscope around her neck and a tablet computer in her hand. She was accompanied by a tall, slender black woman in a white lab coat, hands in her coat pockets, withdrawing one as she approached my bed. Her eyes were brown and kind and hid an intimate knowledge of pain and suffering.

"Mr. Monroe. Glad to see you awake." Her voice was melodious, lilting with some faint accent I couldn't place.

I worked my mouth but couldn't speak. Coughed, coughed, but couldn't catch my breath. Tubes in my nose, my arm, a catheter. I was so weak, unable to lift my hand, even my fingers. Someone came with a tiny bottle of water and a straw. I drank slowly, greedy for the water but unable to do anything quickly.

Throat wet, I tried to speak. "How…?"

"How long?" Dr. Miller said. Her name was embroidered on her lab coat, along with a string of letters, Ph.D.s and other such things. "You've been unconscious for a little over a week. You lost a lot of blood, Mr. Monroe. Too much. You needed an infusion. You underwent several surgeries. We'll go over all that later, though. How are you feeling?"

How was I feeling? I didn't know. "Hurt. Weak." But I hadn't meant to ask how long I'd been out. "Ever? How is…how is Ever?"

Dr. Miller's features went suddenly placid, a mask falling into place. "Just try to rest, hmm? You've been through quite an ordeal."

I twitched, struggled. "No…Ever. How is Ever? Tell—tell me!" I coughed, hacked, my throat raw. "Just—tell me!"

"Please, stay calm." Dr. Miller laid a hand on my arm, and her face went even more still, even more featureless and expressionless. "Your wife is in a coma, Mr. Monroe. She sustained very grievous injuries to her head, I'm afraid. She has undergone many surgeries as well, but...she has not woken up as yet."

I couldn't find a reaction within me. It wasn't real. It was a lie. But I saw the truth in her eyes and hated her for it. "Will—will she?"

Dr. Miller shrugged, a tiny lift of one thin shoulder. "I...I do not know." Her brown eyes searched me. "Truthfully, I don't think so. Her brain was badly damaged in the crash, and I am not very confident that she will wake up soon, if ever." She seemed to sense the inevitable gaffe in speaking that word, *ever*, that name. "I am so sorry. You never know what will happen, but the chances...? Very slim. If she does, her memory could be damaged. She could be...vegetative. There is simply no way to tell this early."

I closed my eyes, felt a tear slide down my cheek and into my ear, tickling and wet. "Ever...*god, no, Ever. Please, god. Not Ever. Not her, too."

It was too much. Too much.

But she wasn't done, brave Dr. Miller. "I'm... there is more, I'm afraid."

"More? What more?" I peered at her, dread gnarling my stomach into knots.

What else could there be? My wife, the love of my life, was in a coma.

Dr. Miller opened her mouth, closed it, and then tried again. She couldn't meet my eyes. "She...your wife—she lost the baby."

the end

a preview from the next book,

after forever

Shock hit me so hard that I blacked out momen-
tarily. "*What?*" I couldn't get my eyes to focus on
Dr. Miller. "She what?"

"Your wife was pregnant, Mr. Monroe. Eight
weeks, perhaps? Maybe less. She…she hemorrhaged.
Lost—had a miscarriage. Before the EMS even
arrived, she'd lost it. There was nothing to be done.
I'm—I'm so sorry. I can't tell you how sorry." I finally
was able to see straight, and the torture I saw on Dr.
Miller's face was…nothing short of profound.

How many times had she delivered such news?
How did she stand it?

"She was pregnant?" The words were nearly
inaudible particles of sound falling from my cracked
lips. "She—she had an IUD. Just—she just got a new
one put in. She didn't…she never told me."

Dr. Miller closed her eyes briefly, which I sensed was, coming from this woman, the same as a sob from anyone else less stoic. "Nothing is perfect, Mr. Monroe. Even IUDs can fail, and indeed, most pregnancies that occur in a patient with an IUD occur in the first few months after implantation." She sighed deeply and stood up. "As for not having told you? I think perhaps she did not know. It was very early, and she may not have noticed any symptoms to get tested."

A cry escaped me. "God...Ever."

"I...if she wakes up, due to the nature of her injuries, not just to her head, which are the most severe, but to her abdomen, it is unlikely she will ever conceive again. I'm...I'm so sorry again, Mr. Monroe."

I heard her shoes scuff on the tile, and then stop abruptly. I opened my eyes to find Eden standing behind Dr. Miller. She'd clearly heard the conversation. She was shaking her head, tears falling in a torrent from her chin, onto her hand, her mouth.

And suddenly, looking at Eden was impossible. I tried to look away, but all I could see were Ever's eyes, jade green, and her nose, her mouth, her lips. Eden approached me.

"Caden...how did this happen?" Her voice broke.

Mine was worse. "I don't know. It was so sudden. It happened so fast."

Then Mr. Eliot was there, too, behind Eden. I couldn't meet his eyes. Had he heard, too? About the—the baby?

Dr. Miller came back in with a clipboard and a pen. "I need you to sign this." She extended the clipboard to me. "We need your permission to do some further testing."

Mr. Eliot took the clipboard, assuming she meant it for him. "What tests?"

Dr. Miller reached for the clipboard. "I'm sorry, Mr. Eliot, but…I was speaking to Mr. Monroe."

Mr. Eliot let her take it, shocked. "Him? Why? I'm her father, her legal guardian."

The doctor looked at me, seeming to understand.

I swallowed hard. "Because she's my wife," I said. "We got married three months ago."

Fury made his face go red. A vein throbbed in his forehead. "You—you *got married?* How—she—how did I not know this? Why didn't she tell me?"

"We eloped," I explained. "It was…how she wanted it."

"But—but—" Mr. Eliot stammered, stumbling backward, anger warring with shock and confusion.

Eden took him by the arm. "Come on, Daddy. Let's go get some coffee, okay?"

He let her take him, but then turned to look back at me, as if I'd stolen something from him.

When he'd left, Dr. Miller said, gently, "No one but you, and your sister-in-law as well, it seems, knows that she was pregnant. Maybe that's important to you."

"Thank you," I said, and the doctor left.

Ever had been pregnant?

I would have been a father.

Never conceive again.

Probably won't wake up.

I'd lost her.

And if I thought that I'd been broken inside before, I wasn't. It was Ever who had healed me, and now the accident had ripped off the bandage and shattered what was left of my soul, irreparably.

songs, artists, albums

Montgomery Gentry
"Kashmir" by Led Zeppelin
"Purple Haze" by Jimi Hendrix
Surfing With the Alien (album) by Joe Satriani
"Springsteen" by Eric Church
"Paint It Black" by The Rolling Stones
"The Sinner Is You" by Volbeat
"Hoppipolla" by Sigur Rós
"Sketches of Spain" by Miles Davis
"House of the Rising Sun" by the Animals
fun.
"Delicate" by Damien Rice
"Just A Kiss" by Lady Antebellum
"Awake My Soul" by Mumford & Sons
"Bulletproof Weeks" by Matt Nathanson
"A Thousand Years (Part 2)" by Christina Perri ft.
Steve Kazee
"Flapper Girl" by The Lumineers
"If You Want Me" by Glen Hansard and Marketa
Irglova
"Little house" by Amanda Seyfried
"Pitter Pat" by Erin McCarley
"Cosmic Love" by Florence + The Machine

about the author

New York Times and USA Today bestselling author Jasinda Wilder is a Michigan native with a penchant for titillating tales about sexy men and strong women. When she's not writing, she's probably shopping, baking, or reading. She loves to travel, and some of her favorite vacations spots are Las Vegas, New York City, and Toledo, Ohio. You can often find Jasinda drinking sweet red wine with frozen berries.

To find out more about Jasinda and her other titles, visit her website: www.JasindaWilder.com.

28985100R00228

Made in the USA
Lexington, KY
10 January 2014